SAVANNAH BLUE

Other books by William Harrison

The Theologian
In a Wild Sanctuary
Lessons in Paradise
Rollerball and Other Stories
Africana

SAVANNAH BLUE

WILLIAM HARRISON

RICHARD MAREK PUBLISHERS
NEW YORK

Book design by Iris Bass

Library of Congress Cataloging in Publication Data

Harrison, William, date.
  Savannah Blue.

  I. Title.
PZ4.H3223Sav [PS3558.A672] 813'.54 80-15436
ISBN 0-399-90081-0

PRINTED IN THE UNITED STATES OF AMERICA

For insights and help, my thanks to
Bob McBrien of the Department of the Treasury; Lou Sims of Interpol in Washington; Kamante Gatura for hospitalities at Hog Ranch; Sabra Hassel for stories about her uncle; Warnock Davies for items on Rhodesia; Chappy Bowie for notes on the headquarters at Langley; Diane Kincaid Blair for recollections about DC; Peter Vanneman for good conversations; Hayden McIlroy for humor and support; Harry Minetree for anecdotes and long friendship; and to Gordon Parks, Jr., a loving friend who will always be remembered.

PART ONE

Woe to every maligner and scoffer who gathers wealth
and counts it over thinking that it will perpetuate him.

The Koran

PART ONE

1

As the taxi crossed the bridge its passenger gazed out at the lagoon, the harbor, and, beyond, the city of Lagos—a great canopy of tin hovels spreading toward the horizon. Around the harbor stood all the half-finished skyscrapers and the building cranes. The heavy smell of oil rode in the air.

The taxi was on its way over to the big Federal Palace Hotel on Victoria Island where the Ermco Oil conglomerate maintained a suite of offices. There, soon, a particular oil executive would visit, so every day the passenger in the taxi made this trip, checking to see if his quarry had arrived in the city. After crossing the bridge, the taxi moved into streets which were long corridors of commodities: stackedup rolls of toilet tissue, cans of vegetables, bottles of Star Lager, bolts of soiled cloth, bedding, plastic kitchen utensils, and those inevitable pieces of corrugated tin out of which most Africans made their houses and their lives. Each family along each street had its own mini-store, so there were vast neighborhoods of stalls and lean-to markets, everyone a vendor, everything for sale, so that the city, like many cities of the old, dark continent, was an endless and overpowering bazaar.

There was a trash pile, perhaps fifteen feet tall and a city block in size, buzzing with flies, a kind of putrid urban mulch. Children played on it, running with their knees high through the mushy litter, calling to each other. Mammy wagons lurched by, picking up some of the hundreds of people who waited at each bus stop, and on each multicolored jitney or lorry the black boys hung out of the windows, old men rode the bumpers, and the forlorn faces of the women stared out beneath ragged bundles and crates of squawking chickens which were lashed to the top.

The passenger in the taxi thought of Cairo, Tangiers, and all the other places awash with human flesh like this, and a tremor of angry grief came over him. The cities of his continent were sewers. He was at war with the men who manufactured such litter, and he thought of himself not so much as a killer, but as a soldier, an army of one, singular and deadly.

Emerging from the taxi in the big curved driveway of the hotel, the passenger paid his driver and went into the lobby. The room was crowded with money changers, guides, pimps, and opportunists of every kind; there were the usual police informers, too, he realized, but he made his way to the call desk without overdue concern. He looked ordinary enough, like any businessman in his dark suit and tie.

Up on the mezzanine was the sound of rock 'n' roll, an unmelodious blend of electric guitar and drums, obliterating the conversations of all the homesick engineers, bone-tired construction foremen, merchants, drillers, and speculators; they were exiles and industrial drifters, men without a family or place, most of them, cut off from the better parts of themselves, who had surrendered to the warm flow of the sewer which washed them away.

He asked for Bobby Bolling.

The boy at the desk fumbled a stack of cards, trying to locate the name. Then he asked his cousin, an older clerk who stood sipping Pepsi two paces to the rear. They both asked for the name to be repeated.

"Mr. Bolling of Ermco. Is he in?"

"Who is calling?" asked the older clerk with an officious smile.

"A friend of Mr. Paxton's. Is Mr. Bolling registered?"

"Yes, you want me to ring his room?"

The man in the dark suit thought quickly.

"No, just give him this, please. Can you send it up to his room?" He handed the clerk a small velvet pouch. "And this," he said, writing out a name on a scrap of paper. "And tell Mr. Bolling that I'll call again tonight." He wrapped the paper in two banknotes and passed it across the desk to the older clerk.

The clerk turned the little pouch in his hand, inspecting it.

"It's a diamond," the man in the dark suit said. "My calling card. I'm trusting it to you—and to Mr. Bolling. If I make a sale later, you can trust me for a bonus, too."

Impressed, the clerk sent his young cousin directly to Mr. Bolling's room with the pouch. Calling the man in the dark suit by the name written on the scrap of paper, the clerk added, "An acquaintance of Mr. Paxton and a friend of Ermco is a friend of ours, Mr. Blue!" They shook hands and exchanged smiles.

Outside, clouds gathered. The man who called himself Mr. Blue hailed another taxi which took him back to the central city.

He stayed at an unlisted, private hotel operated by a single family. The son, who wore a neck brace, solicited guests at the airport, helping them through customs, carrying their bags, arranging taxis. He understood Mr. Blue when told that absolute privacy would be necessary during the week or so he stayed: no girls, no meals, no attention to the room itself.

The house sat on a side street not far from the cracked, dry fountain in Tinubu Square. In the evenings the lone guest sometimes walked up to the crowded Bristol Hotel and took his meal in the noisy dining room. Sometimes he walked over to the nearby public library where the readers were very earnest and the magazines very old. Usually, he just stayed in his room. He ate quantities of almonds, drank beer, watched the single television channel, wrote in his diary, or worked out chess problems on a small, portable board.

The night after learning that Bobby Bolling had finally arrived in Lagos, Mr. Blue bolted the door to his room, undressed, and began making preparations. He was anxious, so cautioned himself to go slow, to kill time, because his work had to be accomplished, if tonight, late in the evening after the dinner hours. His body sticky with perspiration, then, he went to the window, stood back a little behind the flimsy curtain, and let the breeze blow over him. A slow drizzle had begun. Beyond his room in a vacant lot between buildings hundreds of squatters took shelter; a boiling pot hissed with the first droplets of rain, an old woman

11

gathered a string of gourds, a boy in a visor folded his thin mattress and covered it with a sheet of rusted tin. People began huddling in doorways. A mother held her baby. The men lit cigarettes and stood there like cattle: tamed animals resigned to their pens, docile, grey as their rough shanties out there in the vacant lot, grey as the pools of muddy water beginning to form, grey as the deep twilight sky and the rain itself.

For a white man Mr. Blue's skin was dark, deeply tanned, and in European cities he looked like a sportsman. In Africa, he blent well. He could have been a hunter, a worker, or one of those ruddy engineers on the hotel mezzanine. In hotels where he visited or on that isolated estate far away where he lived, he padded around free of clothing. His body was still hard, his legs strong, the flesh still firm on his biceps. But the hands and eyes were most impressive: fingers and hands like strong cable, and eyes dark green as night, iris and pupil fused together like an animal's.

Rain swept across the vacant lot and the people in the doorways huddled closer. Debris tumbled ahead of the gusts of rain: loose cartons, a straw hat. He stood closer to the window, feeling the rain on his body as he leaned against the sill and damp curtain. Then he went over to his single piece of luggage and resumed preparations.

The bag contained his change of clothes, but sewn into its upper lining under a guard of thick leather were the gemstones: uncut diamonds, mostly, which he loosened with a penknife and slipped into another velvet pouch. He worked steadily, listening to the downpour outside. At last he held a number of the stones in his palm, let them warm there, and allowed his concentration to gather.

Beneath the lining were other passports and ID papers. He spread these out on the bed along with several brochures and newsletters from various international business concerns, the *Financial Times*, an envelope filled with press clippings, a handbook on gems, chess magazines, small bottles of liquid prescriptions, and other papers. The clippings concerned one company and one man: Ermco and Bobby Bolling.

Someone far away—out there beyond the sound of the rainstorm— was playing tuneless notes on a wooden flute. He was reminded of his home country.

Before his bathroom mirror he turned his body into profile, looked at himself, held his genitals.

In the flourescent glare, he set the bottles in a row. The square, small bottle marked DECONGESTANT caught the light; a pearl glow seemed to shimmer inside it.

As darkness came, he still waited. He studied out a chess problem. He decided against writing in his diary. When he stretched out on the worn rug beside the bed, sleep didn't come; he lay still, listening to the flute in the darkness, thinking about how he slept like this back at the estate on the floor beside his father's great canopied bed. A lifelong habit: sleeping or resting on a thin rug beside a bed, as if disdaining comfort.

When he knew that the dinner hours were almost finished, he ate a few of the almonds which he always carried wrapped in cellophane. Then he dressed, packed his bag, and went down.

He told the young man in the neck brace that this was the night about which they had spoken, that he needed the family car brought around. Then he paid the mother, an obese, quiet, smiling woman, and said goodbye. After this, he would find other lodgings in Lagos, or, if business could be concluded, take the first plane out of the country.

By ten o'clock he was being driven out to Victoria Island again through the rain-drenched crowds and traffic. The city seemed like a carnival, every street and alley packed with bicycles and pedestrians. A strong nutty odor scented the air. From the bridge he caught sight of the flashing beacon from the lighthouse.

He told the night clerk at the desk that Mr. Bolling was expecting him. The young man rang Residential Apartment Number Three and announced that Mr. Blue was there for an appointment.

"Mention that I'm a friend of Mr. Paxton's."

The clerk did this. Finally, hanging up the phone, he said, "Mr. Bolling is in conference. You're to leave your name and phone number."

"No, that won't do," he answered with authority.

"Very sorry," the clerk said, turning aside.

The lobby was packed with men in turbans, black women in brightly colored dresses and traditional headwraps, whites in khaki workshirts, others in business suits with starched collars, and the usual porters. At the registration desk there was the continuous arguments over lack of rooms. There were few places in either Africa or the world, he

knew, where the noisy, overcrowded conditions kept one so inconspicuous as in Lagos.

In the magazine rack beside the elevator everything looked worn
and used, read many times, creased, wrinkled, and put back; a copy of
West Africa had General Obasanjo, medals and epaulets aglow, smiling
into the camera.

He went up to the third floor practicing what he would say and
trying to remember Bolling's photograph from the press clippings.

Going along a corridor of high glass windows toward Number
Three, he could see across the lagoon: lights coloring the water from oil
refineries on the opposite shore. A soft, wet, dark evening. Thunder
rolling softly in the distance. He felt weightless and raised up, as if he
could see a thousand miles. Bobby Bolling answered the door himself.
He looked exactly like his photographs: a balding, smallish Texan with a
pencil-thin mustache. If one read the petroleum industry's trade magazines, Bolling was conceded to be a laboratory genius who had switched
to management with unusual success. His specialty within the industry
was recovery procedure—getting additional oil out of old wells and
reserves. He had started as an engineer in Odessa, Texas, had worked for
two small companies, had jumped to management with Burmah Oil, then
had entered Ermco as a vice-president. He was thirty-six years old, but
looked fifty. For company reasons only a few persons understood,
Bolling had scheduled a visit to Nigeria during the time when its chief of
operations, Hillary Paxton, would be in New York.

As they greeted each other at the door to Number Three, Bolling
conveyed a single impression: he was somehow unsure of himself. His
cover for this was a smile and a loud voice.

"You say Paxton knows you?" he drawled, filling the hallway with
his nasal baritone.

Standing there in the corridor, the man who called himself Mr.
Blue tried to keep his speech relaxed. "He told me you'd be coming in,"
he said, and he saw, beyond, inside the apartment, a large, buxom blonde
girl in a white jumpsuit.

"You got merchandise? Gemstones?" Bolling wanted to know.

"Yes, I can show you."

"And you're in no way connected with Ermco, correct?"

"I just have a private business with Mr. Paxton."

"I didn't tell Paxton that I wanted to buy anything," Bolling said, still not opening the door wider.

"No, naturally not. I believe Mr. Paxton just wanted you to have this opportunity."

Beyond, the large blonde girl sipped at her drink.

"Well, I can't say I know enough about your merchandise one way or the other to be interested," Bolling finally drawled out.

"Then I hope I didn't disturb your evening."

"Mr. Blue, is it?" Bolling asked, still neither opening nor closing the door.

"Yes."

"You live here in Lagos?"

"No, Capetown. I come up to Nigeria about once a month. I've known Mr. Paxton—oh, let's see, for a year."

"Well, see, I don't know anything about gemstones," Bolling repeated, and he withdrew the little velvet pouch from his shirt pocket and held it out.

"Let me leave that stone with you. It's uncut, but you could get an appraisal. If you can't get it appraised right away, keep it—and I'll settle with Paxton. You'll find that I ask about half the true value."

"You'll just leave this with me?" Bolling drawled, impressed and smiling.

"That's how any honest independent dealer does business," Mr. Blue said. "Actually, I have about three hundred thousand dollars worth of stones with me. The asking price is less than half that. You could keep the whole lot until tomorrow, get everything appraised, and then I could call again. That's my usual practice with trusted customers."

"I could call Paxton in New York and check you out, too," Bolling said. "Would that be all right?"

"He's probably at the St. Regis. Or with his sister in Brooklyn Heights."

For the first time Bobby Bolling's face relaxed. He took the diamond out of the pouch and hefted it in his fingers. It was a large white—by no means the most expensive sort of diamond—but it weighed several impressive carats. Both men smiled. The part about the sister in Brooklyn had been a fortunate addition.

"I'll keep this one stone and see you tomorrow," Bolling finally told him.

"Good. I'll be in touch tomorrow evening," Mr. Blue said, and as he turned away the two men said good night and the door was closed.

He walked down the corridor toward the elevator. Things had gone well. He pushed the button, waited, then looked back down the hallway to see that Bolling was standing outside his room again.

"Mr. Blue?" Bolling called.

It would happen now. It would be this evening.

As Mr. Blue returned to Number Three, he saw three figures standing inside the apartment: Bolling, the large blonde girl, and a black man in military uniform. The officer stood behind Bolling, grinning, his palm turned up, and the gem nestling in it.

"My good pal, Colonel Eweke," Bolling said, ushering Mr. Blue inside and closing the door, "tells me that this is a very good stone, indeed, and that I should certainly see your merchandise."

"The one I gave you was a nice white diamond with no flaws. But you can't see how really good it is until it's cut, polished, and held up to a good north light," he said, coming in. He detested the way he sounded: like a snobbish salesman.

"Well, dat is still many carats!" Colonel Eweke exclaimed in the usual thick accent, pointing at the gem he held.

"Will you have a drink, Mr. Blue?" Bolling asked. Then: "Get him a drink, Hila, honey, and sit him right down!"

"Sorry," he interrupted. "Bad stomach. I never touch alcohol." As he said this, he began giving the greater part of his attention to the colonel. "If you like that one, look at these. A couple of them are only alexandrites, but some of the others are top Capes. And, of course, this big white is the most impressive of the lot."

"I do not know stones dat well," the colonel admitted, flashing a grin. He reeked of liquor, as if he had spilt it on his uniform.

"Would you have anything else?" the large blonde asked. Her accent was European, though Mr. Blue couldn't place it. "We've got some *bangi*, good stuff."

"Perhaps," he allowed.

"*Bangi!* Hey, sure, man, we ve got plenty of pot!" Bolling said in his loudest drawl. "You a smoker, huh? Okay!"

The colonel laughed more loudly than the situation warranted, and Mr. Blue was suddenly their companion and friend.

Hila, the blonde, went off in search of their stash.

On the table in the center of the room, there along with *Time* magazine, the Ronson lighter, and the American display of Kraft cheeses and Planter's peanuts, Mr. Blue opened the larger pouch and spread out his wares.

The colonel took this opportunity to announce that he was virtually an American, too. "I studied petroleum engineering at Texas A & I," he said. "Dat is why I speak as I do: I am an Oxford cowboy from Africa, don't you see?"

Mr. Blue tried to look amused.

"Look at this," Bolling said, hefting the large white diamond. "How big is this baby?"

"Several. It will vary according to the cut."

"Damn."

"Never have I touched a stone dat big!" the colonel smiled.

"You should come out to the boat," Bolling said. He reached over and touched Mr. Blue's sleeve, as if passing a confidence between them.

"Boat?"

"We were about to leave when you arrived," the colonel explained. "But, yas, I have a very nice ship of state!"

Mr. Blue weighed their invitation.

"Just the four of us," Bolling assured him. "Discreet. You won't run into anyone else—which I know must be a consideration in your business."

Hila came back into the room with a plastic humidor, cigarette paper, and her toothy smile. The colonel let his eyes follow her contours as she strolled toward Bobby Bolling.

"I can't decide what's best," Mr. Blue answered truthfully. The evening had promise, but he remained unsure. He tried to smile at the blonde, who was busy rolling a cigarette, dropping a few grains of marijuana on the carpet as she tried to work her stubby white fingers.

"Assuming all the appraisals go okay, I'll probably buy," Bolling said, trying to persuade his visitor.

"And assuming the price is truly right!" Colonel Eweke added.

"It's a real yacht," the blonde put in.

"Well, if it's only the four of us, I'll be happy to come," Mr. Blue said, and with that Bobby Bolling struck a match, held it, and watched Hila light up her creation. When she had taken a deep drag, she passed it over to the colonel.

Anchored in the harbor and lagoon at Lagos were many cabin cruisers, sailboats, barges, and yachts belonging to the highest military officials of the federal regime. Along with a number of other privileged members of the business community of the city, they lived on the water away from the overcrowded streets of the chain of islands which comprised Lagos. The waterways were hardly beautiful; giant loading cranes thrusting up around the horizon, oil refineries and breweries giving off their commercial stench and glow, fleets of scum-encrusted tankers edging around the channels. But out on the water itself, except for the occasional sounds of distant cars on shore, punctuated by fog horn and bell, something of the peace and ritual of the sea prevailed. Small outboards came and went carrying the officers and businessmen, their families, their mistresses, and their subordinates from the docks. Inside each vessel luxury dominated: stocked bars, full galleys, television sets, elaborate bedrooms. The officers lived well. Most of them had private safes and storage vaults aboard their ships. They were courted by oil executives such as Bobby Bolling, by arms traders, investment counselors, embassy personnel, politicians, and salesmen.

Driving down to the small military marina on MacGregor Canal where Colonel Eweke's crew stood waiting with his outboard, one could comprehend the full sweep of the lagoon: small craft as far as the eye could see, each with its own flashing colored lights, each part of the corona of light which was the true center of the Nigerian nation.

Beside Mr. Blue in the car sat Bobby Bolling, dragging at the last of the *bangi*, talking about his business victories. In the front seat were Colonel Eweke, the blonde, and the chauffeur of the big Mercedes staff car.

Mr. Blue weighed possibilities. No, not tonight, he was thinking. And yet the odd isolation of the boat on the water appealed to him.

Bolling kept bragging. He claimed that Ermco under his directive was making the largest cash investment deal in the history of modern business. He talked about recovery procedures, offshore rigs, and his own genius.

"Understand," he said, "the colonels want only cash. So we're involved with half the banks in the world: Citibank to Credito Italiano!"

"Impressive," Mr. Blue answered.

"I also want to say that I'm obliged to you and Paxton," Bolling drawled. "I've been working damn hard out here, and I was beginning to wonder if there was anything special in it for me."

"A little something," Mr. Blue answered.

"I do appreciate it. And about Paxton: do you sell him much stuff? I wouldn't think he was the sort to deal."

"He's an astute dealer," Mr. Blue assured him. "But I usually sell to the colonels. So I'm also grateful to you for introducing me to Colonel Eweke."

From the front seat, his arm around Hila, the colonel raised a hand by way of acknowledging Mr. Blue's remark.

"He's a Hausa—a mean one," Bolling whispered. "But Hila is a true Dutch milkmaid. Something for everyone tonight, if you know what I mean."

"It seems so," Mr. Blue answered politely.

The government launch took them a mile into the lagoon to the colonel's yacht: a fifty-foot hulk with paint peeling off its sides. The night air, heavy with the dampness of the earlier rain, was filled with the odors of fish, brewery yeast, salt, oil, and excrement. Clouds still billowed overhead hiding the moon. A good darkness. Mr. Blue calculated that the colonel's man who drove the launch and the chauffeur would undoubtedly go home for the night. Around the docks, too, sleeping on the jetties and wharves, lay several hundred of the homeless of the city, but none of them would even look up, he knew, if he later returned alone.

The colonel and Hila stood behind the windshield of the launch as it cut through the waters of the lagoon. His hand was inside her zippered jumpsuit. As Mr. Blue watched them he kept thinking of all the colonels across the continent; there were educational programs, five-year plans, housing projects, new highways, reforms, schools, but mostly there were the colonels with their hands into this or that.

19

Bobby Bolling talked oil facts and figures on the way out. He had the mentality, it seemed, of a lewd little accountant.

Inside the musty cabin of the yacht Mr. Blue was grateful—though not surprised—to find the evening settling down: the blonde stayed in her jumpsuit, the men turned to more drink, and the promise of anything sexual diminished. Colonel Eweke had spoils to display: drawers and boxes filled with wristwatches.

"Here are my Seikos, over here my Rolexes, and here are my Omegas! I even got electrics, see?" He moved from carton to carton, drawer to drawer, in his paneled bedroom revealing his treasures. Colonel Eweke was a large man, muscled and corpulant, with a wide Hausa scar slanting across his left cheek.

After wristwatches came guns. The colonel's arsenal was dated, but sufficient.

"I am very proud," the colonel said, laughing, "to have received weapons during the Biafran war from both the Americans and the Russians!"

Hila laughed least, as if she had heard all this before.

They dutifully filed in and out of a narrow storage compartment where the colonel displayed grenades, mortars, and various rifles of World War II vintage. There was even a rusted flamethrower, inoperable, but nevertheless their host's pride.

"If a man becomes my true friend," the colonel announced, "I will give him a fine weapon! For a good acquaintance, only a wristwatch!"

"Perfectly sensible," Bolling said out of his growing alcoholic haze.

Back in the main cabin, Hila became interested in Mr. Blue's origins. "You look, hmm, I'm trying to figure you out. You look like an American Indian, Mr. Blue! That's it!" The big Dutch blonde was both tall and heavy, perhaps sixty kilos. "And your hands," she went on. "You have very strong hands, don't you?" She reached for him, but he slipped his fingers out of hers with a smile.

"Here, let me do the next round of drinks," he said, moving to the bar.

"You have one, too, and we'll talk about your big white diamond," Bolling said.

"Right, I'm far too sober."

"You certainly are, Blue. You're a dead serious man, I can tell that. Of course, in your business you have to be careful, I realize."

"Can't be too careful," he agreed, mixing another round.

"For pretty girls," the colonel told Hila, "I also have very nice lady wristwatchems—" He laughed at his own slurring speech.

"Wristwatchems?" Hila laughed, too. Then she allowed the colonel to pull her down with him on the windowseat.

Bobby Bolling accepted his drink, his face curling into a kind of drunken half-laugh and snarl. He tossed the pouch of gems in the air and managed to catch it.

"These are worth your price, are they?"

"They're very well priced, as you'll soon find out. The big white is worth what I'm asking for the lot."

He passed the whiskeys to Hila and Colonel Eweke, interrupting their frolic on the narrow windowseat with a toast.

"Here's to all the good and precious things under the earth," he said, raising his glass. They gave him a momentary look of uncertainty as he added: "To oil and diamonds!"

Then, laughing, they drank.

"Paxton never mentioned you," Bolling said.

"I'm a very private source and supplier," Mr. Blue responded. "He naturally wants to keep me for himself."

"I reckon so," Bolling said, grinning.

"Getting black-market stones is a very delicate business," the colonel put in. It was the last thing he said.

"If you buy the big white at my price," Mr. Blue offered, stalling for time, "I'll make you a gift of the rest. How's that? You can have some nice rings mounted from some of those."

"Nice rings, yes," Bolling repeated, his voice flat.

Hila tried to shake the colonel awake. She had an odd smile on her own mouth, as if some deep inner spring had failed.

"His eyes are open, but he's asleep," she said of him, her voice a soft whine. Bobby Bolling's tumbler of whiskey hit the floor, but no one turned.

Mr. Blue sat down and watched Hila. She was almost in tears, but seemed to not know why. In answer to a question he didn't ask, she mewed, yes, she did have a pair of wooden shoes, once, that wooden shoes were not very comfortable, but were nice enough on rainy days. She also added that she didn't know the hour, that she had no idea what time it was.

Then, absently, as if waking from her stupor, she took the colonel's limp hand and gave it a few light slaps, urging him to wake up.

Bobby Bolling's face looked oddly distant, too, as he started across the room in a wobbly pattern. He stopped, turned, cocked his head as if listening, then stumbled forward once more. Meanwhile, a drool gathered on Colonel Eweke's chin and his eyes glazed with filmy tears. He slid off the windowseat onto the floor, falling away from Hila's weakened grip.

Mr. Blue sat watching them.

"Death," he told them, "is really a majestic intellectual moment. It leads us to examine the meaning of life itself. Without death, see, we'd float through an eternity of empty time. But precisely because of death we make assessments."

When Bobby Bolling's legs gave way and he toppled to the floor, Hila made her soft, mewing sound.

Colonel Eweke's head twitched and nodded, then he was gone.

Mr. Blue went to the desk, snapped open the drawers one by one, and peered inside. He sorted through papers. Colonel Eweke was indeed a petroleum engineer: there was his diploma, framed, from that place called the Texas College of Arts and Industries. There was also a stack of calling cards—various suitors from various oil companies—bound with a rubber band. A cluster of invoices and bills. Then he turned and noticed the diamonds strewn on the floor beside Bolling's outstretched form. Slowly, carefully, Mr. Blue bent down, picked them up, counted them to make sure, and put them back in the velvet pouch as he talked to Hila.

"Radioactive breakup is an effect without a known cause," he told her, speaking as calmly as a tutor. "And the physicists tell us that the old laws aren't necessarily laws. So there's really not much cause and effect in society anymore, either, you see. Not anywhere. Nothing holds. Are you listening?"

Bobby Bolling began a long gasping struggle for breath.

When he finished picking up all the gems, Mr. Blue gathered everyone's glass, stepped over the colonel's body, and went to the ship's head where he flushed the liquid away. Returning, working carefully, he refilled the same glasses with innocent whiskey, paying no attention to fingerprints but wanting to obscure the exact nature of the substance he had used.

"But in a world of uncertain laws, Hila," he said, still addressing her in his even, detached flow, "death is the one certainty. A magnificent absolute. So it's the foundation of all reality. It makes existence itself real, don't you see?"

He found only the usual in Bolling's pockets: ID papers, money, passport, keys. The wallet contained no family photographs. Bolling, he decided, just wasn't that sort of a man. Neither Hila's purse nor the colonel's elaborate uniform contained anything of interest.

Time and silence: like the tense moments between moves in a chess game, the mind running all its options and patterns.

When Hila slumped to the floor, Mr. Blue went over to her, sat down on his haunches, and watched her. No doubt of it: a poor, homely girl far from home. Probably, once, the unpopular girl at school who turned whore to get at least a form of love. Her breath began coming in short spasms. Then, suddenly, she managed a remarkably lucid question.

"Who are you?" she asked, her eyes wide.

"Mr. Blue," he lied, speaking in a near whisper beside her ear.

Her eyes fluttered with only a slight awareness.

Then he straddled her body, bent down, and kissed her tenderly on the cheek. A foul, bitter odor on her breath. Her eyes seemed to widen with his kiss and never closed again.

On deck he found rubber lifeboats and preservers: a choice of transportation back to shore. All the knots and bindings on the lifeboats had been carelessly whitewashed, however, and were impossible to untie. Then he found the little dinghy: perfect. He unlashed it, edged it over to the gunwale, and lowered it gently into the water below the slippery deck.

A wet darkness all around. Good cloud cover, still, and moonless. The sound of a faraway harbor bell.

When he returned to the yacht's cabin he checked his hosts and found none of them breathing. Small blood bubbles had sprouted from underneath each of Bobby Bolling's fingernails and from his eyes.

He rowed to shore feeling confident. On the way, he dropped his

23

false credentials over the side into the murky waters of the lagoon, weighting them down inside yet another of those pouches. He was no longer Mr. Blue. At the airport, later, where the boy in the neck brace had secured his bag at the Pan Am ticket desk, he would pick up another identity.

The weakest parts of his mission had held: he had arrived with only the barest information that Ermco's Paxton would be in New York while Bolling would be in Lagos; he had only rudimentary information about the company's hotel suite; he hadn't known if his identity as a gem trader would hold, or, if it did, how long it might take to get Bolling alone; he hadn't expected the colonel or Hila; his boldest lies—a sister for the mysterious Paxton—had worked; his deductions had been correct; the solitude on the yacht had been amazing good luck; he would be remembered by desk clerks, perhaps others, but police operations would take weeks, months, years, and whole governments would probably change, whole systems alter in the intervening period; a great endgame had fallen into place.

Three o'clock in the morning.

The awesome feeling of death was around him again, as if he could feel the whole continent murmuring to him; it rose out of the thick oil stench of this Nigerian harbor and blew his way from the putrid desert winds of Morocco, the Sudan, and the Somali dunes; it seemed to speak to him out of the sweet nutmeg fragrances of the river Congo and its lush tributaries; it came out of that humid veldt above Capetown and those stretches of coastal jungle which embraced the sea toward Zanzibar, out of the high savannahs beyond Nairobi, out of the hovels of Cairo, Kinshasa, Casablanca, and Khartoum; a strong, indescribable feeling out of the blood of the centuries, out of the carrion of reptiles, warriors, insects, ageless mammals, and mortal adventurers.

Death: he wanted those who brought the new century to his land to feel it in the deepest shudders of their nerves and bones. Let them catch it like an overwhelming fever; let them catch it from me, he told himself; the old dark germ, black as black.

2

Charles J. Hazo—the Professor—woke up slowly, trying to figure out which of his rooms he had been sleeping in, for he had many hiding places: his house out in Virginia near the college where he taught, the Pentagon suite, the safe room tucked into the condominium complex off Connecticut Avenue, the guest quarters out at Langley, and, finally, the apartments of his two women friends—neither of whom knew about the other. One friend was the intellectual waitress, a reader of novels and part-time book reviewer, whose single-minded devotion to the Professor was sexual; the other was a widow of a former British attaché, a beautiful woman who owned antiques, went to the theater, had women friends for tea and cards, and possessed Charlie in a curiously domestic way. They slept together, the widow and the Professor, but she was usually the one who fixed meals, worried over his health, and asked all the questions concerning his whereabouts.

When his eyes opened this morning he saw the waitress, whose name was Callie. She was still asleep, but her body curled toward his; she had the very slight odor of pasta about her, yet he knew that in her dreams she dreamt of James Joyce, magazines with esoteric names like *Antaeus* or *Ghent*, and her youthful literary career. Callie was twenty-two years old. Lately, however, like the widow, she had been asking a few questions.

Charlie Hazo got up and dressed—a process which took three

movements, for he wore what he always wore: jeans, the pullover sweater, and jogging shoes. In the bathroom, then, he began scrubbing his teeth—which was perhaps the Professor's most eccentric activity. Callie, curled and warm, hearing the sound and recognizing it in her deepest sleep, struggled out of bed and padded over to the bathroom door to watch. She was still weary from work and a long lovemaking session, but ever curious.

"What're you using this time?" she asked. "Ajax?"

"Nuh," Charlie managed. "Comet cleanser." He rubbed the cloth backwards and forwards over his gums so it made a grating sound—like sand paper.

"You ever try Ajax?" Callie asked.

"Uh huh. And Old Dutch Cleanser. And four or five others." Speaking with his teeth clamped, Charlie's words remained indistinct, but Callie understood. When she leaned forward to get a better look, her nightie fell away from her body; she had no breasts, just rosebud nipples, and a body like a length of pipe. She watched as he rinsed his mouth and spat.

"Why'd you get up so early?"

"School at eight o'clock," he told her.

Callie pressed her temples with her fingertips, trying to relieve the pressure of last night's wine. She tried to remember if this was the day Charlie taught his seminar, but couldn't; she could never get his college schedule straight and only half believed that he bothered with students, deans, committees, and all that. Having known him almost a year, she had few facts straight. He was very kind, she knew, and had money for girls and shows; he also went overseas regularly for an outfit called Africa International, some sort of scholarly research foundation.

He tossed the towel away and took her in his arms. The way Charlie rubbed her sleep-warmed body made her feel voluptuous rather than skinny.

"Fond of me?" she asked close to his ear.

"Yes, very fond," he answered, and she smiled. It was the thing they said to each other. There were times like this when Callie, although she was weary with too much experience, exhausted with love, and sick of men, felt dizzy in Charlie's presence. He was nearly sixty years old, and she sometimes felt that he was made out of scar tissue; there was that indenture in his forehead—where a hole had been and where, now, a thin layer of skin seemed to be pulled tightly across a little window directly into his skull; his body was pocked with wounds, mostly small, the larger ones stitched up and healed long ago; his hands always had fresh nicks or scrapes, though, as if he might be a woodworker or a mechanic or a man who beat his fists against walls. "Just racquetball," he told her once, explaining the hands. "I'm really clumsy at the game."

"I'm very fond of you," she whispered, trying to lure him back to bed. But Charlie Hazo, whose teeth fairly gleamed, had a can of shaving cream in his bunged-up right hand, and she knew he meant to leave.

"Got to go," he said after she kissed him.

"You jogging this morning?"

"Probably not."

"Then I don't think you ought to wear jogging shoes."

"But I always do."

Callie, he realized, hanging around his neck, talking about his footwear, was only delaying his leaving, but he appreciated the effort. Although he had Comet cleanser on his breath, she didn't seem to mind.

"You wore—hmm, not these—that other pair of jogging shoes to the concert last week."

"Naturally. I have jogging shoes for dress occasions."

Her warm breath of laughter fell against his neck. "C'mon to bed," she said.

"Can't do it."

"This your old seminar day?"

"That's right."

"So we can't even have breakfast together?"

"You know I'd like to."

Silence between them. Callie clung to him for a moment longer, but knew she had to let go and did.

As he shaved, she mentioned that she had phoned the college one day trying to locate him. He moved the razor over his lip, not answering. It was unlike Callie to do such a thing; the widow had sometimes become insistent, but of course Charlie was almost impossible to contact through the public telephone exchange.

"My boss gave me that afternoon off," Callie went on, answering the question he didn't want to ask. "I thought we could spend it in bed."

"I wasn't in my office?"

"They said they'd leave a message for you."

"The college telephone operators aren't all that efficient," Charlie said, finishing under his chin.

He felt her eyes on him, but rinsed off his face. There might have been an amount of suspicion in her voice. If she became too concerned about his habits, he had decided to let her find out about the widow. If that didn't work, if she became too concerned about his seminars or his frequent trips to Africa, he would have to stop seeing her. As he slapped on some shaving lotion, he felt her gaze, and he thought of the women in his life, past and present, of Callie and the widow, and of one, Stella, who was now, of all places, in Zanzibar. For a moment he studied his old, scarred, fickle face in the mirror and wondered how he could think of Stella at a time like this. But he did think of her. And for the tiniest instant the hint of her perfume seemed to blend with his shaving lotion.

Twenty minutes later he was driving to the garage on G Street. He pulled his Volvo into the correct upper ramp, parked in his usual place, took the elevator down to the basement, and strolled over to the brown Pontiac.

"Good morning, Professor Hazo," his driver said.

They were soon on the George Washington Parkway, the cliffs gliding by, aprons of ice gleaming off the Potomac River to their right. Charlie used the car telephone, calling ahead to announce his arrival. Then he opened his briefcase, stared in at all the paperwork left undone, and sighed. The river flashed through the trees, then the car curved away from it. The sound of traffic. Charlie sat there recalling the time when he had gone out to headquarters by motor launch, the Navy providing a pleasant ride; it had been late autumn, the air cold, and he had wrapped himself in a muffler, standing on the bridge with a young captain, taking a sip of Navy brandy from a flask; the trees were golden and deep brown, a few bare limbs showing, and he had felt alive and important being transported with such care. And, now, he asked himself, do you feel the years? Do you still feel like turning out more product? Do you feel anything at all? Summoning all his morning energy, Charlie answered himself: okay, sure, I feel fine, I feel ready, here we go again. Like all truly complex men, Charlie Hazo bordered on depression, on the low-grade fever of minor despair, and had to give himself constant pep talks.

The car entered the Central Intelligence Agency grounds at a driveway marked with the sign BUREAU OF PUBLIC ROADS. The pine trees eventually thinned out so that the river made its reappearance, then they were soon at the major parking lot, moving around that gigantic H-shaped building, driving alongside the intramural playing fields, and pulling into the usual parking space.

Charlie went inside at his accustomed entrance, showed his ID, got tagged, and went directly to the locker room. Jamie Vander, with whom he jogged, wasn't there, so Charlie, putting on his sweatclothes, assumed that his colleague was already out hitting the path.

Before going outside again, Charlie stopped at the guard's desk.

"Is Mr. Vander already outdoors?" he asked.

"Yessir," the guard answered. "They've gone down by the river."

It was a young guard with a chin like the poster of all Marine recruits, and Charlie thanked him. Of course Jamie was at the river, that's where he liked to jog, but who was with him?

The air was still icy. Snow blanketed the area, and Charlie's breath preceded him in clouds of white steam. Soon, he entered the path and became amused: there he was on the grounds of the CIA, following footprints in the snow. There were two sets, equal in size, but the strides were different, and Charlie, puffing along, tried to guess which were Jamie's. Then the pain of taking those deep, cold breaths shut out speculations.

Where the path cut down alongside the river, Charlie saw canoes lashed to the dark trunks of trees near the water's icy edge; some of the employees actually rowed to work, coming across the river rather than getting into their cars and driving the long loop down to the bridge and back up the parkway. There were many types and kinds of people at work there: lawyers, linguists, scientists, spies of every size and sex and lifestyle, patriots and unbelievers, full-time careerists and those who, like Professor Charles J. Hazo of the Department of Political Science, Graham College, Virginia, were occasional—and, in Charlie's case, frequent—contract workers. They came to work in their canoes, Chevrolets, and limousines. They took fencing lessons in the corridors at lunch break. They had .45 calibre pistols or Snoopy dolls or love letters in their desks, combination locks on their doors, plastic BURN baskets on their work tables, and a vast variety of motivations for doing the work they did.

On the river path, snow crunching underfoot, puffing, head down as he watched those footprints, Charlie looked up to see two figures jogging toward him. He slowed, stopped, and waited for Jamie Vander and the other man to approach. His lungs burned.

"Want you to meet Kip Culley from Secret Service," Jamie said breathlessly when the three of them stood together on the narrow path.

"Are we having a meeting?" Charlie asked.

"This is it, Professor," Jamie said.

"Let's don't run anymore," Charlie suggested.

Agreeing, they trudged back up the path toward the building as Jamie began talking. "There's a situation in Africa," he said. "Somebody's poisoning our businessmen, some single who seems to have a clear pattern: he's very mobile, very intelligent, and so far his victims seem to be picked at random. We don't know who he is, what he wants, or why he's so busy. Those of us on the African desk don't have any data, and it may or may not be terrorist activity. At the moment, in fact, we don't know shit."

Wishing his lungs weren't stinging so much, Charlie listened. The other man, Culley, who was young like Jamie, seemed to be at complete ease without the slightest sign of forced breath. Indeed, he was smiling as if he enjoyed himself. They emerged on the edge of the intramural field.

"I can't go over on an extended trip right now," Charlie said. "It's final exam time at my school."

"No, it's not that," Jamie Vander said. "There's a little guy in Treasury named Foxx. They call him the Little Buddha. He wants to hype all this up. He wants his own private little organization."

"He called me," Kip Culley said in a strong New York accent. "Wants me on his team."

"And he wants you, Charlie," Jamie said, grinning.

"How has he heard about me?"

"The Little Buddha is wise and inscrutable, I suppose, and knows all."

"Nobody's supposed to know about me," Charlie said, and his tone was so petulant and oddly annoyed that both Vander and Culley laughed out loud.

Inside the big dining room they sat around one of the circular tables and had breakfast. They discussed the Company and its present morale: life under the admiral, new executive alignments, and the vestiges of what was now referred to as the Halloween Massacre when CIA employees were laid off and a severe budget cutback was ordered by the president. Clandestine services were still not doing well, Jamie claimed, and there were new bosses who didn't understand operations. The Watergate scandal, they concurred, though long past, had left its bruise. As a result, product—the raw data and information which made the Company so valuable—was of poor quality, and everybody was mostly in business protecting his job.

"The last thing I want," Jamie asserted, speaking softly, "is an ambitious little prick from Treasury taking advantage. If he wants our African desk as his toy, I say the hell with him. I thought we should meet today and agree on that much."

Charlie, who should have ordered his diet breakfast of juice and dry toast, paid very close attention to his steaming plate of ham and eggs. He listened, but also observed Jamie Vander and Kip Culley: two smart young cockbirds, but climbers, too, if ever he knew climbers.

"Whoever this Buddha is, he knows good men, doesn't he?" Charlie said. "Credit him for picking you two and for finding out about me."

"That's not the point," Kip Culley whined, his Queens accent growing more pronounced with his irritation. "We've got to score inside our own outfits, don't we?"

"Right," Jamie put in. "We can't afford to be locked into some cockeyed independent task force. With things all scrambled inside the Company, I have to be on hand here."

There it was, plainly stated: bureaucrats preferred their own courts and rules to someone else's.

"Where'd you two guys get to know each other?" Charlie asked them.

"Kip and me? Yale," Jamie Vander answered, preoccupied with his bowl of cereal and with being unhappy.

"Did this little man at Treasury know about me or did you tell him?"

"I told him we had a troubleshooter on the African desk, a professor."

"You didn't give him my name?"

"Of course not."

Charlie smirked. His breakfast was fattening and delicious; he sat there feeling drained and paunchy, burned out after having run two hundred yards. Even his scars hurt. And here were these two cockbirds.

"How do we know this is just a single operator in Africa?" he asked.

"I'll show you the folder. A very definite pattern."

"What sort of poison?"

"Cobra venom."

"Really?"

"Actually, we've experimented with it ourselves. Maybe you know about that already. It's a wonderful stuff for assassins. Mixed with the right chemicals, it can just be touched to the skin, absorbed, and that's all there is to it. Or it can be administered internally."

"Damn," Charlie said, trying for a tone of quiet amazement although he already knew about the Company's interest in venoms. Jamie Vander smiled, pleased to dispense expertise to the infamous Professor.

"Another item in the folder," Kip Culley added. "There's a victim still alive. In a coma, but alive."

"The Little Buddha wanted the Company to provide an expensive respirator to keep the girl breathing," Jamie said. "That's actually how I first heard from him: he wanted us to start contributing hardware."

"We should go look at this wonderful folder," Charlie said.

On the way to Jamie's office they passed down a corridor heavily hung with contemporary paintings. One was a composition of white on white and Charlie, who admired total ambiguity, stopped briefly to inspect it.

They sat around in their sweatclothes as Charlie read the contents of the folder.

He sat near the window in a slant of winter sunlight which threw an odd, dark shadow down that indenture in his forehead; Kip Culley found himself watching the hole—a mean little cavern in the craggy face—and those nicked, beat-up hands which held the folder. Culley had been hot to meet Professor Hazo. There was something in Culley which objected to men of high reputation, and in their presence he always wanted to have his own qualifications noted: expert pistol shot, decorated member of the Service, highest ranking man of his age, all that. But now, watching the old man read through the folder, he kept surprisingly respectful and silent.

"Did you provide that respirator?" Charlie asked, looking up.

"Somebody's sending something," Jamie responded.

"Tell you what I'll do," Charlie offered, slowly closing the folder. "I'll call Peter Foxx and volunteer. That way I'll spare the two of you the grief."

"Perfect," Jamie quickly agreed. "You'll really do that?"

"Just get me my usual contract even though I might be working for Treasury. I don't want to be paid off in rolls of freshly minted pennies."

"Consider it done," Jamie said, and glanced at Kip Culley as if to confirm what a successful arrangement this was.

"I thought you had those final exams at your college," Culley added with mild sarcasm.

"There's always room on my schedule when my country really needs me," Charlie told him.

Later, sitting alone in the locker room downstairs, Charlie made some notes for himself. Writing on his pocket-sized pad, he listed the names of Peter Foxx and Kip Culley: he wanted some data on them both. He already knew everything he needed on Jamie Vander—with whom he had been working for several months.

Then he took a shower, standing under the hot water for fifteen minutes. During this time, he tried to gather his thoughts further, but could only think of Callie.

Impulsive, he decided, as he dressed. Why did I say I'd volunteer?

Because of time, because time is running out, and there are only a few promising assignments. Somewhere in this maze of a building there is a camera capable of taking a photograph of the whole of England and Ireland, a photograph of such magnitude and yet such clarity that, blown up, its smallest sections converted into photographs themselves, one is able to read the license plate numbers on automobiles in, say, Bayswater Road or on one of the bridges spanning the Liffey. Machines were making so many of the clandestine services obsolete. Cameras, electronics, microwaves, lasers: all designed to peel away men's dirty little political and personal secrets. So there were few dark continents remaining, few adventurers needed, and fewer mysteries requiring personal attention. Machines, impersonal tapes, computer printouts. The opportunity for anything with any emotional texture to it was rare; being needed was rarest of all. Time ebbed away, taking one's illusions and one's real accomplishments out to sea.

But if life ordained an assignment: ah, there, I'm confirmed again, I have someplace to go, people to see, real conversations to enter. The nomad always volunteers to travel on.

Bending down to lace his shoes, he cursed his short breath.

I'm also lonely, he admitted. Depressed, at times, with loneliness. And that's too often been the real assignment; for a few crumbs of inside information and for a few brief excitements, a hateful solitude is the penalty. No wife, no friends, no children, not even a bright student out at the college who could be told anything personal or real. Why not go out again and again? I won't end up both lonely and bored, by god, and if I'm going to have nothing permanent, if I'm going to stay in the service of cockbirds, I'll get my kicks.

He stood combing his thinning hair. His teeth, bright with Comet cleanser, shining back at him from the locker room mirror, looked good.

I've got to do more jogging, he told himself. Ten years ago at age fifty I could've sprinted along that river path like a gazelle.

He curled his toes inside his jogging shoes, then relaxed them. The metaphor of the gazelle tripped his thoughts once more; he remembered Africa, the feel of it.

Walking out into the winter sunlight again and over to the parking space where his driver sat waiting in the brown Pontiac, he could feel that distant old land in his bones. The bush. Lions. The wide savannah. A good quarry, pursuit, the catch or kill. Time in that place was just a prelude to eternity, and he always wanted to go back whenever he had the chance.

"Where to?" the driver asked. "The college?"

The voice broke Charlie's reverie.

"Indeed," he answered, sounding professorial, as he switched roles and thoughts once more. As the car moved out of the parking lot, his concentration focused on the opening remarks he would soon make at the morning seminar.

3

Sidney Markham Cash, who was once, in happier times, the police chief of Eureka Springs, Arkansas, sat listening to the sounds of Pennsylvania Avenue below his window, the murmur of the city of Washington beyond that, and the incessant buzz and clack of his secretaries and office machinery just outside the thin door which bore his name. Before him on his desk was a Teletype message from the police commissioner of Lagos, Nigeria, and Sid dreaded having to call the Little Buddha about it. The matter itself was interesting enough: evidence was growing that a murderer was loose in Africa poisoning American businessmen, but Sid disliked the Little Buddha and never wanted to tell him anything.

He took a deep breath. It was never in the usual executive manner that he summoned clerical help. "Veronica!" he yelled. "C'mere! You out there?"

Veronica, who was certainly not a pretty secretary, not even modestly so, but who was shapely and pleasant and happily married for the third time, opened the door and made her appearance. Sid told her what extension to phone over at the Treasury Department.

"I don't want to talk to him myself," he outlined. "Just tell him there's a folder en route. And a memo from me. Then send this over by interoffice mail."

"Are you depressed, Mr. Cash? You look depressed," Veronica said.

"I am always depressed, you know that," Sid said. "It's the snow. I'm not used to the winters up here."

"Didn't it ever snow in Arkansas?" Veronica asked, trying to be sympathetic.

"There is nothing in Arkansas, not even weather," Sid told her. "Which is why I liked it so much. Send the folder."

Veronica returned to her desk, leaving the door open between them, still talking. True melancholy swept over Sid; the office was too confining, the snow awful, the secretary too unattractive, the Little Buddha too demanding, the world too sad. The offices where Interpol conducted its criminal investigations looked as crowded and as ragged as, say, an impoverished insurance office in Little Rock or the cluttered premises of an automobile club in Memphis. Loose file folders and bulging file cabinets were everywhere outside his door; the paths between the typists were growing smaller and smaller, so that a big man like Sid, who weighed over two hundred pounds and who was getting heavy in the hips from sitting around so much, had to turn sideways to walk to the water cooler or the telecommunications console. Flat green and grey paint—leftover wash from the Army and Navy, Sid knew— covered the walls. The floors were sticky with spilled Coke and coffee, and Sid had once spied a stale piece of cinnamon roll under the corner of a desk, a remnant of some stenographer's brunch. In the far office was Jack Hillyard: a fine detective, a brilliant Secret Service career officer, a family man and distinguished criminal scholar, rotting away like a scrap of bureaucratic driftwood. And here was Sid: fifty years old, paunchy, the true cop, wasted, afraid of a thirty-year-old tyrant who wasn't even here in the Justice Department, who was way over at Treasury. Better to be back in Eureka Springs, yes, Veronica, where one can get out on the banks of the White River during weekends and where, otherwise, it's the basic necessities of human weakness and viciousness: feuds, killings, robberies, rapes, and all that makes police work grand.

For a moment, Sid considered that African killer. He conjured up a nice psychopath, or, better yet, a psychopathic communist. For the merest fraction of a second, he dreamt of research in exotic places, inductive reasoning, hot pursuit, and apprehension of the beast with the simple cop from Arkansas victorious. Awards, citations, medals, promotions in rank.

Veronica appeared once more.

"You're to deliver the new information yourself," she informed him.

"Who says so?"

"The man at the extension number."

"Did he have a high little voice?"

"Sort of. And I don't want to depress you more, Mr. Cash, really, but he says to get over there for a lunch conference."

Sidney Markham Cash, second man in command of Interpol, Washington Branch, Justice Department, put his head into his hands. He was the son of a United States Marshall; grandson of a famous sheriff who shot it out with bank robbers during the heyday of Jesse James; he was the wit of the coffee shop at the Crescent Hotel back home; he did not deserve, he felt, the indignities of a desk job nor membership in the Task Force on Terrorism over which the Little Buddha played politics.

"I don't deserve to meet that little bastard on his own ground and suffer through lunch," he told Veronica.

"No sir," she agreed.

"That is a hateful little man, and it's bad being around him," he told her. "But there is one thing worse than all the rest: watching him devour food."

"Take an umbrella," Veronica reminded him. "You'll never get a taxi out there in that blizzard."

Not far from the White House, at the corner of Fourteenth and F Streets, stood the Old Ebbitt Grill, where, on the third floor, back in a corner which was usually reserved for his solitary dining, the Little Buddha waited for Sid Cash. The room was packed. At the other dozen or so tables were newspaper reporters, tourists, a presidential aide, a noted lobbyist, six secretaries, two wives, one mistress, and a delegation from a chain of islands in the mid-Pacific. The Little Buddha preferred dining alone in crowded rooms, or, when possible, keeping company with some associate in the Task Force, which was his obsession and his career apparatus. The Little Buddha, who didn't call himself by that name, whose name was Peter Foxx, waited over a plate of oysters. When Sid Cash arrived late—shivering and irritated—his host would order a second dozen on the half shell and never mention what he had already consumed. The Little Buddha was thirty-two years old and weighed two hundred and twenty pounds; this was not so alarming except that he was very, very short—so much so that no one ever bothered to inquire about that dimension.

Peter Foxx read the menu although he knew well what he planned to order. He also read the brochure on the historic importance of the restaurant: how President William McKinley had lived in the house while still a member of Congress, how Teddy Roosevelt liked to dine there, how the old clock with wooden wheels over the doorway still kept good time.

The old clock put Sid Cash at thirty minutes late.

Then Sid arrived, moving among the luncheon tables like a fullback, head down, charging, struggling to get his overcoat off as he came toward Peter's presence. He bumped the elbow of the lobbyist and caused a spoonful of clam chowder to go astray on the man's lapel. Sid's terrible rush and uneasiness were apparent and Peter computed it immediately: here was another drone who called him the Little Buddha behind his back, who cursed the bureaucracy which had permitted Peter to thrive, but who still remained everyone's obedient and solicitous co-worker. Of course Sid was a good man: a man for whom others like to work, pleasant, dependable to a fault, slightly slow witted, but an excellent organizer. The gentle desk cop.

Peter knew he shouldn't be rude with Sid, but he was.

"Thirty minutes late," he said flatly, as Sid struggled into his chair.

"There's a blizzard outside," Sid grunted, and, nervously, trying to find something to do with his hands, he picked up his fork and began wiping it off with his napkin.

Peter snapped open the menu again. "I'm having the oysters. You might want to try them."

"I want a beer and a bacon burger," Sid decided quickly, not noticing Peter's disapproval.

"Got something for me?" Peter asked, and Sid handed over the folder with that scant narrative of events in Lagos twenty-four hours previously.

Peter opened the folder and began to read its contents. As he read, he filled the silence with a tuneless humming. He also lit a cigarette—

which he would continue to do at every pause in the meal—and flicked its ashes into a neat pile just beside the ashtray.

When the waiter came, Sid Cash took an interest in Peter's precise ordering: the oysters cold, the veal steaming hot, the bread toasted, the salad tossed at the table, please, the rosé chilled, the ashes removed. The Little Buddha had a high-voiced machine-like enunciation. Irritating. He raised his nose when he read the data from the folder. Irritating. His tuneless humming: irritating. The stubby fingers fluttering the cigarette, so that it all resembled a small, restless bird's wing: irritating.

"Good," Peter said, having finished the report. He started reading over at the beginning. "Just what the Task Force needs."

"What task force?"

"Ours," Peter said coldly. "The one that will get you off that desk where you're sitting. Wouldn't you like to go to Africa?"

"Yeah, sure," Sid answered, and he glanced around hoping to see the waiter.

"This makes six in five months. We've got a very mobile killer disposing of American businessmen all over the continent. It's not the usual terrorist scenario. I like it."

"We've got a murderer, but maybe not a terrorist," Sid offered, waving his arm in the air in hopes of attracting the waiter.

"Well, there's no robbery. There doesn't seem to be anything personal. If you read the report I wrote for the Advisory Commission you'll remember our simple definition: violence or the threat of violence employed toward an impersonal end. You want the waiter, Sid?"

"I want my beer. Maybe some coffee, too. I'm freezing."

"You should sip a nice brandy."

Peter was reading the contents of the folder again before Sid could reply. Sid fidgeted, tapped the table, and finally began to study the Little Buddha: a Southerner, same as he was, but a coiffed and polished Vanderbilt man, so another breed altogether. Peter Foxx excelled at languages, the well-turned and modulated phrases, social graces; he looked and acted rich—which he wasn't—and, all in all, Sid disliked him about as much as anyone he had ever known.

When the first food arrived—the oysters and salad—Sid watched some notorious table habits. Here, Sid felt, the true Buddha revealed himself; pretense and grace gave way to a sort of slopping of the hog.

Peter virtually ate with both hands and without utensils as if he might starve, pushing one bite in behind the other, rotating his platter of oysters, sucking, chewing, rotating his salad dish in the same way and plucking out every morsel. In spite of this subconscious display, Peter went on reading; his nose elevated, his eyebrows arched haughtily. When Sid's burger arrived, he ate in silence.

"No more information than this out of St. Cloud?" Peter finally asked.

"Nothing yet. We've run a sort of early computer check looking for poisoners, and we've requested the usual collection of passport names."

"What about the prostitute?"

"Name's Hila De Groot. Amsterdam, as you see there. She was in Zaire, once, with a small police record."

"Is she still in a coma?"

"As far as I know. The military hospital in Lagos is still trying to locate a better respirator, but can't find one."

The Little Buddha attacked his veal marsala. "I've been trying to get that respirator. She might wake up, if she's made it this long," he said, chewing.

"I was thinking about posting a guard, too," Sid said.

"Why?"

"The newspapers announced only two deaths: the oil man's and the colonel's. The killer might decide to go looking for Hila again."

"Good thinking," Peter said, and for the first time Sid felt the slightest tinge of generosity toward his colleague.

The Little Buddha wiped his plate with a piece of toast. He had eaten as if trying to set a speed record.

"I want our special group to go after this one," Peter said. "But we need more data. Get out a blue notice. Post a guard. Do the passport thing and give me any information you collect, but for the time being don't tell the locals in Lagos we have any special interest—just general concern."

"Did you mean what you said about getting me off my desk?" Sid asked.

"Naturally. There's nobody else over at Justice I'd want."

"Thanks," Sid allowed himself to say.

"You're the best of a bad lot, if you want my opinion, Sid, and I hope you don't take that wrong. Interpol's nothing to me. Just cops on the phone, cops writing letters and sending fingerprints here and there. What's more, the only reason it was taken out of the Treasury Department and sent back over to Justice was because Justice had some spare offices and idle hands."

Sid stared into his coffee cup. The Little Buddha could be hated most, he decided, for his accuracies.

"Not you, of course. You're the only real cop near the top of the pile," the Little Buddha went on. "And you have a quality I don't: people like you and want to do whatever you suggest. If I get our little group together, you'll be important for that. That's why I tapped you several weeks ago to send me anything that smelled like terrorist activity."

Such stark and bold ambition, Sid felt as he listened. A few short years ago Peter Foxx had been—what? —a VISTA worker for a minor campaign aide to some congressman. But after the Munich massacre and a few unnerving hijackings, Peter had managed to become part of a committee inside a commission inside an agency. Terrorism entered the active vocabulary of Washington, and Peter Foxx became one of its spokesmen, saying the word over and over, writing memos and documents on the subject, insinuating himself, and becoming a self-styled expert. Such a little swine. The face and voice and eating habits of Porky Pig. But if things fell right, he might create his own private sty—even in such tight money times when there were few appropriations for new agencies.

Sid took a deep breath and said, "I'll keep an update on the file and phone Lagos about posting that guard. You're right. I want to get off my desk and into something interesting if I can."

"Of course you do," the Little Buddha told him, and he finished off his glass of wine with a slurp.

On the way down the rickety stairs of the Old Ebbitt Grill, the Little Buddha put on his cashmere overcoat with its fur-lined collar. He looked like a miniature prince, and the waiters and the maître d' who stood near the end of the mahogany bar greeted him warmly. Sid caught a glimpse of destiny: he himself would trudge off into the blizzard, he knew, and never find a taxi; he would probably lose his scarf, the contents of the precious folder would blow away, the phone lines to

Lagos wouldn't work, the Teletype would falter, the floors of his office would reek with candy and cinnamon rolls, his life would go its slobby way. But Peter Foxx would grow serene as the Little Buddha, and his dream of a private task force would thrive; he would ride in the black limousines of happy fate, never spilling his veal marsala on his fur-lined collar, and he would convert his small margins of power into commissions, permanent agencies, even whole departments of government.

"Good of you to come to lunch," Peter said, offering Sid a gloved hand to shake.

"Loved it," Sid managed.

They were standing in the cramped double doorway of the grill. Outside, wind howled around the building, and all the old dirty drifts of snow had turned white once more.

"Cobra poison is such an unbelievable weapon, isn't it?" the Little Buddha asked, looking out. Traffic slowed in the streets.

"It's how we'll catch him, if we get the chance to chase him," Sid said, feeling chilled already.

"I've thought of that," said the Little Buddha. "Trace the source of supply. Because venom is big business in Africa, isn't it, with its patterns of trade all set? So we just run it down."

"Maybe," Sid answered. "Unless the sonavabitch has his own snake."

4

In Africa there is that sudden silence which comes at twilight, as if nature has gone into a trance. Then night begins with all its noises: the nocturnal insects, the call of hyrax, the keening of jackals, the deep groans of the big cats, and the murmurs of the trees in the forests and the grasses on the savannah.

At this time each day he rose from his work in the laboratory and went out into the cool twilight of the screened-in-porch. He liked to stroll around the porch, which encircled the stone, whitewashed building, so that he could view the compound in every direction: the great thorn tree, the stone walls, the arching bridge over to the main house, the pods where the cobras slept. In the distance, beyond the compound, lay the hills. He walked slowly around the porch, taking it all in, and as usual before he had made two full circles Wemba, the housekeeper, appeared on the bridge bringing a glass of iced tea from the kitchen of the main house.

On this particular evening Wemba paused in the middle of the bridge to admire the black mamba, Kali, who stood poised and ready beneath the thorn tree. The master paused, too, and they both watched the snake—which had grown, now, to about twelve feet in length. In the past, Wemba would often go into the yard of the compound, draw water from the well for the snakes, walk barefoot past the cone-shaped pods under which the snakes coiled, and even handle the creatures with a

45

stick—in the way his uncle taught him—but no more. The mamba had grown too fierce. No corner of the yard was safe. If either Wemba or the master exposed himself, Kali would dash out and try to strike. Sometimes Kali would get a running start and strike at the underside of the bridge beneath Wemba's feet as the servant came over from the main house. At times, it would try to climb the high walls—always falling back into the yard off the smooth inner surface. Or it would slither up into the thorn tree, find a protruding limb, then try to swing itself toward the top of a wall nearby. But it couldn't escape, so became more furious and more exciting as the weeks passed.

"Look at him!" Wemba called from the bridge, seeing that his master was watching, too. "You know what he wants? He wants me to fall off, so he can have a nice meal! And I am his friend—who gave him a fat pig only the last fortnight!"

They stood watching the snake for several minutes. It stood erect, balanced on a short coil of tail, raising itself seven feet high, swaying slightly, as it watched Wemba on the bridge. Kali could move across the yard in an instant. They reckoned its speed at about fifteen miles an hour, which meant that out in the bush it could finally run a man down—man being, as always, the slowest animal anywhere.

Wemba made his way off the bridge, stepping onto the upper verandah where the bridge joined the lab. The mamba made a run, but pulled up short, still erect and watching. Then Wemba made his way down inside the house to the porch, passing the big room filled with bright bottles and the door to the bedroom with the canopied bed, draped in mosquito netting, where the master's father, the old doctor, slept in his long, undisturbed coma.

"How is the doctor?" Wemba asked, smiling, as he served his master the iced tea.

"My father's fine, thank you, Wemba," the master answered, still standing there watching the mamba from the protection of the porch.

This courteous exchange was repeated daily when the master was in residence, when he wasn't making one of his frequent trips.

The mamba moved back to the thorn tree as if taking up a sentry position, its head still raised high.

"It wants me to cross the bridge again," Wemba said. "It knows I don't stay out here at the lab for long."

"You think it has that sort of intelligence?"

"Oh, master, yes, no doubt of it!"

"Knows your habits and mine?"

"A great snake like that has powers. It understands your father's long sleep inside the house, surely, and knows many things!"

Wemba was well over sixty now, but strong as wire and as efficient around the estate as ever. Every day he cleaned. When the master was home, he fixed simple meals: chicken dishes, curries, stews. He cared for the sleeping doctor—his old, beloved master—with the same care he had given in the old days. And there was nothing particularly strange to Wemba in their care of the old man in the coma: long ago the doctor had isolated himself from everyone in Nairobi, from the curiosity seekers, from everybody except his son. The other settlers of the region were dead and gone. No one knew if the doctor was even dead or alive. There was no one to care. In life, he had been a recluse until neither he nor the world belonged to each other anymore, so his coma was just an extension of his last years: a magnificent solitude, a nearly mystical loneliness.

The master, smiling, returned his empty glass to Wemba's tray.

"Will you sleep out here again tonight or in the main house?" Wemba asked.

"There are things to do here," the master answered. "And in a few days, Wemba, I'll be going away again. Perhaps for as long as a week. In the meantime—maybe tomorrow—I'll go into town. Would you like to go, too?"

"No, I'll stay with the doctor."

This was a courtesy, too. Wemba was always offered a trip into Nairobi, but never went. Not that the sleeping old man needed constant care. Wemba just preferred everyday life on the estate to the silliness of cities, so he kept his own simple hours and days. And, also, in some curious way he felt that he was in the service of important forces. The mamba, Wemba truly believed, was a fierce and meaningful presence. The master had his great duty nowadays, a duty which required—strange and distant though it was—the skill and bravery of the warrior. And the father even in his wonderful sleep still ruled them all.

When Wemba crossed the bridge again, leaving the compound and returning to the main house of the estate, the snake stayed in its place beneath the thorn tree. Kali the mamba had shifted its attention to the slender, dark figure of the man on the porch.

The master's name was Quentin Clare. He was the heir to the life

47

created and left by his father, the biologist, farmer, schoolmaster, hunter, and conservationist William Clare; the estate was his now and so was the solitude; many of the eccentricities were his; the continent was in his odd keeping; some of the silence and anger were his; and the madness, too, if it was that, belonged now to him.

He began to circle the porch, slowly, once more. As he did so, the mamba edged away from the thorn tree and followed—circling the outside of the laboratory, keeping pace. A breeze was up.

Quentin passed the window of the bedroom where his father's steady breathing could be heard. The window was open onto the porch, so the breeze took the curtains in gentle waves and stirred the mosquito netting which shrouded the bed in white. It was a lofty, imposing bed which filled a small room: elevated in its whiteness with the old man— himself large and awesome—laying inside it in vague outline like an ambiguous object in a shrine.

A spiral of wind blew through the yard, so there was a momentary pirouette of sand. The mamba paid it no attention as it continued to watch Quentin's slow progress inside the porch screening.

Quentin was thinking of his mother, Mary Horne Clare. She had been gone twenty-five years—since those days when Quentin's father hunted every month. They had gone up on the northern frontier again that year in spite of the active presence of Mau Mau; a half-dozen men including Quentin and Bill Clare had set up camp on a scrubby patch of land west of Lake Rudolph toward the South Sudan. There, on the second day of the hunt young Quentin, who was never a steady shot, faced the charge of a water buffalo as his father backed him up. Quentin's first shot struck the thick horn which was lowered in the charge. Even so, he stood his ground and fired again. The second shot caught the beast on the nose, jerking its head aside for an instant, but failing to slow its rush. The doctor then opened fire. His first shot penetrated the body, but the buffalo swerved, staggered and came on. By the time Bill Clare's last shot was delivered, the buffalo was on them. Quentin dived to one side. As the big animal knocked the doctor down and passed over him, Bill Clare managed to fire from underneath it, upwards through the stomach and backbone, killing it. By this time, though, it had raked his shoulder and had broken his ankle.

Against his protests, Bill Clare was admitted to the hospital in

Nairobi, where Quentin and his mother visited for the week of his stay. At the same time the hospital itself was filled with a curious—and ironic—malady. A small American firm in the city, a manufacturer of radio parts, had been the place where a new strain of influenza had · started; most of its forty employees had come down with fever, a generally mild attack, and the virus—a weak, yet annoying variety brought over by some American executive—spread through the Karen and Langata suburbs of the city.

By the end of the week Quentin's mother had the fever, but continued to drive back and forth from the estate visiting Bill Clare. The day after the doctor was released from the hospital, she sat down in a rocking chair which occupied a corner of the kitchen. Her face was illumined by a shaft of colored light which filtered through the stained glass panels of the door. She was listening to Quentin pick out a new melody on the piano when she sat back, closed her eyes, and died.

Wemba, who found her, talked to her for some minutes before he realized that her breathing had stopped. Then he sat down on the floor at her feet and began to wail.

She had been the daughter of a retired British army officer and a woman of mixed Asian blood—mostly Indian. Since it hadn't been a proper marriage for the officer, his prospects in Nairobi never materialized and the family suffered all of Kenya's varied prejudices. Young Mary Horne, even more beautiful than her mother, yet an outsider, had plans to live in Europe or America in her teen years. But Dr. Bill Clare, an outsider himself, by fact and by choice, settled the impropriety of her parents by marrying her, and, curiously, as two social wrongs frequently make a right in white Africa, Mary and Bill Clare were acceptable. The daughter had married an American with credentials (a titled biological researcher), money (a substantial and undetermined sum), and eccentricities (cobras). That he had nothing to do with the British who sipped sherry and pale ale on the porch of the old Norfolk Hotel seemed to make him even more acceptable. He was a silent, brooding sort—and rude. And for those who had treated Mary and her parents rudely, rudeness was a language they understood.

The William Clares, then, built the estate out beyond the hills, that odd place with the tiled-roof manor house and the separate compound set off by high walls containing the laboratory. They bought an old Ford lorry, two oxen, hunting rifles, chemicals, a piano, the most expensive ivory chess set ever sold at the Biashara Street market, hundreds of books for the estate library, the best clothes for Mary, goats for their servants, and riding horses. The Nairobi merchants loved them. They also had two special houseboys: Dobo, who handled the snakes, and his nephew Wemba. Dr. Bill Clare paid the natives to bring him cobras for the first two years. One fearlessly ignorant Masai brought a black-necked specimen to the front door of the manor house and stood there holding it in his bare hands while asking to be paid; when old Dobo came back with the promised money the snake spat venom in his face—luckily missing his eyes.

Having made friends with many members of the neighboring tribes by buying cobras from them in those first years, the doctor began holding classes at a special meeting place in a grove of thorn and acacia trees by a nearby stream. He taught biology, the English language, and hygiene. In order to attract students, he brought quantities of palm wine and homemade beer to his lectures; the natives, who were wonderfully mannered, endeavored to stay sober until Dr. Bill had finished speaking. Over the years, his lectures grew shorter and his reputation large.

Quentin was born. In his early years he showed aptitudes for languages and music. The doctor took up farming with little success because of constant drouths. He took up hunting. He entered a chess tournament in Capetown, taking his wife and son on the excursion. Then, before his wife's death finally sealed him off from all activity and all acquaintances, the doctor began to withdraw; something drove him down into himself. He didn't turn to alcohol or any other isolating vice. He offered no explanations. But the classes beside the stream ended. Except to go out hunting occasionally—and he hunted without much communication to those who went with him—he seldom emerged from the laboratory compound. His contacts became limited to his servants and his son, but these became few, too, and he usually only asked for services or errands.

By the time of Mary's death the Clares were already fiercely isolated from one another, but Quentin, in time, would choose to remember that his parents were very close, very loving, and that his mother's death was what set his father apart.

Standing there on the porch outside his father's window, this was exactly what he remembered. Little matter that it wasn't true.

He had his mother's looks: dark skin, the same thin nose and straight lips. Only the eyes were different, perhaps favoring his father's.

The last twilight had gone, leaving the sky a dark indigo. His thoughts of his mother—which were rare, now—passed away. She seemed to be some long-lost distant part of this place, this land, and his and the doctor's odd, solitary myth and mission.

Quentin turned and moved along the porch once more. As he did, he detected the shadow of Kali, still following in the yard.

He strolled by the windows to the lab. Walking on, he began to undress for the night; his clothes fell behind him, strewn along one side of the porch so that he walked naked, the evening breeze cooling his skin.

In the beginning, he remembered, he fought with his father. At first he seemed to be at war with his father, then with himself. And now: he was at war with all the businessmen and traders who had invaded his domain and, as much as possible, with the century itself. Each war was growing more intense than the last. And each, he assumed, would be lost. Each would claim part of him, he supposed, which he would never recover, and this last larger war would probably take his life, he knew, but by that time his life would be worthless to him, for he would only be a killer and a naked barbarian like the others.

As he passed through the door leading into his sitting room, a loud noise sounded behind his back. Turning around, he saw the large dent in the wire screen of the porch. For a moment he couldn't think. Then he knew: Kali had sprung at the screen—perhaps his shadow on it—and had attacked it.

Quentin spoke softly into the darkness of the yard. "You're angry you can't get at me, aren't you?" He smiled, enjoying the prospect of an enemy out there.

The sitting room featured a large desk, books, a narrow couch, a chess table with all the pieces set and ready at the board, and a thick rug where Quentin slept—seldom for more than three hours at a time. On the desk, lying open to his last entry, was his diary. Beside it were the

51

pouches filled with gems—including the big white diamond he had shown to his victims in Lagos. His stack of current readings rose from the floor beside his chair. In a ragged pile beside those lay an assortment of company newsletters and brochures.

The greater part of his desktop was covered with materials for the forgeries: inks, rubber stamps, drawing pens, photographs, and dozens of passports, visas, licenses, documents, and identity papers. All these he had acquired—ready to be altered—during years of preparation. The forgeries themselves were neither clever nor skilled. Some materials had actually been reproduced on an outmoded Xerox machine at a Nairobi pharmacy. Usually, Quentin tore out sections of pages from various passports, then stapled them in new arrangements, manufacturing originals. Even so, his handiwork had never been questioned. Customs officials, policemen, and soldiers, he had discovered, had always looked into his suspicious eyes, but had seldom inspected his papers closely. All things depended on that continuing to be so.

A chill came over him, so he drew a bathrobe around his shoulders. He picked out a few almonds from a tin inside an open drawer.

His gaze went through the open doorway. That wonderful dent out there on the porch screen: he wished that his father could be called from his bed, that he could come down the hallway and go out onto the porch to see what Kali had done.

Smiling at this, he padded down the hallway to his father's room. The nightly check. All the same: the immensity of the bed, the whiteness, the sweet odor, the steady breathing.

When he returned to the sitting room, he went over to the chess table and studied the board. Players in place, waiting.

Time to change travelling names, he decided suddenly. In the past months he had used colors: Mr. Blue, White, Gray, Black, Green, Brown. Time now to alter the pattern like an alert grandmaster in the event that someone—some unusually intelligent policeman, if ever there was such a person—might be waiting at the next stop.

I'll use chess names for awhile, he told himself. Mr. Knight, King, Castle, Bishop. Let them study a new pattern—if, indeed, they can study anything; if, indeed, they can separate small details from major events or trifles from revolutions.

5

Sid Cash soon worked on the project out of curiosity. It certainly wasn't because of the Little Buddha and his proposed Task Force—which was all a bureaucratic pipe dream, as far as Sid was concerned. And Sid didn't really believe he would get off his desk job for an assignment in Africa, a place he wanted badly to see. He had plenty to do, too, and should have ignored his curiosity, but the whole matter was overwhelming: true, irresistible intrigue.

He sat in an armchair—cotton stuffing coming out of its cushions—in the noisy, littered den of his suburban house in Maryland. In his lap was the folder. It was Saturday afternoon, toward suppertime, and as he read and made notes, he tried to light an old pipe which he seldom smoked; the tobacco, older than the pipe, wouldn't stay lit, and he dribbled pieces of it into the folder. His smallest and prettiest child, Sally, age six, screamed obscenities in the back yard. An oddball sports show was on television. His wife was calling from the kitchen, "Do you want to eat later when the kids are in bed or do you want to eat now? Just say!"

Sid's estimate now seemed confirmed that there had been six killings so far. Six American businessmen, all highly ranked in their separate companies, had met peculiar deaths in a period of five months in half a dozen cities: Durban, Kinshasa, Monrovia, Algiers, Lusaka, and Lagos.

There was some doubt about the specific substance which had poisoned them, but it was probably cobra venom because they had lapsed into the familiar coma associated with that neurotoxin. One executive had died of a kidney malfunction and another of recurring heart attacks, but in each case there had been a collapse—at least from available descriptions and medical reports—of the entire central nervous system.

"Just tell me," his wife insisted, standing over him.

"Later," he answered.

"I'll have to heat up the food later," she argued, although she preferred that arrangement herself. She always liked it when the children were in bed, the house was quiet, and they ate alone. For a moment she stood staring at the back of his head where his hair thinned.

Sid flipped a page of the folder.

She sighed and went back to her bright yellow kitchen.

There was other data. A hotel clerk and a chauffeur in Lagos had supplied a description and name. Mr. Blue: dark-skinned, slender, perhaps forty years old, perhaps a gem merchant, probably South African.

A dominant question: the single killer theory. Sid found himself leaning toward the notion that this was a planned terrorist activity, perhaps orchestrated by a hostile government. But, if so, why these businessmen? He sat there pondering. Then he turned another page, arriving at the computer print-outs he had ordered.

The FBI did nice computer work. Crisp pages of print-outs, neat, readable, official looking. They were a meddlesome, snobbish, paranoid bunch and about as effective as detectives, Sid felt, as a gaggle of army colonels running around in circles saluting each other, but their labs and computers worked well—and they probably had no pieces of stale cinnamon roll anywhere under the corners of their desks.

His finger traced over the data. Soon after the Lagos murders he had acquired a list of airline passenger names from there and every other city where such killings had occurred. Focusing on dates around the time of the crimes, he had processed the list—looking for any consistency which might prove helpful and especially for any recurring name. The computer—bless it—had found something.

He fumbled with the folder, his pipe, and the dry tobacco as he got up, passed through the yellow kitchen, arrived at the telephone in the hallway. He remembered the Little Buddha's extension number over at Treasury precisely because he had tried to forget it. As he dialed the number, Sally, his lovely small one, stomped through the hall.

"Goddamned bitch!" she yelled, clenching her fists. Her father paid her no attention. He was thinking of Peter Foxx sitting alone in his office on Saturday; it was another work break between a fancy lunch and an extravagent dinner, Sid surmised, when the Little Buddha would be shuffling papers and dreaming of his future as a leader of men. He knew he would find him there, all the secretaries gone, answering his own phone, and this was exactly what happened.

"You've got something for me, haven't you?" the Little Buddha said as soon as greetings were exchanged. His voice was tinged with excitement and genuine warmth for his colleague.

"Yeah. I ran some airline passenger data through the Bureau's computer and got an interesting thing. In those cities where we've had killings we've also had Mr. Brown, Mr. Green, Mr. White, Mr. Black, Mr. Gray and Mr. Blue."

"Nothing coincidental in that?" the high-pitched telephone voice inquired.

"No way we're going to get the entire rainbow like that," Sid told him.

"Then we can say we've found a pattern?"

"Sure, we can say we're hot on the guy's tail. We can say any damned thing we want to."

Silence at the other end of the phone. Peter Foxx was assessing the sarcasm. Then, after a moment: "I've put in for funding, Sid. We have a good chance. There are nine different groups of so-called terrorist experts around Washington, but a little scrap of information like this could do it for us. I appreciate the call."

"Just keep me in mind," Sid said.

"You know a professor by the name of Charles Hazo?" the Little Buddha wanted to know.

"Heard the name. A free-lance expert, right?"

"He works out of the African desk at Langley. No detective experience, but he knows what you don't. I'll be in charge of the whole operation, of course, then there will be you and the Professor. I have some other names. There will be followers and leaders. Consider yourself a leader."

"Thanks," Sid answered. He imagined the walls of the Little Buddha's office covered with organizational charts.

They talked about the single killer theory. Sid went over his speculations that such mobility on the killer's part suggested financing, organization, and perhaps hidden political motivation. The Little Buddha disagreed.

"I've studied the file on the victims," Peter Foxx explained. "This last one was rather important at Ermco. The others—well, not key executives. I see a random intelligence at work. And some luck. And some clumsiness."

Not too damned clumsy, Sid Cash wanted to say. Yet he admired the Little Buddha's point.

"Your airline passenger data shows real initiative," the high-pitched voice said. "I appreciate it."

"Just regular cop work," Sid offered. "What's the rainy season in Africa? I don't especially want to go over during the rainy season."

"There are different rainy seasons all over the continent. And sometimes it rains in the dry season. Even in the deserts." This sounded so incongruous and improbable that Sid realized that the Little Buddha must have been doing homework.

They said goodbye, and afterward Sid felt fine. If he wouldn't be the team leader, he would at least be included. Already he considered himself on the case, and the realization gave him a smile.

After the phone call, Peter Foxx sat thinking in his office. The damp basement atmosphere chilled him, but he preferred the chill; in hot weather he sweated and grew nervous, so his mental processes slowed. His thoughts, now, were much like Sid's: he needed a stroke of fortune, preferably something dramatic, if ever he hoped to emerge from these basement offices.

The Treasury Building was across the street from the White House. Peter could watch the President come and go. Dignitaries entered the great wrought iron gate across the way, their black limousines shining; tourists and protesters and government employees circled by; all the world's secrets travelled in the street outside. But the Treasury

Building was, literally, a hole: there were more than five floors under-
ground, most of them long out of use, including the old vaults where,
once, the nation's gold—or the largest part of it—was stored. Peter often
had the sensation that he was sinking into the vaults, as if a cavernous past
swallowed him up, as if the whole anachronistic building with its stale
banking mentality had turned into a sinking ship carrying him down.
Once in some odd, distant past there were G-men in these halls; there
were intrigues and plots and the air of excitement. But now except for the
few souls in the Bureau of Alcohol, Tobacco, and Firearms—very unlike
G-men, real or imagined—the occupants of the building made dullness a
religion. They even ate dull food for lunch: paper sacks with dry
sandwiches, greasy plate lunches down at Walgreen's, or plastic candies
from the vending machines. Dull and unimaginative.

Peter sat before a stack of heavy books, copies of his masterwork
entitled *Disorders and Terrorism: A Report from the National Advisory
Task Force.* It bore the names of several administrators, but he had sifted
the research, written it, and placed it in every agency in the city. Clearly,
he felt, if anyone could read, if anyone wanted to know, the document
established his complete authority on the subject. When published a year
ago, the document—a magnificent 661 pages in length—promised to get
him out of the basement. But international terrorism had waned. The
plane hijackers had been rebuffed by new, capable anti-terrorist military
units; the Israelis had discouraged the PLO; most Latin American terror-
ists were just lonely, crazy, inept kidnappers; the West Germans had
handled their own problems; and in Italy the Red Brigade was a disor-
ganization of winos, Mafia types, oversexed romantics, and political
maniacs, in Peter's opinion, who could think of nothing more devilish
than blowing off a few kneecaps.

But this fellow in Africa: something else. Peter hated the thought
that the murders had been conceived and dispatched by an agency
somewhere. He wanted a single adversary.

Peter Foxx walked across Lafayette Square.

A cool, sobering evening. Early April. The slight odor of the
earth—or did he recall that smell as part of all the old, lost sensations of
his days in Nashville, his days as a student and, later, as a teacher, when
his life and career were so poignantly empty? He had been, he recalled, a
kind of robot: good grades, straight clothes, brittle conversations with

conventional friends, proper moments spread out against a backdrop of endless autumns. Couples had strolled beneath those fragrant Belle Meade trees; on Saturday afternoons, sometimes, he had looked up from his reading to hear the sound, far off, of a cheering football crowd; time had held him prisoner. He was a nobody—inside himself and in the world. Educated, groomed, ready—but for what? Once he entered the side-arenas of politics, he still waited. He worked for a Tennessee congressman, but indifferently: efficient and vague. Then he came to Washington, found his substrata, wrote his heavy study, and waited further.

But no more. Emotion was gathering, the first deep feeling of his life. Like a first sexual experience, he knew and understood that a moment of union was at hand.

Already, there were signs of change in him. He had lately begun to write poetry. There in the dining room of the Hay-Adams, waiters buzzing around, the rattle of silverware consoling him, he scratched out a few lines between courses. Tonight's poem was imagistic and descriptive. Peter liked to think that its emotional strength was subdued and controlled, as once, so he had heard, good poems managed to be. Its subject was a place he had never actually seen, a wide plain in Africa roamed over by beasts, a thin line of mysterious hills in the distance, an exotic arid setting where all things were prey to all others.

A poor poem, he would later decide. But, because of the alias of the man in Lagos, his poem written at dinner that night bore the title which would later be given to the project: "Savannah Blue."

6

For six days the tall, leathery Oklahoman had stayed at Mena House out toward the Giza pyramids, but today he was moving back into Cairo proper and the Nile Hilton. His move aroused notice: he tipped heavily and often, he was an unusually well-known guest whose name appeared frequently in the *Herald-Tribune* as well as several Arabic newspapers, and everyone liked him. He was Herman Carr: rancher, gentleman, diplomat, and former advisor to Lyndon Johnson and Jimmy Carter.

"I've learned how to confuse and confound world leaders," he once told a news conference. "Just tell them the truth." Such homespun opinions, drawled out with a grin, gave Herman Carr a constant advantage with the press; reporters invariably quoted him.

When he first arrived in Cairo, he was invited to dine on a Nile sailboat with Egypt's president. They talked about their children and families, mostly, in that long, soft dusk of the Egyptian springtime. He had recently lost his wife to a long struggle with cancer, but Herman told everyone that Egypt revived him. He loved the heat, he said, and the Arab dishes and the ruins and the long sunsets. He said what everyone wanted to hear—his hosts, reporters, the Embassy officials who swarmed around him—and he meant it. From the sailboat that first evening Herman Carr's laughter had carried across those ancient Nile waters; his presence was noted everywhere and appreciated.

On a Saturday morning, one week after his arrival, he stepped out of his hotel and walked into the Musky Bazaar, that crowded market filled with loud haggling and the same, endless display of merchandise: bolts of cloth, camel saddles, hookahs, rugs, brass pieces, scarabs, and alabasters. Merchants tugged at his sleeves and yelled in his ears, but he remained good humored. A frail Arab child sold him a warm Coca-Cola, overcharging him by three prices, but Herman Carr seemed to enjoy the transaction, then carried the bottle with him everywhere he went.

At a jewelry shop he stopped to buy something for a favorite daughter-in-law back home in Tulsa. There he fell into a conversation about scarabs with the merchant who wore thick, impenetrable bifocals and another customer of the shop, a dark, handsome foreigner who wore an inexpensive—but new—seersucker suit.

"No, no, there have been live beetles turned into scarabs. But the true scarab is usually stone or ceramic. This was true even in the time of the Pharaohs!" the merchant announced.

"I thought they put jewels on real beetles," Herman Carr said.

"That's been done," the stranger put in. "They cover them with various sorts of lacquer."

Herman Carr held up one of the more expensive scarabs and inspected it. "Then they used to set jewels around the bug and wear 'em on gold chains, right?" he asked.

"Your daughter-in-law would love that one," the merchant said, peering over his thick rims and not answering Herman Carr's question.

"If these bring luck, she does need it," the big rancher drawled. "She is a sweet girl, but clumsy. Never seen anything like it."

"All the ancients believed in the magic of gems," the stranger said, and for the first time Herman Carr, who admired men who spoke up with information, turned to get a look at the other occupant of the shop. "The Pharaohs had their cartouches. And wore amulets. They thought that beneficial sun's rays might be transferred into the body of the wearer."

"The Chinese believed in magic jewels," Herman Carr added, remembering a little himself.

"And the Hindus," Quentin said, smiling. "And the Romans—who thought that, say, jade had the power to protect the wearer from the evil eye."

"Jade! The Scorpio stone!" the merchant put in, hoping that all this knowledge would result in enthusiasm for a sale.

Herman Carr, outgoing as usual, introduced himself to Quentin. They failed to shake hands, though for a moment Quentin sensed that the big rancher had the impulse to do so. Instead, they stood in the little shop—flags of colored cloth draped overhead—as Quentin spoke of the neshem stone in *The Book of the Dead* and how stones used for healing and good luck were often passed along through generations of families.

"You're English, are you?" Herman Carr asked, smiling.

"No, no, from Johannesburg," Quentin assured him.

"Well, you're an erudite fellow," Herman told him. "Won't you come have one of those little coffees with me?"

"Sorry I can't," Quentin answered politely. "Perhaps later."

"Are you staying at the Hilton?"

"Yes, the same."

"Then maybe we can have a drink later on."

"I'll look forward to it," Quentin said, and they nodded their goodbyes.

Turning back to the merchant, Herman Carr bought a dozen scarabs, some of the most expensive in the whole bazaar—which, later, would be remembered.

That afternoon the rancher joined a group of acquaintances who worked in the consular services for a long lunch at the Khumais; they sat on embroidered hassocks listening to lute players, and although Herman tried some of the broiled pigeon he wasn't particularly hungry. Instead, for the first time since his arrival in Egypt he was growing tired and began thinking about one of his afternoon naps. After a glass of wine, he started making excuses to get away.

An old acquaintance, Bonny Allen, a former basketball player at the University of Oklahoma who had become, in turn, an amateur archaeologist, a wealthy exporter, and, finally, a serious patron for University of Chicago scholars at Luxor and in Cairo, sat beside Herman Carr at the lunch. His opinion—strongly stated, later—was that Herman was especially tired and on the verge of nervous collapse.

By mid-afternoon Herman Carr left Khumais in the company of Allen. They walked back to the hotel in the heat.

"Are you going to keep travelling around for a while?" Allen asked him.

"I thought I was," Carr told him. "But now I don't know. I've seen the pyramids at last. Wanted to do that all my life. Now, I think maybe I'll just sit and watch the sun go down."

Bonny Allen touched his old acquaintance on the shoulder. They had much in common: they had watched a lot of Sooner games, they were men of the world, they understood straight talk.

"Screw that," Allen told him. "You got lots of juice yet. There were thirty dynasties in Egypt, and I know I got at least that many in me."

Herman Carr was laughing at this when they entered the Hilton and parted each other's company in the lobby.

At the message desk he picked up a wire from his ranch foreman, a man who had agreed to keep in touch about matters at home and whose telegrams were grammatical tangles. Today's communication especially amused Herman Carr, so that he was still laughing as he crossed the lobby to the elevators.

Just as his elevator door closed, the rancher saw a shoulder edge it open again. The articulate stranger from the shop in the bazaar entered the elevator with him and together, alone, they started up.

"Hey, how are ya?" Herman Carr said in greeting, looking up from the telegram. "You find anything you wanted to buy at the bazaar?"

"Just this," Quentin Clare said, holding out his hand.

The ring on his finger was an enormous topaz set in a unique design, so that Herman Carr, struck by its originality, still wanting to be friendly, still mindful of jewelry because of his own purchases that afternoon, bent toward it with genuine interest.

At that moment a stream of liquid hit his eyes and face.

He was immediately blinded.

Staggering back against the rear wall of the elevator, the big man shoved his fists into his burning eye sockets. Even as he did so, his knees gave way.

The mixture in the ring was Quentin's most powerful concentrate to date. He had to be careful, in fact, so that none of it spilled or dripped on his own bare hand; as a precaution against this he had applied a coat of clear varnish to his fingers and the top of his hand, leaving the thumb free to press a release mechanism. But the ring was well designed and deadly accurate; its venom spewed out six or seven feet, about the distance a grown ringhals cobra could spit venom from its fangs. The concentrate itself contained a phosphate-buffered gelatin and a highly absorbent agent which instantly penetrated the skin.

"Now, then, now," Herman Carr said. "Now, now," he went on, as if he might be softly comforting someone else.

Sitting in the corner of the elevator, he was dead by the time he reached the sixth floor. There, Quentin Clare emerged—sending the elevator on up before taking the stairway back to the lobby. As he descended, Quentin got the ring off his finger, slipping it into a plastic bag which he thrust into his coat pocket.

His quickest, deadliest kill. The empty elevator had provided him the opportunity; his impulse to act had again been right.

Then he was loose in the city once more.

Beyond the hotel district the streets of Cairo turned into lanes, then the lanes became narrower, so that the houses and doorways, eventually, were no longer numbered. Soon the asphalt ended and the paths became the uneven surfaces of rock and the ancient mud with its peculiar smell. One entered a maze of plaster buildings filled with human odors: strong coffee, glue, urine, tobacco, cabbage. There, inside the maze, away from the obvious hotels, again, he had found a place to stay. When he reached his destination, he had changed clothing; the seersucker suit had been deposited in a trash bin at a public urinal, and he looked like a laborer in khaki shirt and trousers.

The house in the southwest quadrant bore a simple sign in English and Arabic: Room to Let. The proprietress had been put there by her sons, and the room served as her only means of support; since few came to rent, Quentin was regarded as charitable by her neighbors. She set out a small carafe of wine for him in the evenings and, now, as he arrived for the final time, they exchanged the full ritual of greetings.

"There is no god but Allah!" she exclaimed, patting her heart and nodding her head like a spastic.

"Mohammed is the Apostle of God!"

"Bless be the Prophet!"

"Peace be upon him!"

Afterward, he went up to the roof. Within two hours he planned to be back at the airport with his meager bundle of clothing and an American passport and papers indicating that he was a simple roustabout en route to Damascus. Such oil field workers came and went with regularity, often riding first class in their soiled dungarees and bandanas.

The roof gave him a view of the city. He could see the hotel and count the floors—four, five, up to the fatal sixth.

The minarets. The great mosque. The university quarter.

Cairo wasn't an Arab city, he felt, because Arabs weren't truly cosmopolitan. It was a cancer growing on the sand. Tonight after dark its patrols would be out on the streets looking for the sick and dying, picking them up in wooden carts and taking them to lorries. The stench of the century hovered everywhere. These catastrophes—cities—were the world's sores; in the desert, beyond, men stood out like monoliths—tall and important. The very isolation of that vast space gave them a sense of themselves while, at the same time, humbling them before the ferocity of nature, for they were also just one more grain of sand, less by far than a dune, less than the sun which burned them down into nothingness. But the desert tribes, those bedouin gypsies wandering around in their poetic way, were out there listening, as if they could hear the grinding wheel of civilization which would chew them up. And of course it would, too: the cities grew, the sewers widened.

At sundown as the amplified voice of the muezzin called everyone to prayer above the noise of the traffic, Quentin removed the ring from its container and aimed it toward the dirty rooftop at his feet. Empty.

Herman Carr had perhaps been a good man. But he had long been in the service of business and material politics, so that Quentin had wanted to say to him, even as he killed him, something wildly intelligent; think of me, he had wanted to say, as an extreme social critic. And think on this: in a truly corrupt and evil society only the criminal is moral.

In his small, hot room Quentin rolled his belongings into a bundle. Having washed out the ring, he put it back on his finger. There were few personal items and nothing to arouse suspicion, just the miniature chess set, the diary, and the usual personal papers, which, if closely scrutinized, might prove to be hazards.

He ate a few almonds and went downstairs to say goodbye to his hostess. She sat alone in a room of shadows with his nightly carafe of wine beside her. It was probably all she had for herself. No other food was in sight. Placing his bundle on the floor, he sat with her for a few minutes and took her hands in his.

"Drink the wine yourself tonight," he told her. "Get drunk on it, if you will, and dream of the desert."

She reminded him that she was of the true faith and never drank alcohol. The wine, she explained, was for her lone guest.

"You have been generous," he told her, and he pressed money into her old hands. Instead of looking at it, she looked into his eyes.

"You are into dangerous mischief," she said, guessing correctly. "Are the secret police after you?"

"No, not at all," he assured her.

"I had a favorite son," she told him. "But he was killed in the war. The rewards of courage are very small."

"But daring, unlike courage, is a game played with oneself," he answered. "With rules and risks set down in private."

Whether she understood or not, he couldn't tell. He pressed her hands and went out. Never, he knew, would she answer any questions about her lodger these last days.

The airport had only its usual number of soldiers and policemen. Clearly, no one pursued the killer of Herman Carr.

Quentin stood in the waiting rooms of the airport watching the Egyptian soldiers and officials conduct their haphazard searches of handbags, rolled umbrellas, and parcels. They were busy, but inefficient. He knew that back at the hotel the doctors were probably still arguing the symptoms and causes of death. The curious effect of the venom gave him his greatest advantage in escape.

He could feel the perspiration edging down his body as he sat in the bus being transported to the plane. Then, again, he stood in line waiting to be searched before boarding.

He would not be caught and knew it.

Maktoob. It is written.

In another thirty minutes he was airborne over the desert. There, below, was a gigantic golf course, owned and managed by Ermco, with sand greens. Smog hovered in a thick, brown cap over the city. In the distance was a ridge of sandstone mountains. Already he was planning his next journey.

7

Peter Foxx was phoned at five o'clock in the afternoon, just as the secretaries were fleeing the office. Hanning Wilson, the young presidential aide, told him to prepare himself for a late evening meeting in the situation room over in the west wing.

"Has there been an event?" Peter asked, trying to stay detached and objective while asking an obvious question. He held the telephone nervously and almost dropped it.

"Naturally there has been an event," Hanning Wilson said haughtily in his richest Southern accent.

"Where?"

"You'll be given details tonight."

The situation room. The Little Buddha found himself wondering what sort of furnishings it had. His career was in the balance and he sensed it, so he fought to stay rational.

"If I'm going to be well prepared," he said, "I ought to know what part of the world we're talking about."

"It's Africa, then, but I can't tell you a damn thing else," Hanning Wilson said.

"You have to tell me what groups are going to be represented," Peter said, and his voice broke like a schoolboy's when the words came out.

"Several."

"But which?"

Africa. Already, Peter was elated. Now, he tried to determine who his competition might be. When Hanning Wilson stalled, the Little Buddha pressed further. His voice squeaked with excitement, and he hated it, but he had to know.

"Calm yourself," Hanning Wilson urged him. "There's someone from the African desk and someone else from our own staff."

"Why me? Can you tell me that?"

"The President said you, that's why."

"How did he know about me, though?" Peter asked, his voice getting higher and higher. "Does he know I've been studying Africa?"

"He read your report!"

"He *did?*"

Peter had to contain himself. Cool it, cool it, he warned himself, and his free hand fluttered around his desk and over his clothes.

"Come over about ten o'clock," Hanning Wilson said. "I'm sure we won't be meeting until midnight, but you'll just have to wait."

"I'll be there," Peter said, dumbly. Of course he would be there. His appetite was ferocious, but he knew that he wouldn't be dining tonight; with luck, he would eat only catered sandwiches at his desk for the next weeks while his position in Washington power circles was secured.

When he said his goodbye to Hanning Wilson, he almost danced around the room. He ran into the hallway, as if to tell somebody, but there was no one to tell except a busy janitor. The black and white checkerboard floor held him for a moment—a small, fat pawn on an elongated playing surface—before he rushed back inside and locked himself in.

Then depression came. What if he said the wrong thing? What if, say, everyone in the room knew more about what to do than he did? What if the President didn't like him personally? Few people did. What if he appeared too arrogant? Too intellectual?

Then, in the depths of such pessimism, his hopes began to rise. If the event concerned an embassy or a military establishment he would surely not be summoned. For a while he sat thinking, all right, I'm being called because it's the Lagos thing: the cobra killer. I'm being called because they know I'm already onto the event.

Quivering with anticipation, he pulled out Sid Cash's folder and began to review.

The furnishings of the situation room consisted of a single large conference table surrounded by fourteen chairs. The room was paneled in a light, rich wood. Other chairs sat around the wall. The National Security Council met here as well as special coordinating committees. It was where the President squared off with his advisors daily and where crises—events—were discussed and courses of action were created.

Peter Foxx, his stomach rumbling with hunger and excitement, took a chair which, although he didn't know it, placed him at the President's left hand. By eleven o'clock that evening there was a deputy director of the Central Intelligence Agency, Jack Hillyard (top man at Interpol), Kip Culley and his boss from Secret Service, two military types, the director of Africa International, the Little Buddha, and men from the Foreign Intelligence Advisory Board. The President came in, preceded by Hanning Wilson, who bore three fat folders. A stenographer entered in their wake, set up her tape machine, and in the ensuing introductions, which Hanning Wilson conducted, Peter Foxx took a deep breath of the President's after-shave lotion—English Leather, he decided. Also, Peter looked at the President in this sudden close-up and determined that some few hours before this he had been crying; his eyes were still swollen and reddish. But, now, mainly, he was mad, and Hanning Wilson, speaking for him, reflected the anger.

"The President's old friend Herman Carr has been murdered in Cairo," Hanning Wilson began. "Because of delicacies in Egypt's present relationship to us, the cause of the death has been announced as a heart attack. But Mr. Carr was poisoned, probably with cobra venom concentrate or a similar high-potency neurotoxin, and we're here tonight—you see your names and associations on the list being passed around the table—to set a course of action. This isn't the first of such killings in Africa. Jack Hillyard suggests that this might be the sixth or seventh such event in the last few months—specifically, the assassination of American business leaders. So far no diplomat has been killed, so the State Department hasn't been involved. Interpol itself isn't sure that it has jurisdiction because the killings may be political in nature—and signs do point to that. The CIA has done the lab work for us, but they haven't been involved either—until tonight. Their pathology reports confirm the use of the neurotoxin in deaths in Lagos three weeks ago and in yesterday's murder in Cairo."

The room buzzed with whispers. Everyone looked at everyone else. The Little Buddha, trying to assess matters quickly, opened his briefcase as quietly as possible.

"Are we here to form an investigative team?" one of the men from the Advisory Board asked.

"We're here," the President said, not raising his eyes from the table, "to find out what in hell we can legally do."

"In that regard," Hanning Wilson drawled on haughtily, "one of our group might be in advance of the situation. Peter Foxx over at Treasury, who wrote our long report on disorders and terrorism last year, has already filed some preliminary notes and has applied for funds. He has employed—hmm, let's see—"

Hanning Wilson's finger traced over another sheet of names handed to him by the stenographer. At this moment, the door opened and a servant was admitted with a tray of coffee and drinks.

"Sidney Cash of Interpol," Hanning Wilson went on. "Mr. Cash has finished some first appraisals and has compiled a folder."

Slowly, Peter Foxx rose to his feet. Behind the conference table, he was short and pudgy with that high-pitched voice, but suddenly it had changed and had grown more authoritative. In this moment he seemed to take charge of the meeting without invitation, picking up the beat of the aide's introduction.

"We've already got a good description of the killer," he said, passing around a thin dossier of his own—one he had compiled, stapled, and fitted into neat transluscent folders during the hours he normally dined before the meeting. "You'll find that on page two of this material I'm passing around the table. And, please, can I have a liqueur? Is there any Benedictine?"

The President looked up. He seemed pleased by this sudden efficiency and command.

"We've also run some preliminary data through the FBI computers, and I believe we've established a pattern of name usage by the killer or killers. You'll find that on page two."

One of the military types, a one-star general, cleared his throat and tried to smile as he spoke. "We consider this an obvious clandestine operation by a foreign government or agency," he said. "Do you draw the same conclusion?"

In deferring to Peter, the general lost all the ground he might have gained by interrupting. The Little Buddha smiled down on him with soft compassion. "No," Peter said, "we very probably have a single, lone killer with personal ideological motives. Not that we'll rule out the events as the work of an agency or group."

Peter's dossiers were distributed now, and everyone's eyes fell on the pages. The President and Hanning Wilson read their folders, too, so that Peter Foxx still stood, alone, as head of the meeting.

"Any theory where our killer might be operating from?" the President asked, not raising his eyes from the folder.

"None," Peter said. "That's why the work of the team I'm proposing will be expensive and a lot of trouble."

"Just how do you propose this team to work?" Jack Hillyard asked. "I can't see it as an Interpol operation."

"No, it isn't strictly a criminal case," Peter answered. "Nothing has ever been stolen, for instance—except in a couple of instances where local police have removed items or currency from the victims. But it's not clearly a political case either. Personally, I hope to employ the good will of the Interpol network—among other things."

Jack Hillyard's mouth showed the faintest smile. He well understood how Peter hoped to create an independent team out of the jurisdiction of any agency or governmental branch. Hillyard was a big man, rugged as an old cowboy, whose strong, large hands were folded in front of him. His silence now—his failure to object to Interpol being used— was a sign of cooperation. But of course, as Peter understood, everyone was reading the President's mood, and no one was going to object.

There was further discussion about the single killer theory, but for the most part Peter's authority was accepted. He handled it by citing rough similarities in all of the killings. Then the director of Africa International—a private information gathering organization which worked at various times for State or the CIA or the Ford Foundation or anyone else—put the evening's problem succinctly: "How can we go chasing after a killer legally, though? How can we ask police forces, military groups, and foreign governments—some not too friendly—to work for something we want?"

"That's the thing," Peter admitted. "And the President used the word himself: *legally.* I think we all know this has to be a covert operation."

Silence in the room. Peter drank off his Benedictine.

"It also has to be organized so that all our agencies will be in full cooperation," the President said, looking around into all the faces. "I don't want any unnecessary competition. I don't want any hitches—anyone saying that his manpower or computers or communications system can't be available. Because we want this stopped."

Everyone grunted agreement. Hanning Wilson, the exception, barked a prominent and obedient, "Yessir!"

"Mr. President," Peter Foxx said, still standing. "On the last page of my preparation sheet you'll see a list of names. I've taken the liberty of suggesting a team: one man from each of the various antiterrorist groups—excluding the military and the State Department—so that we'll insure that the team has an intramural character."

Everyone rattled pages, turning to the list.

The principals were Peter Foxx of Treasury, Charles Hazo of Africa International, Sidney Markham Cash of Interpol, Jamie Vander of the Central Intelligence Agency and its African desk, and Kip Culley of Secret Service. The Little Buddha, of course, was listed as executive director. There followed a list of associate team members.

"Good," the President said. It had a final, approving ring to it. When he asked, then, if there needed to be more discussion, there wasn't.

"I think we should commend Mr. Foxx for his work," Hanning Wilson said, rising. "And we thank you, gentlemen, for this late evening session. The President wants to see the members of the Advisory Board briefly about another unrelated matter."

"Good night everybody," the President said, waving. Already, some of the men were out the door.

Then the President turned and put his hand on Peter Foxx's shoulder. Peter was gathering up papers.

"How long do you think this'll take?" he asked Peter.

"Probably weeks, sir."

"Well, I hope soon."

"We'll give it everything we have," Peter assured him.

"Good," the President said. "We want that sonavabitch caught."

Hanning Wilson followed Peter into the hallway after this. His whole demeanor had changed. "Anything I can do for you?" he asked the Little Buddha.

"Phone everybody on the list tonight—for starters," Peter told him. "Except for Charlie Hazo. I'll see him. In the morning, see that my request for funding gets approved. We need to set up offices immediately. I've got room in the basement of Treasury, but I need furniture, staff, and equipment by the end of tomorrow. And there's more. You got a note pad?"

Hanning Wilson fumbled in his blazer pocket, then came up writing notes. The Little Buddha's full arrogance was on display now.

"I want White House clearance on an emergency basis," Peter went on. "I'll use the tunnel. And I'll bring over the daily reports personally."

Hanning Wilson looked up with a grin as he scribbled.

"I want everything on White House stationery, too, with signature. And get me clearance at Langley. And access to all materials at Africa International."

Having finished writing all this down, the aide looked up and said, "You know what everybody will say? They'll say you got this job because you're a Southerner."

"In a month they'll say I got it because I was a genius," Peter answered.

"You damn near were a genius tonight," Hanning Wilson said. "How'd you know and how'd you get ready?"

"Deduction," the Little Buddha told him. "I was the least important person in the room. So, logically, I had to be the most important before the evening finished. Why else would I be invited?"

A staff car drove the Little Buddha across the street to Treasury, then waited while he attempted to phone Charlie Hazo from his office. When he failed to locate the Professor, he was driven home to his apartment. There, he tried again without success to reach his key man.

Before morning, unable to sleep, the Little Buddha took a walk. His fur collar tucked up around his ears, he strolled over toward the fat spire of the Washington Monument, then he turned back toward his little apartment tucked in among the minor embassies up toward Dupont Circle. The familiar neighborhood calmed him: all those nice brownstones with small brass nameplates beside the doors. In this section of town there were a number of baby carriages on the sidewalks every morning. Many large English prams pushed by nannies. And big cars at the curbs: Bentleys and Lincolns. Dogs on leashes. The new leaves on the limbs overhead. All of it gave Peter Foxx a sense of intense pleasure—especially now. He was part of its quiet importance.

By the time he had finished walking, he was thinking about the *Executive Intelligence Report*, a document published by the government and bought at $5 each by every major banker and industrialist from New York to Dallas to Seattle. Should we put in a warning, he speculated, that this killer is out there? How to phrase it?

He decided to ask the renowned Professor, if ever he could find him.

8

"You should have waited in the hallway for me," Peter told Kip Culley. "You heard it said that the Advisory Board members were wanted on another matter entirely."

"It was after midnight," Kip Culley argued.

"After this, try and make sure what I want."

Furious, Kip Culley could only turn away. They stood in the basement of Treasury as workers carried in desks, communications consoles, lamps, and file cabinets; doors were being opened, so that the Little Buddha's rooms expanded into a larger suite.

Sid Cash, setting his desk in order, listened from a far room. He checked his passport, worrying that he needed a yellow fever shot.

"Now this morning," Peter went on, squeaking, "I want you to try and locate Professor Hazo for me. Don't contact him, just locate him. Can you do that?"

"I left word at his college. He's supposed to call me."

"Where does he live?"

"He has several rooms. But he usually only answers messages when they come through his school."

"I want to know where he is," Peter said, trying to calm himself, "so I can go and visit him personally."

"Did he say he'd be on the team?" Kip Culley asked.

The question was ignored. "After you've found him for me—and I hope it isn't too much of a task for one of our secret service sleuths—set your own affairs in order. I expect you'll be in Africa for six months."

For a moment, the two men stood staring at one another. Then Kip Culley stalked out, went into his own office, and started pacing. The floors around his desk were stacked with boxes, so that he had to stomp over and between them. When he settled down, he sat on the desk making calls to Graham College, the Pentagon, the house in Virginia, and, then, when all else failed, to the waitress. Among the many numbers he did not know or try was that of Andrea Sloane, the widow of the attaché, who had the Professor in her garden, enthralled, planting a mixed arrangement of petunias.

A cool sunlight in the garden that April morning: an almond tree ready to blossom behind the high fence, the ground still cold from winter, and Charlie in his jeans with his pullover sweater tied around his neck. Andrea, always gracefully awkward in her movements, like a giraffe, raked leaves into a neat pile; the Professor, watching her, thought how very much like that wonderful animal she was, how she lurched and swayed in a movement which seemed always perilous, then caught herself, turning it into grace. She had small hips, no breasts, thin neck and shoulders. With her dainty brush strokes, she seemed to be practicing etiquette with the garden rake.

"Do you want brunch?" she asked.

He patted the last of the petunias into place.

"That would be swell," he answered, getting up. His grimy hands were held away from his jeans as he started up the back porch steps. "Just let me clean up, okay?"

Andrea smiled across the yard. Beyond them the sounds of Georgetown arrived, muffled and reassuring.

As he passed through the rooms of antiques and oak woodwork toward the bathroom, Charlie shed his muddy clothes. Then, impulsively, he grabbed up the phone before stepping into the shower and called the college. His fingerprints and smudges decorated the telephone, the marble-topped table, the oak frame of the door, and the scars which adorned his dirty torso. There were several messages for him on the dictaphone at the college, most of them from Kip Culley.

After his shower Charlie slipped on an old bathrobe which had belonged to Andrea's husband. They had a brunch of eggs, dry toast, and white wine on that little glassed-in rear porch. The late morning grew hot, so that Charlie opened the robe and Andrea, watching his body in the sunlight, became both sexually aroused and curious.

"Where did you get all those scars?" she asked him for the hundredth time. "Not in battle, I presume."

"It was a car accident," he told her, being partially truthful.

She sat watching him: the flat brown stomach, muscled like a young man's, and the soft curve of his penis in that mixture of dark and greying hair below his waist. Suddenly, as if for no reason, she understood his scars.

"You were in a car that exploded," she said without emotion.

"Why do you say that?"

"You were. Deny it, if you can."

"You're right, then," he answered, admitting it. "A car exploded. It was some freaky accident in the fuel line. Bits of metal went through me like shrapnel."

"When did this happen?"

"Years ago."

He finished his eggs. Andrea's head tilted to one side as she studied him; she saw him as if in a vision, beautiful and far away, dreamlike, and in some remarkable way she knew more than she understood.

"It was a bomb," she said. "Someone tried to kill you, isn't that right?"

"Don't be silly," he said, and he began to stack up the dishes.

"Someone blew up your car." She said it with wonder, confirming many things she had been feeling.

Charlie carried dishes into the kitchen. The house, one of those quiet townhouses lined up in the Dumbarton Oaks section of Georgetown, suddenly felt like a mausoleum. Drawing the robe around him and tying the sash, he went back to the telephone and dialed for Kip Culley. The call had to be transferred. As he waited, Andrea came and stood beside him—noticing all the smudges.

"You're messy," she told him.

He smiled and listened to the static inside the phone.

"And your car had a bomb in it. Someone wanted to kill you."

At this point, Kip Culley was on the line sounding irritable. The story of the situation room was related to Charlie: how the Little Buddha stood up, what was said, how the President behaved, everything.

Now, Kip Culley explained, the Little Buddha wanted to see the Professor. More than that, he wanted to surprise him, unannounced, so that probably he could go over all these victories once more. And they were probably all going to Africa, he said, never to be seen again.

Charlie said little in response except that he would go back to his house near the college and wait. When he said goodbye to Kip Culley, he turned to find Andrea looking at him expectantly.

"You're going away again, aren't you?" she asked.

"Looks like it."

"Are you important?"

They looked at each other. In spite of the sunlight outdoors, Andrea's house was always shadowy English: dim and cool.

"No," he said. "Very unimportant."

But her eyes were wide with a curious knowledge: he was in jeopardy and had lived that way for years; someone, long ago, had tried to assassinate him, and although that particular danger was in the past there were men who would do him ill; he was clearly an adventurer in this odd capital of adventure; and the scars on his body which had once hurt him now, in some deep way, hurt her.

By afternoon he drove along the Lee Highway out toward his place near Falls Church. He was worrying about his library out there. If he went to Africa for an extended period—and he was tired of school and ready—what would he do about all his books and papers? The old farm house was already damp and musty; should he box things up? He thought of renting the place out just so someone would be there looking after it. Summer would soon arrive, he finally decided, and I'll maybe be back for next term.

When the Little Buddha arrived, the two men greeted each other on the lawn, each trying to cover his surprise; Peter was much shorter, much squeakier, than Charlie expected; and the Professor was considerably older and somehow less vulnerable than Peter had supposed.

"I see why you want me to lead the operation, of course," Charlie told him when they were sitting in the study. "You don't know anything about police work—which I don't myself, so that we've got Sid Cash on the team—and you don't know anything about Africa. Ever visited over there?"

"No," Peter admitted.

"You're the bureaucrat," Charlie said, sizing up his guest. "Your big thrill is restaurants and offices. I'm just an academic. Classrooms and research projects in libraries. We're neither of us completely fit for this job, but I do love Africa. It's a liquor I get drunk on. So, sure, I'll go."

They sat on the floor beside the coffee table; a yellow light encircled them. On the large desk, stacked up haphazardly on the leather inlay, were the notes and jottings which comprised the beginnings of Charlie's memoirs—a project that he well knew would never be completed. There was also a Persian slipper on the desk—bright and embroidered—with a zippered top. It contained a little pot, a little cocaine. There were hundreds of felt-tipped pens, Charlie's favorite writing instruments, and books, half-read, with markers sticking out.

"Of course I'm going to be very loyal and very grateful," Charlie said.

"How do you mean? Will this project help your career?"

"Career? What a curious word is *career*."

"How will it help you, then?"

"It will take me back to Africa for months, if we're lucky, and I imagine we will be—because I don't think we'll ever catch our man."

"Why not?"

"Catch a single man in all of Africa?"

"You think he might be all that clever?"

"He wouldn't have to be clever! Just not terribly stupid. If we've got a man with forgeries, he could go on forever."

"I believe we'll catch him."

"Don't be silly. Ask Sid Cash or anyone else at Interpol," Charlie said. "They catch approximately one-tenth of all international criminals—and most of those fit very well established categories and patterns of behavior. You know, credit card violators—that sort."

"So we'll fail?" Peter asked.

"Probably. But a year, perhaps two, will be granted us. The President might be out of office by that time. Herman Carr will long be forgotten, I tell you that for sure. And I'll linger in Nairobi, maybe go back to Zanzibar, which I love, and you'll eat every day at the Sans Souci."

"What about the cobra venom? And the description! We have a description of the man! And he's using a series of similar names—we know a lot toward apprehending him." The Little Buddha's voice grew squeaky with excitement.

"Forget it," Charlie said. "You don't understand what you're dealing with."

"Think what success would mean!"

"The odds are too great," Charlie told him. "You don't know that continent, not at all."

"You have a poor attitude," Peter whined, his voice ever rising.

"I'm going to make you look good," Charlie promised him. "That's all you need to know. And maybe we'll get lucky. But don't count on luck. Africa is not a place one gets lucky in."

PART TWO

"It is their forest and they can hide from us whenever they want to."

A village chief along the banks
of the Ituri River, speaking of
the Pygmies

9

Two weeks had passed since Quentin's journey to Cairo, and he was preparing himself once more.

Most of the time since his return had been spent at the workshop which occupied one corner of the lab. There he washed, sanded, and polished the gems which comprised the Clare fortune; one by one, he had sold them off to travelling buyers on lower Biashara Street or to Mr. Rhamadi, the owner of one of the better shops up near the New Stanley Hotel.

His father had taught Quentin to cut stones. At first both of them practiced cutting inexpensive quartz crystals and moss agates, so that now Quentin felt confident cutting the best diamonds and alexandrites in his collection. With a good, uncomplicated table cut and highly polished his stones brought fair prices and paid for all his excursions and expenses at the estate. Prices varied from month to month and from buyer to buyer, but no matter. There were enough stones to last; he planned no heirs, nothing for anyone to inherit when he was gone.

Today he was cutting one of his best diamonds, a fine white. Not a feather or flaw. He had only two better: the large white and one fancy—which bore a bluish tint. But the one he prepared to cut he admired a great deal. He worked with slow patience.

One flaw in the wrong place in a cut diamond is reflected in every facet. Equally, he thought as he worked, I have to stay prepared in the trips I take; my diet must be right, my transactions in Nairobi must be discreet, and all my plans must be careful.

He prepared the stone in the vise for the cutting after testing it against his cheek. It didn't feel too warm, so was in no danger of burning. If he cut correctly, the stone would stay cool and the wax around it firm.

Slow, careful.

Pace mattered entirely. Like all his work, the gem required great care and, then, after slow preparation, the hammer raised, a single, quick act of violence.

Hesitating, he looked around. Everything was ready: the carborundum cloth for sanding, the paste of tin oxide, the polishing wheel, the good piece of leather Wemba had provided—damp with paste—for the final polishing. But his thoughts weren't right, and he felt uneasy. Wait, he warned himself, until the right moment.

He strolled around the lab. Hammer still in hand, he decided against making the cut on the diamond just yet. Instead, he would go into the city.

Wemba, again, refused to make the trip, so Quentin drove the Land Rover out that long stretch of dirt road until it joined the Langata Road heading toward Nairobi. Bushbuck and wildebeest grazed in the adjoining fields. Driving along, he thought about his father, ruined by values he had tried to flee: that crippling American passion to succeed, to turn life into progress, to win recognitions and honors. The doctor had left America because he had failed to get along with his university administrators, had settled in Kenya, had temporarily thrived, had married, but had never achieved what he had hoped. Among those natives who listened to his lectures and who drank his palm wine he was always the eccentric. Between he and Mary something in the sexual machinery had failed. He had made some money by collecting, processing, and selling venoms, but that work only compounded his reputation as an oddity and had never satisfied him. From his mother Quentin learned a high regard for culture and knowledge: he played the piano, studied languages, worked in the lab, read. He came to appreciate his continent's legacies: the wild nature, the primitive undertow. But his father was always a westerner: bedeviled to make good in the world's eyes and doomed to obscurity on that scraggly estate back in the bush.

Near the city there were pedestrians alongside the road, their heads loaded with swaying calabashes.

Uhuru Highway, then, and the boulevards.

Behind the fact of his present mission lay all this curious history and unruly logic: his father's frustration and solitude, his mother's love of Africa and her untimely death, Quentin's own aimless loneliness, so much. But the contest itself now had him in its keeping, he knew, and old reasons or old angers didn't matter; a man might go to war because he believed in a cause, Quentin felt, but once he is in battle such early passions disappear and he fights because he is physically there—involved, equipped, unable to leave, and proud of his soldierly skills.

He walked along Kimathi Street toward Mr. Rhamadi's shop.

In his thoughts was that first time in South Africa. In Durban. He had struck up a conversation in a downtown bar with an American accountant for a group of companies dealing in chrome. He had followed the man into a public toilet. A simple business. And the game had started.

"Mr. Clare, you look bad, What's the matter?" Mr. Rhamadi said, greeting him. They stood beside the jeweler's workbench at the rear of the shop. Lost in thought, Quentin hadn't fully realized that he had arrived.

"I was thinking about my father," he said, making his excuse. "How are you today?"

"Ah, the good doctor! Peace to him! Have you got something for us again?"

"I'll have a stone ready soon. Today I want to know about prices. How's the market?"

"A good time to sell! Bring the stone! Don't go down into the market with it! You know you'll get a fair price here!"

"I know that, yes."

"You remember how you came by all those stones?"

"Yes," Quentin said, "I remember very well."

"How many years did your father sell venoms? Twenty?"

"Many years."

"And built up his fortune. And came to me that day and said, 'Here, buy me precious stones! I don't trust the banks!' You recall I told you this many times?"

"Yes, I remember."

"He didn't trust the banks! Good! And the gems I sold him that day have increased in value, have they not?"

The old merchant was pleading, Quentin felt. Yet he had no animosity toward Mr. Rhamadi or any other friend or acquaintance of the family who had dealt honestly with them.

"I will always sell through you, Mr. Rhamadi," Quentin told him. "Have no fear."

"Your father left the venom business just as it got good," Mr. Rhamadi went on. He was a small, Indian man with a nose like a Persian. As he talked, his hands met prayerfully under his chin.

"Yes, you've said that many times."

"Because it is true! Ah yes, he could have been very wealthy—like the men who opened the Institute. Let's see, how long has he been dead now?"

"He's been gone more than twenty years," Quentin answered.

"A long time. And the venom business—like the gem business—has grown so much. Who could think it?"

"Remarkable," Quentin agreed. He found himself watching Mr. Rhamadi behind the workbench, thinking, he knows and remembers a great deal—enough to incriminate me and lead any pursuer to the door of our estate.

"It is very precious, venom. Nowadays it brings many hundreds of pounds for every ounce, does it not?"

"I don't keep up," Quentin told him. "Look, Mr. Rhamadi, I'll bring you the stone next week. It's a fine white. You'll have cash, won't you?"

"How many carats?" Mr. Rhamadi asked, very interested.

"After the final cuts, perhaps twenty."

A smile creased Mr. Rhamadi's face and his hands saluted in prayer once more. "Not to worry," he said. "I'll have the money in an hour, if the stone appears."

After leaving the shop, Quentin walked over to Government Road where the United States Information Agency library was located. The magazines there were up to date, the books were well kept, and if one could ignore the atmosphere of propaganda, Quentin felt, it was easily one of the better public libraries on the continent. It was there, of course, that he found his targets. Among the many corporate magazines and brochures, in the pages of the *Wall Street Journal* or the financial sections of other major newspapers, he located his potential victims: managers of American companies, visitors such as Herman Carr or Bobby Bolling or other corporate dignitaries.

The reading tables were almost all filled. All around, hopeful black faces. They dreamt of El Dorado, each of them, he knew, and came to the library as if it were a dream factory.

For an hour he sat and read. Nothing of striking consequence. Then he saw the first mention of his exploits, an article in the *Herald-Tribune* on the death of Herman Carr which indicated an investigation had started "on the remote possibility of foul play" in Cairo. The newspaper was more than a week old and sent Quentin looking around the crowded room for more recent editions. He found two other editions, but no further mention of the case. After a search, he found a *New York Times* article on Carr's death from which the *Herald-Tribune* notice had been extracted.

He walked over to the Thorn Tree Cafe. There, he bought the last available editions of American newspapers and sat down at one of the outdoor tables searching for further information. Nothing. He ordered a coffee and sat there thinking.

They were after him. Good.

All sorts of speculations bombarded him.

He would never kill Mr. Rhamadi, he decided. He would never again kill anyone except the quarry. The poor Dutch whore and the obnoxious colonel in Lagos: he felt badly about them. Their deaths subtracted from the meaning of his work. Nor would he murder—like some common criminal—to cover his tracks. If Mr. Rhamadi told some investigator that, yes, years ago Dr. Clare kept snakes and sold venoms, and if this led to his capture, so be it. The game was itself: it should be played ever more skillfully, more cleanly, more perfectly, and without such simple-minded vice.

He looked around the cafe at all the tourists and regulars of this most popular town center. It was not his place. Not once in the last ten years had he sat here—nor had the doctor ever allowed himself this. It was never possible. Did that make sense? And, now, it was after the fact of such vanities. Now he was their enemy and destroyer. With his cup of coffee untouched, he left.

As he drove back to the estate that afternoon after his last errands, his thoughts went back to the newspaper item. He went over the elevator sequence and recalled nothing left undone. Had they determined, at last, that venom was used? Probably so. It would be on Herman Carr's clothes. Would they link the death with those in Lagos? Was there anything overlooked there? He decided against undue worry. Too much was in his favor: the size of the continent, the years of planning, the ineptitude of African police detection, the chaos of governments, and even the random choices of victims.

There was only one place where weakness could occur: inside himself. Keep steady, stay prepared, he cautioned himself, and the game is yours.

Back at the lab, he went to the stone, quickly prepared once more, raised the hammer, aimed, and brought his stroke down. The diamond—earth's hardest substance—split. A perfect cut.

It was evening again, and he freed himself of clothing. In the yard beneath the thorn tree, Kali waited.

"Stay where you are," he said under his breath. "I'm coming out."

He unlatched the screen door on the porch. The door lay beneath the shadow of the bridge which led from the upstairs verandah over the wall of the compound and back to the house. As he slipped outside, then, his first, slow movements were obscured.

Another game. The question, clearly: how far away from the door can I move before Kali will come after me? How many steps will I need in retreat? Who will be faster?

As he took a step from the shadow beneath the bridge, Kali's great head raised up. They both waited.

Few mambas exceeded ten feet in length, so Kali was the finest, largest specimen Quentin had ever seen or heard about. It was also perhaps the fastest. Its venom, like its cobra cousins, was a glycerinelike combination of proteins and salivary acids, and the neurotoxin these produced would of course attack the central nervous system, immediately affecting heartbeat and respiration. Diaphragm paralysis and suffocation would follow. A hemotoxin also would cause severe clotting in the blood. Usually, death would occur in a human in from five minutes to two hours, but Quentin himself had improved on that. By creating a concentrate—very much like employing the process for making concentrated frozen juices—and by adding two basic chemical agents, he had managed to get a product which would act in seconds.

He took another step.

Kali had been found near Kilimanjaro. Wemba's brother-in-law, who lived near the border of Tanzania, had brought him to the estate and had been paid two Kenyan pounds for the specimen when it was newly hatched.

One more step. The last one, he decided, that he should take.

Kali raised up, its head some seven feet high now.

The doctor—long before Kali's appearance—used to walk in the yard among the pods where the cobras slept. Casually fearless. He milked the snakes, too, with the help of old Dobo. Many were taken into the laboratory, fixed in the vise, held, and their upper lips turned back to expose the reservoir which secretes the poison. This little sac was then cut and the poison drained. The process was repeated time after time with the same cobras, and only on certain occasions were the fangs or the sacs removed entirely. When these last operations were performed, a hot iron was applied to the inside of the upper lip, so the sac wouldn't repair itself. And almost always, Quentin remembered, the removed fangs grew back.

In the old days the cobras in the yard were indolent and lazy, Quentin recalled, and very unlike the magnificent Kali—or any true mamba—who would attack anyone or anything without provocation.

One more step now, Quentin knew. Slowly and deliberately, he took it.

Kali came for him. Darting to his side as he slammed back through the screen door, it was so agile, so violent and quick, that Quentin could hardly think. As he stumbled through the door, Quentin brushed a banana tree; its leaves still shook as he stumbled back onto the porch, so Kali, furious, attacked the insolent plant, biting and striking at it over and over.

Quentin had always heard stories of how cobra poison killed plants, even moderately sized trees, so he watched the banana tree for some time afterward. The plant survived, but he noticed that as he watched it—each time he came close to the screen door—Kali was also closely watching him.

10

The Egyptian detective who met with the Professor, Sid Cash, and Jamie Vander at the Nile Hilton was named Hamid Al-Hamidi; Sid, trying for friendly familiarity, called him "Ham" at first, but a glance from the Professor assured him that this was inappropriate.

After a lunch at the Kursaal—mixed meats, arak, even a noontime belly dancer—they finally got down to business by mid-afternoon, sitting on the open balcony outside Sid's room. They could see the river and a hundred minarets. As they went over the autopsy report on Herman Carr, Jamie Vander was clearly looking out on the shimmering horizon with his mind blank.

"No major damage to the heart," Sid said, reading aloud. "The walls of the kidneys were slightly ruptured and some blood escaped from the cortex into the capsular cavity. The liver had lots of ruptured cells and was totally wrecked. The muscles all over the body were necrotic—which means, roughly, that their fibers were broken down. In the muscles and throughout all the major organs the fatty tissues were destroyed."

"A very dead man," the detective said wryly.

"Of course he died—or quit breathing—because of shock," Sid said, finishing up. "A hell of a dose."

"The venom was squirted on him," the Professor said, reflectively. "How was it squirted, I wonder?"

"Surely, a ring," Hamid the detective said.

"We have the report from the merchant in the market," Sid Cash said, rattling through papers in his new folders. "Does he sell rings in his shop?"

"Make a note of that, Jamie," Charlie said.

Jamie brought himself to life and made a note. "God, it's hot here," he said. "Could we have some lemonade?"

"Lemonade, good," cried Hamid, getting up as if he was hosting a party and disappearing toward the telephone. "I'll call the room service."

"Please," Charlie asked. "Don't appeal to his sense of social duty anymore. We have to quit eating and drinking and make our list."

It was the end of a week of such detours. The doctor who performed the autopsy went on holiday before filing his findings. Days were spent in introductions with everyone trying to explain each other's presence. The dead rancher's friend, Bonny Allen, told the ambassador, an Arabic newspaper reporter, the police, and the President of the United States that Herman Carr had died of a heart attack, nothing else, and that he couldn't have been murdered because he didn't have an enemy in the world and wasn't robbed. The desert heat made Jamie so listless that he could hardly talk. The Professor disappeared for two consecutive evenings—Sid Cash looking forward to a meaningful organizational discussion—so that he could sample Egyptian womanhood. Kip Culley, who was in Lagos, was on the phone constantly, but never had anything to report.

"Are we all right politically?" Sid Cash had asked the detective at one point.

"Never," Hamid answered. "All things here are political and religious—even stealing fruit!"

By way of proving this assertion, the doctor who performed the autopsy and then went off to someone's private oasis, being a Coptic Christian with an assortment of predjudices against Moslems, would only release the report to Sid personally. This made Hamid angry and delayed matters for another day.

By the time their Egyptian detective called for lemonade and made a few personal phone calls, they had two lists. The first was a rough plan:

1. Kip Culley would stay in Lagos where he would guard
   the survivor at the hospital, interview everyone who had
   seen Mr. Blue, and try to bribe the police toward full and
   future cooperation.
2. Sid Cash would go to Nairobi and set up the main headquarters.
3. Charlie Hazo and Jamie Vander would stay in Cairo until
   the latest investigation was complete, then join Sid.

The other list, hastily drawn, gave them more work than fifty men
could easily accomplish. Sid wanted a list of all gem dealers, venom
wholesalers, known forgers, and known murderers who used poison.
Jamie Vander's special pursuit would be the active terrorist groups, such
as the PLO: did they have such a killer in the field? Did they know of
any agency or group which did?

They already had a list of known radicals in several countries.

"It might be one of these, but most of them are too disorganized and
too local," the Professor determined.

"Is our killer rich?" Sid asked, thinking out loud. "How does he
finance himself, if he's independent?"

"The rich hire mercenaries," Hamid answered. "Who would bother with such strong feelings himself if he lived in luxury?"

On and on, their afternoon conversation turned into a series of
evening monologues. At last, the detective suggested dinner and a
cabaret.

"Don't you ever go home?" Jamie asked as tactfully as possible.

"What is there?" asked Hamid, shrugging. "Only my wife and
children!"

After dark, they dispersed. Jamie had a rendezvous with the local
CIA agent, so Sid and Charlie got away for dinner together at last. In the
street not far from the hotel they ran across a snake charmer. There he
was: his cobra, hood flared open, edging out of the wicker basket to notes
played on a crude wooden pipe. The Professor had seen this a hundred
times, but Sid insisted that they stop.

"Can you imagine being bitten by that thing?" he asked in awe.

"Come on, let's go get whacked," Charlie suggested.

The charmer, within easy striking distance for the snake, played and moved his body slowly from side to side. A crude alcohol lamp provided light for his onlookers who tossed down a few coins when the show finished. Sid, very impressed, was among the last to leave.

They went to the Cafe Nefertiti. There, Sid tried to get down to business during his first drink, but Charlie would have none of it.

"In search of the lands of myrrh and gold, the Roman general Gallus led a force of ten thousand men into this desert," Charlie said. "It was 24 B.C. and the poor Arabs—never having seen such a wonderful army before—just kept out of sight beyond the next dune. The elements went to work. The expedition never fought a battle and was completely wiped out."

They sat in silence for a moment, sipping their aperitifs.

"We're not going to accomplish very much, are we?" Sid finally asked, already disappointed.

"Above the Sahara," Charlie said, "we have a kind of passionate misunderstanding and misdirection. Below the Sahara—as you'll see when you get to Kenya and elsewhere—we have a sort of mystic confusion. Between these, in Africa, there is nothing—except the desert sand."

Sid looked at his new colleague. Then they ordered dinner.

"Tell me about the intelligence network," Sid said later on during the second course. The music drifting in from the Nefertiti Lounge was executed by electric guitar and drum, neither of which paid attention to the other.

"The French, who are always chauvinistic and ravenous for personal and national gain, have the very best resources," Charlie said, chewing on his steak. "Especially in North Africa and, of course, in the Congo and along the west coast. Next, the South Africans. Their agents are everywhere, and their secret police pay well. The informer network, you see, is the thing: you've got to get the local police on the payroll somehow. Our CIA runs a poor third. It mostly reprints and redistributes whatever African intelligence the other two sources provide."

"And the police?"

"Hopeless—almost everywhere," Charlie said. "And of course the Third World countries are too poor to have spies, true policemen, or even bona fide regular armies."

"Wait a minute, then," Sid said. "What do we do? Bring in our own people?"

"Impossible. Where would we put them? It would take a year—even in a good, stable, modernized place like Nairobi. There would be jealousy if we accomplished anything and laughter behind our backs if we didn't. If we spent forty million dollars we couldn't stop this guy from pumping venom into another dozen victims during the next six months."

"So what are you going to do?"

"Go to Zanzibar," Charlie sighed. "I know a woman there."

Sid paid elaborate attention to his entree, thinking as he pushed food into his mouth. The dish before him was a strong curry, for which he would pay a price the next three days.

"I think we'll find something when we check out the venom dealers and the known forgers," he finally asserted.

The Professor didn't answer.

"And we have the whole goddamned Africa desk out at Langley," Sid went on. "And outfits like Africa International. We've got every scrap of intelligence on the whole continent!"

"Intelligence told the President that the South Africans were going to detonate a hydrogen bomb in the Kalahari Desert," Charlie said, not even looking up from his steak. "The President believed the reports and went straight up in the air. But no bomb. Even when our boys get a scoop, they usually get it wrong. The best thing is to say nothing. Which is what they usually say."

When they returned to the hotel there were no less than four messages from the Little Buddha. Peter Foxx, who was far away—in both distance and understanding—wanted daily written reports.

11

The Little Buddha made a short address on terrorism to a gathering of colonels and guests out at the War College at Fort McNair. Afterward, at the buffet, he let it be known that his presence was demanded every day at the White House. He intimated that he was an expert on African affairs, too, which resulted in his being invited, later, to give another brief address at the Stanford Research Institute—an organization, like Africa International, with ties to the intelligence community.

He issued a memo to the office secretaries—six in number—that they were getting too fat.

He arranged for private instruction on the pistol range in the sub-sub-basement of Treasury.

He began lessons in Swahili at the Gardner School of Languages over on 14th Street. Once, after attending class, he came out famished and rushed across the street to the People's Drugstore, where he consumed a lunch at the cafeteria. The food was so appalling that he arranged a later lunch at Tiberio's.

Another printing of *Disorders and Terrorism* was ordered.

The only member of the Task Force he could reach with regularity was Kip Culley, who reported from Nigeria that he needed, by his estimate, $50,000 for bribes.

An achievement was lunch in the Senate Dining Room, replete with the famous bean soup and Peter's senator from Tennessee. The

Senator wanted terrorism stopped. The Little Buddha wanted a souvenir of one of those big Senate ashtrays with the seal set in the middle.

More and more, too, he found himself making policy decisions for seniors and directors at both Treasury and other branches. Deference was paid him for two obvious reasons: he was in the White House on a daily basis, and, also, the men at the other branches seemed too busy to care. Peter, as one of his own bosses on the third floor at Treasury put it, had "good legal ways" which everyone seemed to appreciate. He turned out papers, studies, documents, preparations and briefs; he worked long hours.

Between lunches and buffets and his same elaborate evening meals, he added weight. His belly protruded so much that his genitals were cast in permanent shadow.

He suffered insomnia which increased his poetry output.

He became obsessed with Charlie Hazo's dossier and improbable life style. He wanted to find out facts beyond the latest and altogether superficial security check on the Professor—included, in summary, in the dossier—but he didn't know who to ask for more information. He found that he was unduly interested in the old boy's sexual history.

Finally, a reporter asked for an interview—based on knowledge of rumors that Peter Foxx was a new expert on anti-terrorist activities, had some special relationship to the White House, and was part of a covert group. The reporter, an aged newspaperman named Fielding Blanks, whose beat was the Treasury Department, had an indelicate sense of humor and had dubbed the appointed newsroom in the building the Aaron Burr Memorial Office. But the Little Buddha, hearing that a request for an interview had occurred, informed the fattest of his secretaries to set up an appointment with Blanks.

"What exactly do you do?" Blanks asked him, sitting in Peter's office the first thing on a Tuesday morning.

"You want an interview with me and don't know what I do?" the Little Buddha answered, being coy.

Shocked by Peter's high-pitched voice, but stifling a grin, old Blanks made a wild guess. "There's been an event, I know that much," he said. "The public doesn't yet know about it. You're involved. Right so far?"

"Yes, the death of Herman Carr in Cairo," Peter said, confirming the wild guess.

"And so you—" The reporter, weary, wary, unaccustomed to anything of news value in his daily rounds, sought a phrase. "You go over to the White House personally every day. And so—" He was thinking fast. "The President has appointed you to investigate Herman Carr's death. Correct?"

"You said it, I didn't," answered Peter, being so coy as to be obvious. Fielding Blanks had a notepad in his lap now, but his mind raced along to so many possibilities that he failed to write anything.

"Herman Carr was probably murdered," the reporter said flatly.

"Probably," the Little Buddha replied.

"How would you describe the makeup of your investigative group? Is this a Treasury investigative unit?"

"Oh no, hardly," Peter said with a thin smile.

From this opening gambit, the character of events in Africa altered. The next day Fielding Blanks went to his editor with a story resumé; both of them quickly understood that they had something extraordinary.

"How do you want it handled?" Fielding asked his editor.

"See if Foxx will let us do a full interview," the editor suggested, wise in matters concerning political egos and careers. "Promise him—oh, featured coverage in the Sunday edition. See what he says."

Peter Foxx, the Little Buddha, not only said yes, but divulged his nickname, the nature of the Task Force, its new code name, certain preliminary activities in Africa, and everything except the names of those who worked with him from other agencies. The only name attached to Project Savannah Blue was his own.

After the publication of the article, Peter found that the White House cooled toward him. His reports, he was told, could be sent over once a week. But having been firmly planted he found that his prestige had taken root; he was respected, even feared a little, at Treasury, where no one ever received publicity, and, clearly, in a city where there had once been many groups of anti-terrorist experts vying for recognition and control, there was now only one voice. The Marine Corps guard, which traditionally protected overseas diplomats in times of crisis, established a liaison officer who sat in the basement offices among the fat secretaries. The Pentagon asked Peter to diagram the precise chain of command for authorities in anti-terrorist activities. He was appointed to the board of directors of Africa International. Copies of his huge report were distributed once again.

The headwaiters of the city knew him on sight.

12

Wemba and Quentin spent the afternoon playing their favorite—and separate—games.

Wemba's game had no name, but Quentin referred to it as hole-in-the-ground and assumed that it had rules. On a patch of earth outside the compound and near the kitchen door of the main house, Wemba dug two rows of six parallel holes. These two lines of holes contained assorted pebbles—favorite stones of Wemba's worn smooth by so much playing. The game was played all over the continent in every tribe, on almost every street corner of every city, in every village. It had various names, some close to the one Quentin gave it, and since it was a game whose object and rules varied it was mostly an occasion for argument. An elder would shout at a younger player, "Stupid! This is not how we play in our tribe!" One player, thwarted in collecting all the stones of his opponent or in getting up one row of holes and down the other as he had intended, would become furious and throw his opponent's prize pebble into the bush. Another player would scream at his opponent that tradition or religious dogma or respect for parents were not being observed.

The blacks of the continent sat on their haunches, their bony knees thrust up around their shoulders, their arms dangling in the dirt, and played the game or its variations for hours.

The extraordinary thing about Wemba's playing was that he played alone, talking and arguing only with himself. Quentin accepted this as part of the character of the estate: loneliness here was intense.

Quentin's game was chess, diversion from his work in the lab and at his desk with the forgeries, and he played it alone, too. He had several variations, all as much of a mystery to Wemba as hole-in-the-ground was to Quentin. Lately, he had gone to the chessboard with books on some of the classic games of Paul Morphy, Capablanca, Fischer, and others to replay their strategies. He often played against himself, but found this tiresome. He wished, sometimes, for an opponent far away, a pen pal and distant adversary who could send his extraordinary moves in reply to his own. He loved chess—or, at times, as he decided, the idea of chess. One of his favorite books was a dual exercise in poetry and chess problems—the poems witty and vague, the chess problems amusing. A favorite novel concerned a chess master who went mad after his defeat in a crucial game.

Thinking of his father in all this, how they used to play the game together, he got up and went down the hallway. Peering inside at the old figure in the bed, he decided to enter.

The day's work was finished. Wemba had turned the doctor over, applied medicine to an old nagging bedsore, emptied the plastic bag at the end of the yellowed catheter, and changed the sheets. Two scents dominated the room: the familiar sweet odor of cheap disinfectant and the pale, subtle smell of gardenia which drifted in the open window; gardenia bushes lined the front road beyond the high walls of the compound. The night breeze was blowing just right, so that the scent was brought indoors.

Quentin took a chair beside the bed. He sat for a long time looking through the netting at the chalky white face on the pillow.

On their hunting expeditions together, Bill Clare usually tinkered and repaired. He took apart their rifles, the motor of the Land Rover, their cameras, and anything else mechanical and not in perfect order. On those annual hunting safaris up to the northern frontier the doctor often sat alone in the tent all day, parts of engines or equipment spread out on a greasy cloth before him, while Quentin and some of the *watu* went shooting on the surrounding savannah. They owned a short wave radio, not a bad one, but it was always disassembled, the doctor's permanent toy, so that back at the estate Mary never expected her husband's promised calls. During one period after the long rainy season when there were plenty of snakes brought in and venom sales were good, Bill Clare saved enough money to consider buying an airplane, but mother and son only had a good laugh over the prospect; it would always be scattered in pieces, they told each other, laughing, with a wing here and a strut there and most of its parts left on the greasy cloth whenever the doctor wanted to fly it.

Vivid memories: the laughter of Mary Clare and the concentration of the doctor as he sat cross-legged on the floor, his old cloth spread out before him.

Those same inquisitive skills were with the doctor in the laboratory, too. He peered inside birds, reptiles, insects, and other animals like an augur; his dissections smelled up the place, and the bowels of all his poor creatures were spread around like those mechanical parts on the old cloth, as if he searched out secrets in all the mess around him—omens and answers.

What happened to his father?

What stopped his restless questioning?

Did he find answers or give up the search?

Once, near the base of Mount Meru the doctor and Quentin had spied, they decided, the legendary old elephant. They had heard about him for years. Now, moving across the high grass on a plain strewn with acacia trees, they saw this monstrous creature, fourteen feet high at the shoulders with those great, uneven tusks, one of them more than eleven feet long. The huge elephant had to hold his head up and tilted to one side so that the longer tusk wouldn't plow the earth as he moved.

"Is it him, do you think?" Quentin remembered asking. He had been about fifteen years old at the time.

"No doubt of it," Bill Clare answered, and they stood watching from their vantage point on the slope as the beast glided slowly through the singing grass in the afternoon breeze. The elephant was named Juju—magic—and the blacks told wondrous stories of his age, stamina, and exploits.

It carried in its body more than a dozen pieces of spears, the metal shaft of one weapon protruding from high on its rear leg and bearing, at times, small leafy limbs or vines picked up in its travels. Legend declared that more than one hundred bullets were in its body, too, and this seemed confirmed in everything Quentin saw as a boy, for the beast appeared to be made up of scar tissue—a shuffling, slumping hulk of pain and majesty. They talked about the bullets, Quentin and his father, fully aware of the hideous truth of them: mindless men from far away had come to destroy nature itself. But the magnificent Juju, its blood marking a trail wherever it walked, or so the natives claimed, would not die. Its territory was awesome in size, from the Transvaal to Kenya, from the desert to the sea—although it seemed to prefer the central lakes, Victoria, Tanganyika, and Nyasa, and crossed rivers and virtually impassable areas without regard. Nothing of what seemed its natural boundaries held it. Legend increased it. Time magnified it. Each assault it survived, so it began to reclaim in mythology and history all those who attempted to belittle or destroy it.

Then it was gone. Dead, perhaps, although no one really knew.

Twice it had charged and killed hunters—that much everyone knew, for those stories were documented in the white men's newspapers. In both instances, it charged, taking their rounds point-blank as it came, shaking its head so furiously that the tusks flashed white, then running them down. Once, after being stalked by a hunting party of natives near the village of Kibondo, it fought off their coordinated attack, taking many spears then running away. That night, a moonless night, it stalked them in return. And, curiously, none of their dogs barked warnings. Juju charged into their helpless village crushing huts and people, trumpeting and goring, ramming trees and kneeling on victims, until thirty men, women, and children lay dead. A party of men went out at dawn seeking vengeance, but the fight had gone out of the warriors and Juju had vanished.

Some believed that the bullets finally weighed it down and killed it, so that it found its appointed graveyard beyond the eyes of mortal men. Yet others claimed that it was still wandering alive and free, gathering small herds with it from time to time, as was its habit, then moving off on its own again. But few if any men would lie about seeing the beast now; real and verifiable knowledge of it was too important. And where stories surfaced the storytellers were usually questioned and discounted. Did you see the uneven tusks? The bluish scars over its body? The shaft of the spear sticking out? The glaring eyes? To be unsure was to be disgraced, so the tribes, eventually, even began to let the legend alone.

Quentin never saw it again and scarcely heard of it. Yet neither did he forget. It was an awful thing, immense and terrifying, wonderful: Africa itself carrying the spiteful, thoughtless iron of the modern world inside its body.

Darkness had come as he got up from the chair in his father's room and made his way out onto the porch. Wemba, who had hours ago stopped playing his game, occupied one of the rockers out there in the evening quiet. He stood up when Quentin appeared.

"Are you wanting supper now?" he asked.

"No, I'm not very hungry."

"I came to the doctor's room, but you were sitting with your thoughts," Wemba said, making no judgment and asking nothing.

"In two days," Quentin said, "I leave again."

13

The Professor and Jamie Vander were still in Cairo when word came through the police teletype that Hila DeGroot had emerged from her coma in Lagos.

After midnight that night they sat in the Cairo police headquarters—a vast stone and pillared cavern which reminded Charlie of a train terminal. At desks where Hamid had secured them permission to go through some of the local criminal files, they tried to use the telephones.

"Get us a plane to Nigeria," Charlie said. "See if your buddy with the CIA can find us anything tonight."

In spite of the late hour, everyone was having dinner. So the place had the look of a pharoah's tomb, a mid-American terminal, a secretarial pool, and a restaurant. Desks were turned in all directions like boats in a regatta; the odor of garlic and the clacking of antiquated typewriters dominated; around the walls were frescoes and hieroglyphics which looked strangely authentic; detectives, clerks, thieves, and prostitutes passed documents back and forth to each other.

Jamie got on the phone, stuck a finger in one ear and clasped the receiver tightly against the other.

Charlie tried to explain to the Cairo teletype operator to call the Kenyan police so that Sid Cash could be located.

Hamid and the chief inspector of detectives sat nearby eating fruit. The inspector was a small, oily man who winked at everyone.

"This new witness," Hamid called to Charlie. "She is well enough to talk with you now?"

"Maybe, don't know," Charlie called back.

Hamid looked smug, as if mystery would surely triumph.

Perhaps it would, too, Charlie thought. It was now the end of April, and the task force had been slow developing. Idi Amin had been deposed in Uganda, the peace treaty had been signed between Egypt and Israel, the first gasoline shortages annoyed the Californians, and Sid Cash had gone off to Nairobi to set up their main base of African operations. Meanwhile, Charlie and Jamie had remained in Cairo to try to find out if any Arab government or intelligence source would admit knowledge about such a killer. None would, although many of them were at least checking on each other. In Washington, the Little Buddha had given a long, controversial interview to a newspaperman. Kip Culley, until this evening's message, had almost been forgotten in Lagos.

The teletype operator seemed unable to understand exactly who Charlie wanted to call in Kenya. He kept talking about unauthorized personnel. At last, Charlie gave up the effort.

Jamie came back from his phone conversation to report that they could probably hop an empty Air Force carrier to Lagos within the hour.

A vendor came through selling sandwiches, so Hamid and the inspector abandoned their paper bag of fruit and bought some.

"Let's get out of here," Charlie said, so they gathered up their notes and left.

They drove out to the airport in a night of soft moonglow. The level sands looked like snow, and the sky glistened like hard enamel. Charlie sat back and enjoyed the drive, but Jamie was excited and talking about prospects.

"We got nothing in that final report from Interpol, so this is really a break," he kept saying. "Interpol has decided this is definitely political, so they won't help much from now on. They did come up with one poisoner, a French kid who worked the hotels with his girl friend in Hong Kong and who managed to poison a whole tour group. But their big computer check on hotel and airline lists got nothing."

"They didn't even find a man whose name was a color?" Charlie asked absently.

"Not even Lime or Beige," Jamie answered.

As their driver guided them out of the city, the odor of the smog stung their nostrils. There was no reason for it, but Charlie began to think about Stella Kane, a woman he hadn't seen in months; it was the feel of the night, the moonglow, something, that made him recall her so vividly. Jamie was still talking on.

They entered the military gate at the airport and drove along toward a lonely area where a few silent helicoptors were silhouetted against the moonlight. The desert night reduced everyone to soft words and whispers as they said hello to the three-man crew.

"By the time we hear from Sid," Jamie was saying as they climbed on board, "I'll bet he has a survey of all the venom farms in East Africa."

Charlie nodded and smiled.

They took their seats and buckled up. He couldn't understand this strong feeling about Stella, but he no longer wanted to see Callie or Andrea or anyone else; he only wanted Stella Kane, who had been an improbable acquaintance and lover on and off for years, who had an improbable job with the tracking station in Zanzibar. He could feel his body beginning to ache for her, as if she were some lost limb throbbing with nerves.

A young lieutenant came through with box lunches, coffee in plastic cups, and peppermints, all of which Charlie and Jamie accepted and held in their laps until takeoff. Then the engines revved up and they were off, Jamie's voice rising and still making words although Charlie wasn't listening.

It was a long flight, and the Professor slept fitfully. He and Jamie sat facing one another, their knees almost touching across the narrow aisle, and the empty plane rattled and often woke him up. When Jamie found him awake, he always began talking again.

At one point, Jamie was talking about meeting Kip Culley at Yale. They had been recruited by the CIA, had taken their polygraph tests, had gone through military training together. He had gone to work for Clandestine Services, moving from one dull job to another inside the Technical Services Division, he said, and had never moved into counter-intelligence as he had hoped. Kip Culley was a Queens Irishman and his background, Jamie said, was strictly Manhattan. The Professor didn't care. He slept, nodded, tried to listen, tried not to listen, and finally didn't care which of these two cockbirds were which.

Near the end of the flight the Professor was staring into the depths of his box lunch while Jamie continued.

"You know how it works," Jamie was saying. "Both Kip and I went into this work because we felt we'd see—well, some scope. But we only get to work on small pieces of puzzles and never see the whole pattern. That's how operations are designed, as you know. But I figure you see whole contexts. You always have a big picture, right?"

It took the Professor a moment to realize they were having a philosophical discussion.

"There aren't any contexts," he finally answered, rummaging around inside his box lunch, but not eating anything. "We don't know the meaning of this case we're on. We may never know."

He tried not to notice Jamie's fallen expression.

"I mean, who's going to tell us the significance of these murders? Some deputy director of yours out at Langley? Some historian? My own view is simple: seek a few facts, get an occasional description of how things work, and never worry about the greater political metaphysic."

"So you're not interested in whether or not we've got a brilliant revolutionary or just a madman killer?" Jamie asked.

"Well, if we had a foreign agent, his murders would have probably indicated a political pattern by this time. But there isn't one. None of the victims fit together, so we've got an independent."

"Yes, I see that," Jamie said.

"So it will take a lot of time. Months. We'll see if Hila DeGroot can give us a lead. Sid Cash will be thorough. And when we've exhausted normal procedures I think we'll probably get down to business and lay a trap."

"Put out decoys?"

"Our killer has access to information and seems to know who the important executives are," Charlie pointed out. "We'll probably do better in the long run if we use his awareness."

"Put an ad in the *Wall Street Journal?*" Jamie asked with a smile. He watched the Professor with renewed admiration.

"A few months from now the President will want results, the Little Buddha will be screaming his head off, and all of us will be tired and want to go home. So, yeah, I think we'll try it."

The carrier banked into its final approach. Looking out of the window behind him, Charlie found his thoughts had drifted to Stella again. Curious and wonderful. He wondered if she happened to be thinking of him, if they had linked up in some strange telepathic frequency.

Jamie was still talking, mostly to himself. "How does he find out about these executives? And how does he get so many passports? And we need to work on motive."

Losing altitude, the carrier settled down beneath the scattered clouds. His thoughts astray, Charlie continued to gaze out; divided by a thin white strip of beach and surf, the world below was all sea and jungle.

14

Kip Culley pushed his way through the early morning crowds along Marina Street toward the Iddo Hospital where he would meet the Professor and Jamie. A tinge of nausea stirred inside him, so he fretted that his body, now, as well as his work, might go bad on him. He also worried whether or not Hila DeGroot would get awake enough to reveal anything to them, whether the little recorder he had taped to her bedside would work, if the guard had stayed at her door as ordered, and if the plane from Cairo had been on time.

Crowds at every bus stop. This strange distant ghetto didn't work for him. Nothing here worked. He suffered daily diarrhea, homesickness, anxiety, and indecision.

In the lobby of the hospital Kip was spotted by Dr. Apaka, a large Ibo with a hiss for a laugh: "Sss, sss," as if a bit of happy steam escaped his lips as he spoke. Dr. Apaka wanted only one thing from Kip, the weekly bribe. Kip paid regularly because for a mere $25 weekly Hila's room was cleaned, a soldier stayed at the door, the respirator was checked, and Dr. Apaka and the orderlies strolled in and out on a somewhat irregular basis.

"Tomorrow is payday, yes?" Dr. Apaka asked, greeting Kip.

"Yes, I'll have it. How are you?"

"Fine, but you don't look so good."

"Stomach upset again," Kip told him. "Seen my colleagues? The ones who are coming to see our patient?"

"Sss, sss, nobody here who isn't deathly ill," the doctor said, making a joke which seemed true enough to Kip.

Kip went upstairs, feeling his body ache with each step, and the soldier at Hila's door got up with a grin as he approached. The American's visits meant that the guard could go take tea in the hospital snack bar with the nurses.

Hila looked calm. Her hair was spread out golden on the pillow, and the respirator whirred gently so that her lips, in response, opened and closed, moist and inviting; she seemed always about to say something, and, now, occasionally, she did. She spoke in English, Swahili, Dutch, and in broken sounds of no language at all.

Kip checked the little tape recorder. Watching her, he slipped a new cassette into the recorder and switched it on. Her eyes were open halfway, one lid sagging more than the other.

On her bedside table sat Kip's notebook with all its simplistic entries.

> *agriculture*: yams, cassava roots, maize, groundnuts (peanuts), cotton, peppers, cocoa, palm oil, rubber, gourds
> *tribes*: Yoruba, Ibo, Hausa, the nomadic Fulani, Nupe, Tiv, etc.
> *creatures*: little gecko lizards, mud fish (catfish) in the rivers, tarpon in the sea, tsetse flies, leopards in the hills, cobras & pythons, etc.

Standing there, he felt his overwhelming lack of preparation. He had no languages, no mysticism, and no capacity at the moment to understand anything except his own hamburger and Coca-Cola style. The walled compounds of the surrounding villages were forbidding. The eroded hills looked strange. The people crowded each other off the sidewalks into the slow swirl of traffic, so that they were like the surly masses around the stadium after Yale had lost a football game; except these people were curious and oddly distant from him. And his work was impossible. He couldn't organize or accomplish goals and found himself moving with the crowds, drifting from the brewery parking lots to the racecourse to the hospital to the railway station, endlessly moving but going nowhere.

The steady whirring pulse of the respirator filled the room. He wanted Hila DeGroot to wake up and to have one of her more lucid moments for the Professor. He wanted to feel healthy. He wanted to be home with his wife in Centerville, Virginia, in bed with the sheets smelling of Arpege and sunlight.

He picked up the bedside phone after half a ring.

The receptionist asked permission to send up guests. Charlie and Jamie had arrived.

They greeted one another in the corridor. Each commented on how awful the other looked: Jamie and the Professor wrinkled and weary, Kip pale and nervous. They managed a laugh about it before moving inside Hila's room and circling her bed.

"She awake or asleep?" the Professor asked.

"Don't know, really, but she starts talking sometimes," Kip said. "So far I've got nine cassettes—mostly mumbling, but I figure somebody in Washington has a machine which will decipher it all for us."

They talked to each other, but focused on Hila.

"This isn't what we expected," Jamie said, gazing at her.

"Communications are always going to be terrible," the Professor sighed. "Phones won't work. Telegrams don't get delivered. We'll work on our system once we get established in Nairobi. But don't think we came here for nothing, Kip, because we had to see for ourselves, and you were smart to tape this little recorder next to her."

Kip smiled weakly.

"What next?" Jamie wanted to know.

"Dump the cassettes in my briefcase," Charlie said. "I'll take them to Nairobi. You should get a long-playing recorder in here. Have you tried questioning her?"

"Yeah, yesterday," Kip replied. "She babbled all day, but I don't know if she heard what I asked."

As they stood watching her, a bubble of drool formed at the corner of her lips. After a moment, they all began to turn in silence and go, but Hila spoke her words thick and labored and meaningless to them.

Charlie turned to look at her lips forming the words.

"*Een ogenblik*," she said.

"What's that? Dutch?" Jamie whispered.

"Listen," Charlie said, hushing him.

"*Verlovingsring*," she said clearly. "*Diamant!*"

The men looked at one another

"*Zuid*," she sighed, and seemed to drift into sleep again.

"It was like this yesterday," Kip offered. "Maybe she'll come around in the next day or so. Dr. Apaka seems hopeful."

They stood in the corridor talking after this, going over their plans for the evening and next day, when Kip staggered over to the wall, slumped against it, and began to sink. He went down so quietly that neither Charlie or Jamie noticed him at first. Then, sliding down the wall, his legs melting underneath him, he breathed a heavy sigh which caught their attention.

"What's the matter?" Jamie asked, trying to lift his old schoolmate, but not succeeding.

"I think the killer got me," Kip replied, and it sounded for a moment like a witticism, but it was seriously meant. He did think so. He had decided that only some potent venom could weaken him so much. His feeling, at that moment, was that the killer would get the guard, Hila with her feeble drool, Dr. Apaka with his hissing laugh, the whole continent, blacks and whites, and that nobody would ever know how or why.

"Steady," the Professor said, as they lifted him up.

For a while his colleagues held him there in the corridor. A nurse passed with a tray of food and medicines. An orderly went by, promising to send help. At last, Dr. Apaka himself appeared, and Kip Culley was admitted without formality to the room next to Hila DeGroot's. They laid him out on a bed without sheets, and as the Professor's cheek brushed against Kip's in this transaction he noticed that the young man was burning with fever.

That night Charlie stayed at the hospital, sleeping on a stool pushed into the corner of Kip Culley's room. Kip tossed around and suffered nightmares in his fever, and in the next room, her respirator still whirring, with only a few cassettes left of her last efforts, Hila DeGroot lapsed back into her deep coma, spiraling down and down beyond anyone's reaching her, and died.

15

Scotch-taped to the desk in his new Nairobi office was Sid Cash's list.

1. coming: list of forgers
2. flowers to Kip
3. venom farm: dealers & sellers
4. rings that squirt: dealers in antiques, etc.
5. jewelry & rings
6. airport name scan
7. Kenyan police & military: put somebody on the $ and say howdy
8. one secretary daily: written reports to DC
9. budget for Jamie & Professor

Sid was fond of lists and believed that anything much more elaborate, such as written reports or sentence outlines, was obscene. In this particular list there resided a month or more of hard duties; done correctly, the airport scan and the surveys of jewelry dealers and venom sources might really require the fifty operatives Peter Foxx wanted on the job.

That noon Sid and his driver, Ngomo, were going toward the car. It was a bright day, the sun not too warm, and the Thorn Tree Cafe was packed with tourists, mostly blonde kids with rucksacks and eager looks. The giant tree trunk which made the place famous stood covered with safari notices and scrawled personal memos, and everything was very British, holiday-like, and spirited.

They drove north toward Lake Naivasha.

As they went along the foliage thickened and changed, and the animals appeared. Away from the city their herds and groupings became so numerous and amazing that Sid began to count: thirty species, once, in nine miles of highway viewing. Giraffe, hyena, wildebeest, zebra, baboon. Then, later, as they entered the forest, the creatures became shy, but by this time Sid's eye was sharper and he spotted the monkeys, the eagle, the tiny dove; silver deadwood and pools of water off in the forest reflected the afternoon sun, and, finally wanting to say something, Sid remarked that he would like to go wading out there in the cool shade. He was thinking of Arkansas and his boyhood, and the look he got from Ngomo said plainly, "Go out there, boss, at your own risk." There was death and terror out there, everything from nasty thorn pricks to the calm stare of the leopard.

Silence for awhile. Their Jeep had a definite rasp in the engine.

Already something was happening to Sid which he only faintly understood. He was deeply happy away from his office work in DC, from his family, from all those things he had worked to achieve, but more than that. In the drive up to the Institute, he knew that his whole life had come to this strange assignment; he would never be the same. Impala, an ostrich, some large white bird he couldn't name: the animals kept coming.

New emotion flooded into Sid. It was important for him, for he had come to the end of an old self—one he had wanted to abandon for several years—but it would result, now, in oversights.

Along a dirt road through the forest, some one hundred yards off the highway, the Institute sat surrounded by giant cottonwood trees which sent their airy particles floating down around Sid and Ngomo as they got out of the car. Sid felt at home, too, with this familiar tree. Having been away from nature for so long, he felt inebriated. As they walked up to the porch of the rambling log house built in the trees, speckled with afternoon shadow, smelling of wild jasmine, he felt like a guest—and had already lost some of his old inquisitive toughness.

That his contact turned out to be a woman, a pretty one, who served him tea first thing—he was hungry—disarmed him, too.

Her name was Daphne Brent and her father, who was away, was the founder and owner of the business.

"Lemon or cream?" she asked him, and he liked the way she said it. Her accent, like everything else, pleased him; from the dry grasslands around Nairobi he had entered this green seclusion.

He explained his purpose, and over tea—Ngomo sitting on the edge of a hassock, his knees up, balancing his cup and eating cakes with them—they began discussing poisons.

"There are deadly poisons got from plants here," she told him. "Two kinds of poison lilies, an amaryllis, and two Apocynaceae are used for making poisons to tip arrows. You know all that, I suppose?"

"Yes, but I'm only interested in a neurotoxin—and very probably the deadlier sort from the cobra or genus *Naja*."

"Some plants do produce neurotoxins," she said.

Sid smiled. "Yes, I've been studying." Daphne Brent was not particularly charming, but tough and brittle, he decided, in an interesting way.

"Well, we keep a number of snakes—hundreds. They only live in captivity, usually, from six to eight months, so the farmers and hunters bring them in, we keep buying, then we milk them and sell the venom."

"Do you have a list of names of those who bring you snakes?"

"No, we keep few records," she said. "We know many of the handlers personally. My father has usually known their fathers. They've come here for all the thirty years we've been doing this."

"Are you a scientist?" Sid asked.

"No," she answered, not elaborating. Sort of defensive. He didn't ask about her father's credentials as he planned a return visit.

"And the cobras are collected around here?" Sid continued.

"For very many miles around. Some have been brought to us all the way from the Gedi ruins. And from beyond Serengeti. The price of a good specimen is about ten British pounds, you see, which is approximately a tenth of the annual wages of most blacks in the country. So it pays them to find the creatures—there's naturally some danger involved—and to transport them up here."

"The specimens usually come delivered by the handlers personally?"

"Almost always. We received some shipments, but many snakes die en route or there are accidents or we've even refused to go down to Nairobi and accept delivery."

"I can understand why."

"Quite. More tea, Mr. Cash?"

"Thanks, no. And you do have a list of those companies you sell to?"

"There are only three clients," she said. "Ninety percent goes to the Pasteur Institute in Paris—with whom we have an informal relationship. Then there's Allen and Hanbury's in London. Then only occasionally we've sent venom to your Central Intelligence Agency. Are you really with them?"

"No, with Interpol—as I told you."

Daphne Brent sipped the remainder of her tea. She was having a political thought, Sid decided.

"And, say, at the Pasteur Institute," Sid went on. "Do they make serum with the venom? I never have understood exactly what's done with it."

"Horses can be innoculated with venom," she said. "It's a slow process, but, yes, they can transform horses into serum factories, so to speak. But most venom is used in laboratories. It's such a very strong toxic chemical, you see, that it has the effect of causing the various elements in chemical compounds to separate from one another. So it's used in analyzing compounds—breaking them into their component parts."

"Are there middle men?" Sid asked. "Anyone between you and these clients in Paris, London, and Washington?"

"No, we package and ship directly ourselves."

"Someone at the post office could intercept, though?"

"Always possible." Her smile indicated that she wasn't enjoying herself. What did she do up here all day, he wondered, and what sort of life was it?

"How many employees here?"

"Fifteen or so. I have made a little list of those, as your secretary asked me to do."

"You understand that this is important, I hope," Sid said. "Innocent people are getting killed with cobra venom. We'd like to know where it's coming from."

"Quite so," she answered. Defensive still. Daphne was not a nice person, no, he decided, yet he wanted to be no place on earth except in that room: her dry enunciations, the cottonwood particles drifting by the window, the black shape of Ngomo on the hassock, the lush green shade surrounding them. It was not an office with snow outside in the streets. The room, the people, the job had texture again, as if for a long time he had lost the sense of touch.

"And who are your major competitors?" he went on.

"The largest outfit nearby is down in Dar es Salaam. There are others in Rhodesia—all over, for all I know. But, of course, we're the largest here."

"No small, minor competitors?"

"The business was very loosely organized for years. Individuals— doctors, missionaries, those sorts—extracted venom. At times, the market was good, so my father tells me. But we finally got things organized. There are a few collectors who handle transportation from, say, Mombasa or from Lake Rudolph—agents, so to speak. But we are the Institute."

"I see. How many people altogether in this whole network?"

"I couldn't guess," she said, smiling coldly.

"Try."

"Hundreds, then. They're naked black men, most of them, Mr. Cash, and they lift up rocks at the edge of the desert or go barefoot into ruins where the cobras like to gather. They catch them with forked sticks or their little nets, and they bring them to us. Some of the natives appear in the driveway with virtual monsters in their arms. For the money, you see. And they have names you probably couldn't pronounce and live in huts or caves or on the ground—with no addresses or permanent locations. You're not in the twentieth century here, and they aren't either. And personally I don't believe you can locate them, not in any sense. Not physically, not spiritually, not in any way."

"Quite so," Sid said, deliberately borrowing her phrase. "Can we see your setup now?"

"Come into the yard," she said, and they went outside.

The yard was a pit hewn out of rock and hard clay: some twelve feet deep and possibly sixty feet square, its bottom covered with stones, some of them in neat piles, and dotted with white, cone-shaped pods made of light plastic. The snakes were mostly inert, but impressive; Sid resisted saying anything or giving off the long, low whistle he wanted to give. Ngomo stayed back safely on the steps leading into the house, his cup and saucer still balanced in his rough hands.

Two men, naked to the waist, were raising a particularly fat cobra with a long bamboo pole fitted with unsharpened hooks.

Sid stood at the pit's edge seeing what he could. The snakes wore markings. Beyond one of the stacks of stones there was a pool of water, an open tap above it sending down a steady stream, rivulets running out its top.

"I'd like a brief interview with your employees today," Sid said. "Just a minute or two each, if possible."

"They come in shifts, and you've already missed one," Daphne said, walking the edge of the pit. "But, please, help yourself."

"Someone will have to come back. The odds are poor, as you say, but we want to be as thorough as we can."

She smiled back at him, shading her eyes from the sun's glare. The smile, he momentarily felt, was more genuine, but her voice was rich with irony when she said, "Someone out there in our world has really disturbed yours, right, Mr. Cash?"

He didn't answer.

In the laboratory, a separate frame building down a path behind the pit, there were other specimens in glass cages. There they could be observed up close as they awaited milking.

"Are venomous snakes immune to poison from other snakes?" Sid asked, thinking of another question. She seemed most content, he decided, explaining things.

"No," she answered. "They're not."

"If you kill a cobra, will its mate come to avenge it?" he went on, stating the old myth.

She gave him an amused glance. They walked between rows of the glass cages now. Through a glass door Sid could see two attendants milking a cobra in the next room. The lab was air-conditioned, and Sid could also hear the slight noise of a distant gas motor from off in the forest behind the building.

"Does anyone get bitten here?" he asked.

"We've had one death and quite a few survivals from bites," she said. "One old employee, bitten in the face and convinced he had only a few hours to live, asked that we have a party. We stopped work for the day, opened all the beer and wine on the premises, ate every scrap of food, and he lived. He slept for a few days, then he was mostly embarrassed, I think, over the whole incident."

In one of the cages there were newly born cobras.

"Immediately after birth the young raise up and open their hoods," Daphne told him as they passed.

This information somehow gave Sid a shudder.

In a special pit in the side yard, Daphne showed Sid the only mamba owned by the Institute.

"They're a very nervous snake," she said, "and can be alerted by a nearby footfall. This one knows we're here watching it. Their chief area is to the west. There are many in Rhodesia. They lay eggs. They're the largest and deadliest—mostly because they have so much poison in their bodies. But they're also more savage. They attack almost anything. Want to know more?"

Sid and the mamba seemed to exchange stares.

"Is he watching me?"

"Oh, yes," she answered.

Back beside the large pit they saw Ngomo still on the steps, sitting down in the shade now, waiting until this disturbing tour had finished. Sid watched his hostess, trying to assess her politics; colonial, he guessed, but another one of those who consider any brief visitor an outsider. Lots of ironies there. She was a truly beautiful woman: not much makeup, her black hair pulled back, the sort one finds on magazine covers, he told himself. In contrast, he was aware that he was large, even corpulant, and sweating. She doesn't like me, he found himself thinking, because I'm not particularly beautiful. Odd, that such knowledge would lurch in.

Down in the pit he saw one cobra strike at another. The lunge missed and the snake fell clumsily in the effort and had to regain its coil.

"The man using venom as a weapon isn't a black man," he told her as they strolled back toward the Jeep. "I think he'll be easier to find than not—once we have more information. And we have other unique scraps of data. It won't be as though we're looking through your whole network of employees, handlers, and agents."

"We wouldn't mind if you did," Daphne Brent assured him. "It's just that—well, I don't think you know what you're saying. You have no real comprehension."

"How do you mean?"

"We estimate the animal populations in this country by flying over them in airplanes," she said. "Two people sit in the back of a plane, you see, and talk into tape recorders as they look down. This represents scientific method applied to the continent. Of course, they never have any idea what the size of an elephant herd is—much less how many antelope or monkeys there are down there. They talk into their microphones, saying, 'Six elephant, one giraffe, a dozen zebra,' and so on. But the estimates are frightfully inaccurate and never agree with other estimates."

"The continent is large, I know," Sid said. "And my job's hard."

"Impossible, not hard," she said. "You surely know that you're applying western methods in a situation where they truly can't work."

"I believe they will work," Sid said, and even as he did doubts sprang to mind. "This is my first visit. I can see there will have to be a larger staff, more interviews than we anticipated, more travel. Then there's—"

"But can't you see what you're saying?" she interrupted. "And this is only one part of the continent. There are other venom laboratories, a whole trade in Europe, and nature itself is the commodity—so there can never be any real inventory!"

They stood beside the Jeep, Ngomo waiting for them to finish their argument. The deep greens of afternoon gathered around them. Sid tried to smile at Daphne, to pacify her, to assure her with his calm that in spite of all her objections there would be solutions.

"Sorry to have bothered you here," he said awkwardly. "It is a necessary procedure toward—"

"I'm not annoyed by the interruption, please believe that," she told him. "Nor by you personally. Please. It's just the—innocence. The magnificent innocence!"

Stiffened by this, Sid opened the door to the Jeep. Ngomo took the signal, got inside, and started the motor.

"For any annoyance, I apologize, Miss Brent," Sid said. "But, even so, I'll have to come back and start an investigation in earnest. The Institute seems to me very important in all of East Africa. We'll have to run down every lead."

"Mrs. Brent," she corrected him. "I have a husband. My father's name is Bryan Wilton."

"Is your husband here, too?"

"No, in Europe. We're separated. Sorry, he's not your white man. Try again."

"I wasn't thinking that," Sid told her. He was thinking it, though, and as they said their goodbyes, having come to this impasse, and as the Jeep pulled away with them giving each other slight waves of the hands, Sid was still embarrassed that his thoughts showed so clearly.

Going back along the highway toward Nairobi, bouncing so that he could barely write, he began another list. Ngomo stared ahead at the road, saying nothing.

Images of the pit remained with them both. Ngomo, who had not even peered over its side, had seen snakes like that before and had no interest in reviving any old nightmares. Sid imagined the insides of those cone-shaped pods gleaming in the sunlight; there would be coils of cobras underneath, he knew, entwined with each other, impossible to distinguish. Beneath that cone of domed plastic, lying in the shade, a ball of deadly movement: the individual cobras blent into one.

His list grew long and complex. There were footnotes and asides: things to do, tactics, staff, money, methods. He had never made such a long annotated list in his whole career.

16

Zanzibar.

She met him at the airport, threw her arms around his neck, and took his mouth with hers: a long kiss, bold, in the sunlight, taking his breath away, and when they finally parted they were both laughing.

All around him, this favorite place of his: the overpowering scent of cloves, the aquamarine sea, sex, and a rampant craziness. Stella was part of the craziness.

The curiosity, as he once admitted to her and as she agreed, was that they didn't fit; their bodies were mismatched and their rhythms were off, so that although they had good sex they never enjoyed successful sex. But in all other ways they were companions in humor and in trust. Stella Kane, who worked for the satellite tracking station on the island, who had led the Professor to the place years ago, stood looking into his eyes that afternoon, crowds jostling them as they held each other, and said to him, "Okay, here's one: America has been importing urine from Haiti!"

"Why?" he asked, throwing back his head in laughter.

"Because for some needed experiments in Florida! American male urine was found to have too many proteins! They couldn't use it!"

Stella was a collector of idiocies.

They went directly to her bed where, as usual, they performed with an enthusiasm which dwindled into quiet stroking.

"God, I missed you," he told her.

"I love you so much," she answered. Then she added her favorite, forlorn, comic refrain: "Oh me, pain and misery!"

Afterward, they walked along the sea wall.

Around the harbor of Zanzibar Town lay a strip of grass shaded by palms and adorned with japonica. Beyond were all the traffic and market noises, but Stella's house—she was lucky to have it—was out there on the green. Nearby, an old Arab house had served as the British consulate, once, and there Burton and Speke had fitted themselves for their expedition up country toward the huge inland lakes and the sources of the Nile. In that house, too, Livingstone's body had been laid out.

They walked and talked, catching up. With the tide out in the harbor all the fishing boats tipped at odd angles, their masts askew, going this way and that. Another craziness. Then, as they walked, the old palace loomed into view.

Out at sea a single dhow sailed the horizon, a lonely visitor from across the Indian Ocean who waited for the tide.

"Seems crowded in town," he said to her.

"Not an available room," she said. Nothing unusual registered with him, for he was watching her mouth as she spoke. "There's a big Trade Mart bringing in people. The President speaks tomorrow. The clove market is going full swing. And it's a holiday of some sort, so all the fishermen are in port."

He told her his business, all about the Little Buddha, the killings, and how he had cut short another school term to go on assignment. Stella sensed the maniac logic in all of it; she had lived in Washington and knew.

In reply to all he was saying, she gave him another from her collection.

"Guess what Greta Garbo said this year?"

"What?" he asked her, grinning with anticipation.

"After all these years of saying she wanted to be alone, she said she was lonely."

"Is that it?" he asked, as they kept walking.

"I've got others," she said. "It's really been a pretty good year for non sequiturs."

Charlie took her hand in his. Their whole lives, he sometimes felt, had gone akimbo: their jobs had often sent them to separate cities, Vietnam had claimed month after month, other romantic interests had occurred for them both, nothing had fit. He was sixty years old, she was nearly forty, time had ebbed away. Now here they were again at this cuckoo island at the bottom of Africa, a place with a leper colony, flying squirrels, a rain forest, Chinese goods, Russian military advisors, Persian women, and two people in the minor key of love. They had known each other for ten years—and even at the beginning nothing had matched, not their ages or their destinations. In his own affairs there had been Callie the intellectual waitress, Andrea the attaché's wife, five or six others, but there was always Stella, who loved Africa, who loved craziness, who loved him—how did he even know this?—and so on his various African assignments he managed to get to Zanzibar. Again and again. And here she was once more.

For Stella, the sight of Charlie Hazo stepping off the plane from Dar es Salaam meant more than she could ever tell him. There he was: jogging shoes, dark sunglasses, gleaming teeth, and all that scar tissue. He was getting older. He was the ultimate absurdist. But her heart exploded beneath her heavy breasts like a schoolgirl's, and all the orifices of her body opened to him in that hello kiss. She would make an effort to keep matters light, preparing to say goodbye again soon, finding jokes wherever possible. And, true, they were a mismatched set. And, yes, other lovers had crowded their lives and nothing had ever worked, not even their most acrobatic sex, but her blood rushed around in her veins when he spoke to her. And he was in love with her in some fortunate romantic way—how could she know this? how?—which she would never betray that she understood.

"If there's a new headquarters for this big operation being set up in Nairobi, why are you here?" she asked him, squeezing his fingers.

"Because you know I don't like Nairobi. Too civilized. Give me this muddy dump anytime."

"You've got some business here? Going to invent another little seminar?"

"No, I've got no business this time. This is time off for planning strategy. I've come to think things out."

"Can I help?"

"Definitely."

"Wanta go to dinner over at the new hotel?"

"No, I'd like to think in your bed."

"We just came from there."

"I've missed you, Stella."

It was the dearest thing he had ever uttered, and she thought she might cry. Instead, she turned him around and they walked back the way they had travelled, hurrying their steps a little this time.

Rain fell most of the night, and they watched its shadows off the contours of each other's bodies. Again, their sexual futility resulted in a strange, deepening tenderness. Four times, too, they started quiet, brief conversations before lapsing back into sleep; once, she asked him about the scars, those old pocks in his torso, just as all his women asked him, only this time, surprising himself, he told the story. Fifteen years ago he had owned a nice Jaguar car, he said to her, green in color.

"And you wrecked it," she sighed, guessing.

"Just listen, okay?"

He had gone out to his garage in DC: a small wedge of locked car space in a row of others on the back alley of some town houses.

He usually opened the garage through an inner stairway which led down from his kitchen, he told her. He usually came down, started the car, then pressed the garage door opener—which automatically raised the outside door and admitted him to the foul Washington weather. But this morning he went outside into the alley, taking out an overflow of trash, and opened the door with his key from the outside. That had saved his life.

The bomb, like the car, was a small, deadly little package. Had he started the motor inside the closed garage, as usual, the concussion probably would have killed him, but this way he just caught flying metal. Everything burned as he crawled outside—on fire and losing blood over his whole body—and threw himself in a pile of dirty winter snow to extinguish the flames.

"That place on your forehead," Stella whispered. "You got that in the explosion?"

"No, that's another story."

"Liar."

"No, really, I'll tell you another time."

They lay in silence for a while until the inevitable question arrived. The warm rain, the clove-scented sea air all around them.

"There's the strange part," he said. "I have no idea who might have done it. There was an investigation which even covered all my neighbors—checking to see if they had such enemies and if I might have been hit by mistake. But nothing. My trips to Africa had been far more routine then. You know, small academic conferences—that stuff. I had never made a single run for either State or the CIA. Nothing personal anywhere—at least, it was assumed that none of my former girl friends were clever at making car bombs. It was almost like an accident except, of course, it wasn't."

"And since then?"

"Nothing else. But it was an incident which threw a shadow. I'm still—scared."

"You don't act scared," Stella said softly, kissing another large scar high on his shoulder.

"Not terrified, not just cautious either," he said. "Somewhere in between. I got sobered up."

They fell asleep again. Sometime later in the night he awoke with her breath against his cheek and neck; she had pulled herself so close against his body that they were drenched in perspiration. He lay awake with an assortment of musings and half-thoughts. A Swahili saying: "Where fate is accepted, grief is short." The early gods of the island: tree spirits. Historical fact: there was a creek running through the old Stone Town where they used to throw corpses. Everything was monstrous accident, he decided; fate, nature, malevolence, all of it. It didn't matter if you took a fever from being pricked on the finger with a thorn or if you were slain by your arch foe or if you died of heartbreak from lost love; death was so unruly and real. The ultimate idiocy, Stella: things die on us, we die on each other, we die of ourselves.

The continent, shaped like a question mark, ancient and terrible, was a death mask to put on; you held it up to your face to test how it felt. You walked on death here; the mulch of the centuries was underfoot; the loneliness you felt was death; these islands, these rivers, these sea breezes blowing off the remains of the old slave markets and battlefields and deserted ruins whispered death.

Charlie Hazo, lying in bed in the arms of a woman whose love with him had died over and over, reviving at times only to die again, had entered into his last intellectual period: he would ponder and wait. Death was with him, all around. His very own. So that even his sleep was a metaphor.

In the morning, of course, he was better.

There it was: a bright yellow tablecloth, the sanity of toast and coffee, Stella smiling, and a cloudless sky.

She gave him a good morning hug and made that small sound under her breath, saying, "Oh god, pain and misery!"

"You aren't having fun?" he asked her, sipping that strong bitter island coffee she served.

"When you come see me, I ache," she told him. "I think it's simple yearning—that sort of ache. But I don't sleep and my bones hurt."

"Let's go do something today, then, and forget your bones." he suggested. "Let's go into Stone Town and walk around."

"I'd like that. I'd like to show you off."

"Show *me* off? You got some island boyfriends who are easily impressed?"

"You're impressive. You are," she said, and she plopped down in the kitchen chair across from him, put her elbows on the table, her chin on her fists, and adored him. He felt very alive.

By noon they were walking in the overcrowded town. In the narrow, winding streets the crowds overwhelmed them, and in spite of themselves they both complained.

"It's the damned Trade Mart," she told him. They stopped for tea they didn't particularly want just so they could sit in a doorway.

Charlie read an old copy of the *London Telegraph*. Together, they watched the flow of pedestrians, the Arab women in their purdahs, the black women in their bright kangas, the Americans in slacks.

"Aren't there a lot of Americans?" he asked, once.

"And they've all brought their wives," she said. "Look at all of them."

Still, nothing significant registered.

After tea they took another walk, passing the old clove warehouses, cutting along the edge of Ngambo, the black quarter, then moving back into Stone Town with all its Arab and Indian stalls. Old consul houses peeked out from clusters of weathered palms around the edge of the harbor. All the European nations had outposts and embassies here in the old days, hoping to snare the rich Indian Ocean trade, but since the drab new socialist regime the city and island had faded into ruin. The American embassy had closed, and only the Russians stubbornly remained in their big grey compound.

During the walk, Stella talked about her job. Her work at the tracking station was a weak cover, she admitted, and her reports had slumped into routine. She gave Langley no news, no fresh insights, and no intelligence, she said, yet they kept her on. She expected to be transferred soon.

They passed a headquarters house for the Communist Youth League. Outside its ornate door, studded with brass nails, a coffee hawker clinked his empty cups together to attract trade. Toward the sea wall once more, they looked out on a great swelling of thunderheads.

Then there was a band.

"Is that what I think it is?" he asked.

"Yep, John Philip Sousa," she said, smiling, as if to say, yes, this is the idiocy for today's collection.

Stars and Stripes Forever came brassing out of a crumbling pavilion in the big public area beside the harbor. Walking toward the commotion, they saw a cluster of flags, a tattered marquee, rows of metal chairs set out on the grass, and what seemed to be a thousand men and women—white, European and American, starched—wearing dark sunglasses. As they strolled closer they noticed that a number of blacks, Indians, and orientals were sprinkled through the throng, too, disguising themselves in western dress. The black band members were robed in green with golden trim—except for a single, good natured trombonist who wore a soiled T-shirt and the trousers to his army fatigues. Everyone sported plastic name cards; the women were bedecked in corsages; a table with a punch bowl and a microphoned speaker's stand adorned the front of the marquee. A dozen soldiers tried to look inconspicuous around the edges of the crowd.

Stella knew exactly what was going on. "I was invited to this," she admitted.

"The Trade Mart," Charlie said flatly, remembering.

"A wholesale cloth alliance, no less. The women at Saks or Bergdorf's next season are supposed to buy fabrics from the east."

"We could crash the party," Charlie said, as they walked on.

"Yes, and I could introduce you to J.J. Barney. He's a manufacturer and entrepreneur from Ohio. There, the tall one near the speaker's stand."

Charlie looked, but saw no one who looked like an entrepreneur.

"I thought Tanzania's head man was coming for this," he said, and as he said it his thoughts tripped.

"The President's address is tomorrow. By the way, I have to work tomorrow. No avoiding it."

They strolled on. The band changed tunes to something less robust, but Charlie wasn't listening to either Stella or the band anymore. Suddenly, a tiny crease of worry: this publicized event, the President, all the Americans. He slowed their pace.

"Something wrong?" she asked.

"No, nothing," he answered. Deliberately, he put his worry out of his mind by drawing her body against his.

"I forgot to tell you: I've got a present for you," she said, and they were into another zone of awareness again.

"Something to wear? Jogging shoes?"

"No, something to drink. A guaranteed aphrodisiac!"

"Really? Where'd you get it?"

"From an old woman who works on the cleaning crew at the station. She's been watching me, she said, and she decided I needed love."

"Only one thing to do. Let's go try it."

"It's supposed to be from the wizards of Pemba Island," Stella told him. "Pure white magic. You have to drink it down, but I only have to rub it behind my ears."

They were laughing as they moved away from the music in the pavilion. That afternoon, then, they went back to Stella's house near the sea wall, undressed, started to bathe before going out for the evening, but fell into bed once more. Later they made omelettes and settled in for the night.

They were searching for a last bottle of wine when the phone rang.

"It was a friend over at the station," she told Charlie when she rang off. "Remember the entrepreneur?"

"J.J. Barney," he said, pronouncing the name.

Surprise showed in her eyes that he remembered. "Yes."

"Something happened to him, didn't it?" he asked abruptly.

"He's dying," she said, reading his face. "Heart attack, something, they don't know." And suddenly she understood his hesitation during their walk; she knew what had crossed his thoughts.

"Where?" He hurried the buttons of his shirt. Stella could only repeat what she had heard on the phone.

"In the park," she managed. "Where we were—"

The Professor was already scrambling into his jogging shoes tucked beneath the edge of her bed.

The pavilion where the Trade Mart was being conducted still swarmed with people: delegates walked around and clustered in groups underneath the palms, soldiers idled near the marquee, and the band members stood around with their clarinets and trumpets in their hands. It seemed like the end of a long, drunken party. Hurrying, Charlie made his way toward the group of men beneath the marquee. An army officer stopped him.

He tried to explain his business, but found it difficult.

"Official or not?" the officer kept asking, holding Charlie's sleeve.

"Yes, official!" Charlie finally lied, and so was allowed to pass. The body of a policeman lay sprawled on the grass, abandoned, while everyone knelt around someone else who Charlie couldn't see.

"Who's in charge?" Charlie kept asking everyone.

"Please," someone said to him, as if he were an annoyance.

"Tell me what happened," he kept saying. "I'm an American authority." He used that ambiguous word consciously, afraid that anything more specific or less powerful would have no effect.

A late evening breeze was rising, so that the lanterns and naked light bulbs hung in the palms around the pavilion caused tendrils of shadow to be thrown across the grass. The flags grew noisy. From across the park came the sound of laughter.

"It may be that a murder has been committed here," Charlie kept saying, making his way toward the center of the group.

"Murder?" someone replied vacantly, repeating the word.

"Tell me what happened! Please, excuse me. I'm an American—"

A man in mirrored sunglasses stood up and greeted Charlie, but would neither introduce himself nor let the Professor come closer.

On the ground, propped up against a tent pole which held the marquee, was J.J. Barney. The sight was grim and amazing: he was bleeding from the eyes.

Stella Kane, meanwhile, came hobbling across the park in high-heeled shoes. Hurrying and stumbling, she was dressed in a dour grey two-piece suit, her most severe social uniform.

Everyone talked at once. A doctor prepared to unbutton J.J. Barney's coat, but Charlie Hazo yelled at him, "No, don't do that! Don't touch him!" There were curses and shouts and explanations. The man in the mirrored sunglasses, who would turn out to be a police commissioner, placed his hand on a small revolver which he wore inside his coat. Only after this did the confusion lessen. The policeman on the ground, someone explained to the doctor and to Charlie, had carried J.J. Barney from the speaker's podium to his present position at the tent pole, then had dropped dead himself. This was hardly expected, the narrator added.

"Yes, there's very likely deadly poison on both these men," Charlie explained, and everyone took a step back.

A pleasant black man in green robe and golden braid stepped up to the commissioner of police and asked, "Will that be all for the band tonight, sir?" Workers, at the same time, were beginning to dismantle the marquee under which everyone stood. And it was beginning to rain.

As an army colonel arrived—someone else to take charge—Stella glimpsed the condition of J.J. Barney and gave a short gasp. Charlie pulled her away.

"Help me here," he told her. "We've got to close the airport and the docks at once."

"Yes," she said, trying to reason along with him. "Stop the ferry."

"Exactly. Stop all of it. You understand, don't you?"

The army colonel, the doctor, and the commissioner stood talking about the situation as workers continued to fold up chairs and lower the marquee. The dead policeman, Charlie noticed, was lying in the rain now—all evidence probably being washed away into the grass beneath him. At last the commissioner interrupted his conference to order the workers to stop.

"Now, please, who are you and what do you want?" the colonel said, coming over to Charlie.

Witnesses, at the same time, recounted events to the commissioner, Stella, and the doctor. Mr. Barney, they recalled, was among a number of guests around the punch bowl. They were all shaking his hands and talking loudly. Then, as he moved toward the speaker's podium for the evening address, his legs became shaky and he took ill.

As rain began to fall harder, a black man in a business suit stepped underneath the marquee and took a photograph of J.J. Barney with a small camera adorned by cube flashbulbs. Droplets of bright blood continued to form in the eyes of the business leader; except for the photographer, now, no one paid any attention to the stricken man, for he was clearly unreal and gone.

"You want to close down the island?" the colonel asked Charlie. "But naturally this is impossible, you see."

"It's an *island*," Charlie insisted. "We've got him! He can't get off, if we shut down all the transport right now! Don't *you* see?"

"There are many steamships and ferries," the colonel said, smiling proudly like a representative of tourism. "Also many planes, commercial and private! This is quite cosmopolitan here. Have you been here before?"

"If we act quickly, we've got a chance to catch him," Charlie told the colonel. "But you'll have to take responsibility!"

The colonel laughed out loud.

"If what you say is true, we can possibly catch such a man," he said, amused with Charlie's urgency. "But close the island—oh, no, not possible. Not all of Zanzibar, not hardly!"

17

Minutes after his appearance at the pavilion, Quentin was aboard a sixty-foot rusted commercial boat sailing toward the mainland. Its load was cloves and its destination was Bagamoyo, a harbor forty miles north of Dar with less traffic and a sleepy Arab town with few European amenities. The ship stank of rancid bilge, so that Quentin, sitting underneath a yellow slicker on its deck, was glad for the soft rain washing over them. There was only one other person on board, the ship's owner and captain. He had been paid ninety British pounds for his services—a sum arrived at through an hour's bargaining earlier in the day.

The owner usually took two or three deck hands on his journeys over to Zanzibar, but well understood that Quentin wanted to go alone—and that the price was for both the fare and the solitude. The business of these waters was often shady or worse: piracy, smuggling, black marketeering, even some occasional white slavery—usually of an impulsive sort these days, as the owner told Quentin, in which some white European girl was kidnapped and whisked away to be raped and sold, if selling could be arranged, or to be murdered if no available buyer turned up.

On the return trip, the owner wanted to talk about all this, but Quentin under the slicker, kept his silence.

"There are men who will pay in money or women," he boasted. "They tell me this!"

His laughter made Quentin sullen.

The rain fell silently, a thick misty brine, and the sea around them seemed to disappear.

Since reading that single tell-tale line in the newspaper about possible foul play in Cairo, Quentin had planned with a new caution. This trip had been made without air transportation, accommodations, or much time spent in Zanzibar. In a day's time using a forged name and vehicle papers he had driven his own Land Rover across the border at Namanga, then had driven through the mountains down to Bagamoyo on the coast. There he had gone directly to the harbor to strike a deal with the boat owner.

He had known about the Trade Mart from the Nairobi newspapers because Kenya had sent delegates. He had learned about J.J. Barney only after his arrival on the island; it had been easy to learn the identity of the event's principal man. He had struck with impunity. Now he had escaped. As they made the journey across that narrow stretch between island and mainland, he was already thinking of his next excursion. Salisbury, he thought. After that, Nairobi itself. Then something far away on the west coast.

Darkness still lay over the little harbor when they arrived. He paid the owner—who had stopped talking about white slavery and had turned wary and afraid after they docked—and made his way along the narrow back streets toward the Land Rover.

Someone had stolen his spare wheel and tire off the rear rack and had slashed open the tarpaulin. For a few minutes he stood in the darkness, listening. Then, deciding that matters could be worse, he climbed inside and drove away.

By noon of the next day he arrived at the Namanga border station again. This time, though, things were different: soldiers were everywhere.

Braving it out, he drove the Land Rover into their midst. The patrol house, flanked on each side by driveways for cars coming and going, overflowed with soldiers and customs agents. Tourists and visitors were being questioned inside.

He stood beside the Land Rover trying to think what to do. A young soldier nearby smiled at him.

"What's going on in there?" he asked the boy.

"Mon, I don't know," the young soldier sighed.

Even if they weren't looking for him, they would take a long look at his clumsily forged papers, he concluded. He thought of turning back into the country he wanted to escape. Over there—fifty yards off—was Kenya and safety. He thought of bribing someone. He could drive into Serengeti, then later cross the border at one of those isolated back trails in the national park. What to do?

Quentin made his way to the porch of the patrol house. Around him, the soldiers stank of sweat and stale beer. But he was excited with the game. Aloof, he walked through the soldiers and customs guards and entered the station.

An American couple, man and wife, argued with a border official. She was particularly strident, insisting, "No, I won't! You won't search me!"

The guards and soldiers found her very amusing.

"Just go in the bathroom and—"

Her husband's careful explanations infuriated her.

Quentin fixed himself against a rear wall in the crowded room.

"You will not get through this station without searching!" the border official proclaimed. Laughter from the guards and soldiers. A small white dog moved underfoot, sniffing at Quentin, sniffing at someone else.

The American husband raised his voice.

At the far end of the counter which halved the room, another uniformed customs agent raised a rubber stamp, then brought it down with authority on someone's passport. Again, laughter from all the soldiers and guards.

They have sealed the borders, Quentin reasoned, and probably have the airports, bus terminals, and train stations under close watch.

The American wife said something shrill, then broke into laughter of her own.

Quentin waited. From his position, he could see that the gate beyond the patrol house was wide open. As he drew closer to the window, he checked all the guards: they were talking to each other, drinking bottles of Tusker, passing cigarettes around. Outside the station, he decided, nobody asked for one's passport or papers and just assumed that the officials inside had tended to business.

Boldly, he walked back onto the porch. He breathed a heavy sigh, as if everything with the agents had been an ordeal. Folding his papers back into his pocket, he walked straight for the Land Rover.

Distant laughter again: the Americans and the soldiers.

When he started the motor, its sound startled him. His hands on the wheel turned moist and cold.

Then he drove through the gate and into Kenya.

Again, he felt that everything was on his side: luck, nature, even the vain bureaucracies of men.

18

"Perfect. Couldn't be better," Peter Foxx told the Professor.

"But I really couldn't get the harbor closed," Charlie pointed out. "I couldn't close the train depot. I couldn't even explain who I was or what the hell I wanted."

"Take my word for it," said Peter, "What happened in Zanzibar fits into everything very nicely. Our man was on the spot. Almost caught the killer. If the police and army hadn't bungled, we would have. That's all anybody here needs to know."

"But it wasn't like that. We didn't almost catch anybody."

"Officially, it was a near miss. Would you like some lunch?"

"Where?"

"Someplace powerful. Cosmos Club. You earned it, so you name it."

Charlie Hazo had flown to Washington to report, and now after only four hours in the city he was ready to return. There were too many dreaded loose ends. In the month of May his seminar students left plaintive messages in his college mailbox asking if he would please read their term papers, allow them makeup exams, and attend to their personal lives; it was Callie's birthday, so she would want the collected works of T.S. Eliot, say, bound in leather and delivered with a kiss; Andrea would want to cook leg of lamb, then ask him leading questions about his recent whereabouts and love life; the people renting his house would want to break their lease; the life of the Little Buddha would ensnare him.

He had kissed Stella goodbye at the Zanzibar airport, that sand-swept configuration of chug-holed runways and bleak Arab houses.

"Oh god," she had said, nuzzling his neck. "Pain and misery."

"I want you to come to Nairobi and work on this thing with us," he had suddenly told her in response to that familiar low moan.

"How could I do that?"

"I'll try and get you a special assignment. You work on getting a leave. We'll say you're needed."

"Am I needed?"

It had been such a pointed question, designed to bend the Professor into uncharacteristic sentimentality.

"Well, I need—do need you. Want you," he had stuttered. "Sure."

She had broken into laughter, burying her face against his shoulder. She smelled like cloves and Jontue.

It had been a good year for idiocies, whatever, she had told him, and she had enjoyed seeing him again. The comedian Jerry Lewis, she reminded him, had been nominated for the Nobel Peace Prize that year; Anwar Sadat, who had actually won the prize, had announced that all infidels of the true faith in Egypt could be subject to execution; major religious wars were still being fought in Lebanon and Ireland; some Arabians were planning to float an iceberg to their desert homeland; and, again, Stella and the Professor, mismatched, had met and parted.

Charlie, unable to say anything remotely sane, bit his lip.

When he was in the plane flying back to DC, he decided to make a real effort to arrange Stella's temporary transfer. Life was short and love was shorter.

After their first briefing, Peter took him to the Jockey Club for lunch. There, Charlie watched the famed dining habits of the Little Buddha: hands aflutter, eyes shooting this way and that toward dishes being served at other tables, appetite on display. Peter, Charlie noticed, ate a piece of chocolate mousse pie in three bites, halving the pie with his fork and devouring that, then turning the dish sideways, halving the remainder, and gobbling down those two portions.

The Little Buddha was now mildly famous. His mother and father had come up from Cumberland, Tennessee, in fact, to see their son receive an award—made up for the occasion, from the sound of it—from Treasury. But the source of his fame was the article by Fielding Blanks which had adorned the Sunday edition of the newspaper; in it, Peter Foxx was extolled as a genius who "played a series of cunning gambits in a deadly chess game with a maniacal killer." The article, reprinted and mounted in a little glossy folder of its own, had been sent around to all those offices which possessed copies of *Disorders and Terrorism*. Having sent out his own best-seller, as an editor of the city remarked, Peter Foxx was now sending out his own reviews.

"Will Sid catch our man?" the Little Buddha asked Charlie at lunch. "Or do you still think there's not much chance?"

"Not much chance," Charlie said, forking veal into his mouth.

"So what should we do?"

"There are lots of possibilities."

"Name the most expensive one. Nobody here will understand anything except the cost anyway."

"Well, we can put an obvious target in the field."

"Good. What will this require?"

"Publicity," Charlie said. "But you seem to have the knack for it."

Peter, in spite of himself, smiled proudly. Then, thinking ahead, he began to work on the scenario. "Obviously, we don't set up camp in a single African city. We give our decoy an itinerary and follow him around, don't we?"

"Exactly."

"I like it," Peter said, snapping his fingers at a waiter. "Let's get going on it."

At this moment, gliding between tables, her graceful neck executing its soft thrust, Andrea came toward them. Charlie put down his napkin and stood up while the Little Buddha gulped down the remainder of his coffee.

"How long have you been in town?" Andrea inquired.

"For six hours," Charlie told her, manufacturing a smile.

At this point, Peter Foxx was trying to get his belly out from underneath the edge of the table. In doing so, a water glass, mostly empty, tipped over, and in the midst of all this introductions were made.

"You will be coming by later?" Andrea asked, fixing her eyes in Charlie's.

"Tell the truth, I don't think so," Charlie replied. "I have a flight out early in the morning."

In the silence which the three of them shared, the Little Buddha tried to clear his throat, but burped ever so slightly.

"Well, then," Andrea said, "I just thought I'd drop by your table and tell you that your petunias are doing fine."

"I'll call you," Charlie promised.

"Nice meeting you, madame," Peter said.

When she had gone the two men sat back down. Charlie felt oddly miserable, and the Little Buddha wanted some Amaretto.

"Handsome woman," Peter said, trying to console the Professor.

"A wonderful woman," Charlie agreed.

"Let's see, you're sixty years old. A marriage, once, long ago. Lots of girl friends. There was another one in Zanzibar, right?"

"You have an unnatural interest in sex," Charlie said, offering a wry joke in his own defense. But, of course, the Little Buddha took this personally.

"Not so unnatural," he argued. "To be inactive isn't necessarily the same thing as being unnatural. For that matter, an overactive gland could be considered—"

"I didn't mean to bring this up," Charlie interrupted.

They sat in silence for a few minutes until the waiter delivered the liqueur.

"All right, I want several things," Charlie finally began. He sounded more determined and decisive than necessary, for the Little Buddha would agree to anything he asked. "I want a woman on the embassy staff in Zanzibar as my personal aide. I want the State Department to furnish a decoy—with first-class care and attention. I want an open budget. After plenty of publicity, we'll start a tour of, say, a half dozen cities. I want men from secret service to replace Kip Culley—crack shots and top detectives—who will stay with the decoy day and night. No slip ups. A top operation."

146

"Done," said the Little Buddha, like a god granting a mortal favor.

"Can you organize all that?"

"Of course. But about the decoy. Who should we get?"

"I thought of playing the role myself," Charlie said.

"Shouldn't we get a bona fide business leader?"

"I've been giving the whole thing some thought. And now, yes, I believe we need someone who can be checked out. The killer seems to have his sources. I wouldn't be surprised if he's not looking up his victims in Dun & Bradstreet. He's clever."

"A real live businessman, then," Peter said. "Shall we tell him he's a decoy?"

"I've thought that over, too," Charlie said. "We'll have to decide. But, you know, I don't think so."

"Top notch," Peter said. "The bastard won't even know the game."

"We shouldn't do it that way," Charlie admitted. "But it has a certain beauty. And I think it would be more effective."

PART THREE

In the highland lives a hairy giant, one side flesh,
the other stone, who devours mortal men lost in the forest.
It carries a great club and can be heard knocking on trees
                                                as it moves along.

                                        Masai folk myth

19

The decoy's name was Olin Lockridge.

His business was heavy machinery: cranes, front-end loaders, back hoes, drills, and lifts, all described and illustrated in a company brochure of his own design. His offices were at Fox Lake, Illinois, outside Chicago, but in recent years his company had opened international subsidiaries in Kuwait, Tel-Aviv, Alexandria, and Rabat.

"Our growth focus," he had explained to Charlie Hazo, employing his usual vocabulary, "has been the Mediterranean and North Africa."

He had welcomed the State Department's overture to send him around central Africa—Lusaka, Nairobi, Salisbury—selling his machines. Africa, as Olin Lockridge understood it, needed his equipment. There was a lot of land there, as he told Peter Foxx, and it probably all needed to be moved.

The Little Buddha, in turn, explained that a certain amount of danger and precaution was involved.

"As you know, American businessmen have even been murdered lately," Peter said, closely watching Olin Lockridge's eyes.

Lockridge was a man of average size, deeply tanned and healthy looking, who seemed to suffer mild aphasia as he began to speak. His features would contort, his fingers tighten, and he would seem lost in momentary thought. Spaced way out, as Jamie Vander described it. Troubled, as the Little Buddha generously viewed him. A man of high intelligence, as the Professor summed it up with his usual sarcasm, who could not easily bring all his complexities of thought together.

"I welcome this opportunity," Lockridge replied to the Little Buddha, brushing danger aside.

Lockridge received a week's briefings and preparations at the State Department during which time Peter, Charlie, Jamie, and Stella put together the protection unit. Six secret service men—two each for the daily eight-hour shifts—would have full bodyguard duties. Everyone would be wired to talk with everyone else. Two full-time intelligence engineers would control electronic surveillance. An armed, plainclothes marine sergeant would be the unit driver. Two advance men would check all hotels, airports, and physical settings for business appointments. Jamie Vander would direct the tour. The Professor would keep close watch, it was agreed, while he and Stella directed larger operations in Nairobi and across the continent—meaning that they would join the entourage only on occasion.

During this break, Charlie went out to the college in Virginia. He met with his seminar, hired a grader, and arranged to have the semester close without him. His dean, again, was both helpful and—because Charlie had tenure and brought some small measure of prestige to his department—helpless. He called Callie, who was not home. He hoped for a new boyfriend for Callie, one who wrote poetry or delicate short stories with lyric endings.

Then he stopped by Andrea Sloane's house in Dumbarton Oaks.

"I didn't expect you," she admitted. He followed her through the dark panels of the old house to a small room with a reading lamp where she had been sitting alone, reading and drinking. His quick estimate: the drinking had won out.

He told her that his work in Africa had grown complicated and that he had little time.

"You like projects," she said, and her voice, tinged with accusation, also said, you prefer them to people, to love, to normality, to me.

He said that he couldn't stay long this visit because he had to go by the Bethesda Medical Center to see Kip Culley, a colleague who had been brought back from Africa.

She took a sip from what appeared to be a weak whiskey. "You've killed me," she said suddenly. "You've murdered me."

"What are you talking about?"

"You raised my hopes," she said, her voice cracking. "And now you're gone, I know it."

"Don't say that. Please."

"It's true. I would've done very well, but I got my hopes up."

Charlie felt guilty, then defensive. How could such a scene as this go on—into the last decades of his life?

"We will always be together," he told her. "Friends don't leave each other. They don't divorce. We're going to be great friends for a long time."

Andrea thankfully did not cry.

"You're going to be too busy, I know it," she said in a hurt whisper.

"I'm going back to Africa, yes, and I know we won't see each other for months. But we will again."

"I don't believe that," she whispered.

He reached over and took her whiskey glass from her hand. Then he drank it off. He needed it.

He noticed her scarf, her tailored skirt, the costume necklace: clothes bought carefully, tastefully, in little boutiques on the quaint sides of malls. A beautiful, tailored, civilized woman.

They stood at the front door. She accepted his reassuring lies, then he kissed her cheek and walked away.

The next days filled up with details. He met with several of the thirty men being sent to Sid Cash. Selected from all branches of the detective, protection, and intelligence services, they would spend most of their African duty running down the known forgers—there were seven altogether on the Interpol list—and investigating the network of venom handlers, agents, and clients.

He had looked forward to days and nights with Stella, an extension of the pleasures of Zanzibar, but had to settle for her efficiency; she set up the training office for Jamie, arranged the conference with Sid Cash's men, and seemed to have real zest for the project.

"What about the killer?" she asked him, excitedly.

"Hell, I don't know. What about him?"

"Don't you have a profile of him? Some mental picture?" Her eyes flashed with intrigue.

"In my worst moments," Charlie told her, "I fear that he's far smarter than we are. And I know that he's single and organized while we're many and confused."

Once during that week of briefings and preparations Charlie went down to the pistol range in the sub-sub-basement of Treasury with Peter, who had an assortment of weapons for everyone, including a little Beretta Jetfire .25 for Stella's purse.

At the firing line, the Professor couldn't hit a thing. The weapons seemed to jump in his hand. The Little Buddha stood there with his belly out, though, and blew away the bull's-eyes.

"I ordered these Army Lugers," Peter said. "I've been down here during my lunch breaks setting the sights and balance myself. Old Georg Luger's weapon has always been good, but gunsmiths are always trying to convert it to fire the standard .45 ACP cartridges, and they usually rebuild the frame, modify the trigger, and make it a top loader. I've been designing my own custom model. Here, hold it. Feel the difference."

Charlie hefted the Luger and tried to react with appreciation.

"My model has a new barrel. And it's yours. Take it to Africa and shoot our killer."

"You have a lot of talents," Charlie managed. "But be serious. I'm no hit man."

"Please, take it," Peter said, and his little hands fluttered around the display of pistols laid out before them on the firing counter. "I believe your plan will work. I think you'll meet your man. But I want all of you armed and ready."

Together, they went up in the elevator to Peter's offices.

"A man who uses poison, well, he's low, very low," Peter said, as they ascended. His drawl had deepened. "As I see it, he must get close to his victims. He talks with them and deceives them, then attacks. And so poison is a very personal, deceitful method, don't you agree?"

"Yes, that's so," Charlie answered.

"Poison is cowardly."

"Yes, it is," Charlie agreed.

"Beware of this fellow. I figure him to be the lonely type, Charlie," the Little Buddha said. "And loneliness makes a man fierce."

20

Sid stalked around his inner office talking to himself.

On a return visit to the Institute up at Lake Naivasha he had met Bryan Wilton, Daphne Brent's father. On impulse after their day of interviews he had asked Daphne to dinner in Nairobi.

Her polite refusal had thrown him into terrible introspections.

What came over me? Why, he asked himself, did I ask? He felt that Daphne belonged to this country and that he was an imposter of the worst sort; she was a physically attractive person and he was impossibly wrong; she was right to warn him and to be dismayed with his job. Besides, he told himself, I'm married, happily married, and miss my wife and children every hour.

"I wasn't even thinking of that sort of thing!" he told his empty office. "And, then, *she's* married, isn't she?" He thought of her absent husband, who was probably thinner and somehow less sweaty than himself.

Outside Sid's office Ngomo sat talking with the secretaries. He could barely hear Sid's voice through the closed door, but understood that agony was being personified and addressed—a familiar tribal custom.

The desk on which Sid rested his fist was covered with memos and reports. One was a recent memo from Sid to the Little Buddha suggesting that a United States Information Agency library was the probable source of the killer's information. Sid himself had visited the one on Government Road in Nairobi and had determined that materials on the visits of both Bobby Bolling and Herman Carr to Africa could be obtained there. Another report on the desk was a new, comprehensive assertion from the CIA that no cobra killer, including Russian or Chinese agents, was at work from inside the intelligence community. The document also suggested that entrapment might be the best solution. This did not make Sid feel better. The Professor probably had the best strategy, he was starting to concede, and would probably get the man, and, if so, the killer might well turn out to be a common criminal— mildly resourceful—who Sid or any decently competent policeman should have caught.

"I only asked her to dinner!" he told the office furniture. "So why do I feel embarrassed?" He felt as though he couldn't go up to the Institute and work on the investigation anymore.

He put on his new Colpro safari jacket.

Does this coat look stupid, he asked himself, or does it not? It looked like a theatrical disguise, but he had bought it so he wore it.

He opened the door, went through the outer office without speaking to anyone, and left. Ngomo watched him go.

In the elevator Sid unfolded his list of shops. For days, on and off, he had surveyed a number of jewelry stores personally, looking for an antique ring of the sort described by the merchant in the Musky Bazaar in Cairo. The merchant had told Jamie about such rings and had provided a photo of one which, in turn, Sid had recently reproduced for all his men surveying shops in other cities. The merchant in that shop had provided only a scant description of the customer who had stood beside Herman Carr that day, but his excitement on the subject of rings with compartments for poison had led the investigative unit on a whole new line of pursuit.

Sid stood in the lobby outside the elevator reading his list. Then he walked out into the sunlight. Across the street was Mr. Rhamadi sitting at his work bench.

"Oh yes, many times have I sold such rings as that," the old proprietor said in his high, Indian voice.

"Exactly like this one in the picture?"

"Very almost exactly the same," exclaimed Mr. Rhamadi. "But

years ago, naturally, for these I have not seen in a long time! They are true curiosities now! Very expensive, if you have one! I would buy it from you for an agreeable price!"

Sid had no squirting rings for sale, but wanted to know if Mr. Rhamadi might recall any customer in recent years who had purchased one.

"No, these have not been present in my shop for so long," Mr. Rhamadi began explaining again. Sid made a note, marking this shop off his list.

As they talked, Quentin Clare appeared at the front door to the shop. Seeing the big man talking to Mr. Rhamadi, Quentin idled around the counters, pretending to inspect an assortment of jade. In his pocket, tucked into the little velvet pouch, was the diamond he had promised— cut and polished.

He waited several minutes while Sid explained to Mr. Rhamadi that he was an international policeman, that the questioning was important, and that he should report any such ring turning up in his shop. The old man listened courteously. When Sid walked out of the shop, passing Quentin without raising his eyes to him, Quentin went back to the work bench and presented his gem.

Mr. Rhamadi weighed the diamond on his small brass scale— carved, Persian, beautiful, and inaccurate—in order to get a rough esti- mate of its carats. As he did this, he remembered that Bill Clare, years ago, had purchased the kind of ring Sid Cash sought. A sudden bump of memory: two customers in a row, one seeking what, once, the other's father had possessed. He told this amusing coincidence to Quentin.

"Was he a policeman?" Quentin asked.

"Oh yes, very much so," Mr. Rhamadi answered, smiling.

Better to ignore this, Quentin decided. But as he watched Mr. Rhamadi record their transaction in the old leather-bound ledger, grave apprehensions started: they're here in Nairobi, they're looking for leads, they're coming after me. And the worst apprehension of all: how much do they already know?

Turning, Mr. Rhamadi placed the diamond inside the heavy old safe, green and tarnished, which sat behind his work bench. He handed Quentin a receipt.

"Your money will be here in two days," he told Quentin. "As

always, I will show you the chart on how your stone grades out and the weekly rate. A fair price, very fair, you know that."

"I'm sure," Quentin replied.

"Your father," Mr. Rhamadi said, still remembering, "was such a very intelligent man who made many purchases here. But your mother, oh: I consider her to have been among the most beautiful."

"Thank you," Quentin said, accepting the compliments and the past tense for both parents. Folding the receipt into the pocket of his khaki shirt, he walked back outside into the crowded street. He had other errands and now, since seeing an investigator, a special item to buy.

A few blocks away on Biashara Street bright *kakois*, brass pots, and poles laden with colored gourds adorned the market stalls. Quentin bought from an Indian butcher, refusing, as he always did, to frequent any of the new supermarkets around the city. Next, carrying his packages of beef, he visited a safari outfitter, another Indian, like virtually all of the merchants in the shops and stalls, who called his store Benghazi.

Quentin bought a German-made pistol, an SIG 9mm weapon which the clerk insisted carried the strongest firepower of any handgun in the store.

"We have a bothersome lion around the place," Quentin explained. "Odds are that I'll run across it at night or sometime when I haven't got my rifle, so I want something to knock him down with a single shot."

"For you might not get another, correct?" the clerk asked, smiling through his soft Indian cadence.

"True," Quentin said. "And give me a shoulder holster for this and a half-case of ammo."

He hadn't talked firearms or thought of ammunition for years. With his memory jogged, he remembered hunting safaris with his father again. They used to sit around the fire at night determining by the sound of a lion's roar how far away it was. "The roar of the lion," he remembered the doctor saying to him, "is the loudest sound on earth produced by an animal." Surely it was, too, for they used to stare into the fire's last embers, drinking one more glass of wine before retiring to their tents, and listen to those faraway booming calls; from miles across the savannah, from the far reaches of Quentin's young imagination.

"Ammunition," the clerk said, talking to himself as he brought a box down from the shelf.

Another image crossed Quentin's mind: he saw himself shooting a man. A startling thought. They were after him now, so he wondered if he would do it to keep the mission going and the game alive.

Carrying his packages, he started back across town toward the American library. Another distinction came to him: he would never kill Mr. Rhamadi or any of his own, he knew, because that wouldn't do. But he would take the lives of the invading businessmen, their protectors, or any of those who served them. This was no personal duel; it was a larger war, revolutionary in tone, and greater than a single individual or a private grudge.

An important point, then. He felt more confirmed about buying the pistol.

By the time he reached the library a cooling rain washed the streets. Running the last steps, he held his packages over his head.

Inside, the reading tables were packed.

At the periodical shelves he sat and read. There, eventually, he turned to page three of the *New York Times*: a manhunt by order of the President of the United States himself, the formation of a task force, the Little Buddha, and all the politics and sensationalism.

He read the article through twice. Caution, but also some real elation swept over him. His work abroad—much of it as distasteful as any soldier's duty—had gained wide attention. Nothing had been in vain, he felt; his war was theirs and their destinies had entwined.

21

Quentin recalled an argument.

It was one of those days during drouth: another rainy season in which it didn't rain. The bush dried up around them, the creeks cracked open like sores, the savannah became raw. The Masai, who usually burned off their grasslands so that new green grass for their cattle would spring up after the rains, saw their blackened fields remain black. Animals gathered at the few shrunken waterholes, making temporary truces with one another in their desperation. Farms and plantations went into bankruptcy. The natives, who lived at subsistence levels on their meager farms, dug deeper and deeper into the ground for the last sweet roots; they devoured their dogs; their children, like wiry black insects, clung to their mothers' shoulders.

"You haven't wanted me to farm, but I want to do something," Mary had told the doctor.

"It's foolish to farm out here. Look what a single drouth season can do. There was a coffee plantation over there—you remember it? Gone to drouth. There were the little farms on the hillsides. Gone. The markets in Nairobi have even dried up. No one can farm—least of all another woman looking for something to keep her from being idle."

"Let's collect venom again, then, and sell it to the Institute."

"We won't do that either. That's settled."

Quentin had listened to the conversation from where he sat on the piano bench. The window beside him was open and his parents were in the yard, tending vegetables—their small supply—in the beds which could no longer afford the luxury of flowers. Quentin had been playing a prelude. He had stopped at the sound of their voices as they came around the side of the house.

"But I've got to have something for myself," Mary argued. "I'd rather it be something practical—something to help pay expenses."

"Tend the vegetables, then."

"Something more. I want—"

"The Institute has ruined the old business! You know what I feel about the whole subject! I won't be a supplier in another long commercial chain which goes back to the Europeans and the Americans! There was a certain—well, romance to the work, once, but I'm not going up there to the Institute with my hat in my hands to quibble with some snippy Englishman over prices and the way things get done!"

"I'll do it," Mary said. "Let me."

"Our money is safe—put away and well invested, if I do say so myself, in gems of good quality which will always appreciate in value. We'll sell them off for the next thirty years, if necessary. We don't need you working."

"But suppose I need it—for myself?"

"Why should you?"

"Because Quentin's education is finished. I'm proud of it, but it's finished for me. Now I need something else."

"An education's never finished," the doctor argued. "Give me the spade."

"But you have him in the laboratory now. You have him out hunting. He's going to be yours, more and more, not mine. Don't you see that?"

"You can be a great help to me, then."

"No, I can't be that either," Mary said. "You have your work and your politics. You're more and more—" She stopped, weighing her words. Quentin could hear the sound of the digging. His fingers rested silently on the keys. "You're very cut off," she said, finishing.

Another silence.

"Look at these scrawny beans," the doctor said. "Not enough here to make a full pot."

The small sound of Mary's sigh.

"We could plant out around the compound, of course, but I think the nocturnal animals—as hungry and as thirsty as they all are—would eat the whole crop soon as not. And, by the way, you should keep a rifle loaded. I think we'll have more and more scavengers."

His mother's silence.

Years later Quentin would place that argument into new contexts. It was a natural alteration on his mother's part, he realized; she hadn't so much turned away from her husband as just to herself, her own need to have purpose and work. But Bill Clare took her anxiety and search as rejection. Soon he was sleeping alone out in the laboratory in the compound.

Between Quentin's eighteenth and twentieth years he took his father's political obsessions as his own. The western world meant to take away culture, adventure, personal freedom, the arts, true science, nature, and any wild spirit; it meant to instill efficiency, production, conformity, comfort, and the consumer mentality. It believed in material salvation. It wanted Africa—and all the poor people of the earth—for its exploitation. And it would prevail over any protest, too, and would finally win out, the doctor claimed, because men even when they fancied themselves not so materialistic could still be bought.

"If I had absolute mobility on the continent," the doctor said to Quentin one day, "I'd go to the capitals of every country and shoot the bastards. I'd never let them in."

Quentin never forgot this. They were working in the lab with some of the old venom containers and equipment, trying to clean up. The doctor had also made the observation that many simple household acids, mixed with gelatins and lyophilized venoms, became contact poisons. A touch to the skin, even so much as a drop, he remarked, could kill a man. Those statements, then, linked together as they worked, stayed in Quentin's thoughts.

Mary had been dead for some time, the doctor would seldom come out of the compound, and Quentin's pain for his parents—his only real bridge to the outside world—had filled him with emotion.

Not long after that afternoon together in the lab the doctor decided to destroy the remaining cobras in captivity in the yard of the compound. He and Wemba, working carefully, overturned the cone-shaped pods and separated the coils of cobras with a long bamboo stick, then used a rifle to dispatch the snakes one by one.

There was one king cobra, very shy, which had been delivered to them almost a year before. On arrival the specimen was still young, no more than six feet long, and Wemba told the doctor he had never seen it in the yard. Their guess was that it had occupied one of the pods by itself, perhaps died, or, if not, lived as solitary as the remaining Clares themselves. They had only occasionally accepted snakes over the last years as favors to old handlers they had known—men with families, usually, who had brought specimens in the past, badly needed money or food, and took what they were offered. The king cobra they had accepted because two Kikuyu boys had captured it, walked miles with it, then learned that Dr. Clare was no longer in the business. They discussed killing it, but the boys—no more than eleven years old—were so pathetic that Quentin had intervened, had paid them two shillings each, had instructed Wemba to feed them, then had sent them on their way. It had been a particularly poor specimen, lying around in the yard of the compound for days before finally going to drink and crawling off into one of the vacant pods.

Many of the other cobras uncovered that day were already dead, so when Wemba and the doctor came to the king's pod they fully expected this of it, too. Quentin stood on the bridge, watching. He had offered help, but the doctor had wanted only Wemba—and less movement— among the pods.

The attack was sudden and unexpected.

When Wemba threw the pod back with his bamboo pole, the big king—which must have been feeding regularly at night and had grown to more than twelve feet in length—came directly for Bill Clare. The doctor fired from the hip, missed, and dropped the rifle as he was struck in the face. By the time Quentin vaulted over the bridge railing, the creature had turned on Wemba. Backing off, keeping it at bay with the pole, Wemba had finally bumped into the wall of the compound, his heels digging at the loose sand at the base of the wall as if he meant to scurry up its side, when Quentin recovered the rifle and blew off the snake's head with a clean shot.

The doctor had been struck high on the cheek and in his left eye. The strike had knocked him down, for the big king had charged upright, moving forward like its cousin the mamba, so that its head was nearly as high as Bill's face when the blow was delivered. The large fang entering the cheek had left a small bubble of blood; the one which had penetrated the eye, however, had torn the eye from its socket on exiting, so that the doctor's eyeball hung loose on his face by the threads of nerves and small blue veins when they carried him into the lab.

"Stay with me," Bill Clare said. "Stay here at home with me!" In his growing delirium his words sounded like a plea and a prison sentence all at once. And these were his last and only words to his son.

Quentin could only nod in reply.

The doctor entered his coma still asking for love.

Short of his twenty-second birthday by a few months, Quentin took over the estate. For a while he tried some of his mother's last practical thoughts toward putting the whole operation back on a paying basis; he bought cobras now and then, whenever hungry natives brought them to the compound, but never contacted the Institute or made arrangements to extract venom; he planted during the next season and the crop was fair, but he and Wemba neglected to harvest anything except for their own table. He sold off the first diamond to Mr. Rhamadi and for months did nothing: a little piano, some reading, visits with his father in the room Wemba prepared out in the laboratory, the first solitary chess games, learning about those gems left to him in an assortment of velvet and leather pouches.

He was his mother's son: quiet, intelligent, detached, and wanting a purpose he did not have. His talents impressed him very little; the diary, which he started, he disregarded as anything significant, as just a means to record the dreary passing of the days. Often as not, he saw his father's familiar ravings loom up off the pages. And as his father lay there draped in white, Quentin discovered that he missed his mother more and more; he missed their lessons, the feel of her thin body beside his on the piano bench, the sound of her movements in the main house where her dishes and bric-a-brac still sat on the shelves.

She did not love his father at the last, he knew, but wanted to. Their lives had been set apart from the world, so it was painfully ironic that they set themselves off from one another. The estate, like a fortress hidden beyond the hills, had him in its keeping. Within two years he felt that he had gone mad with solitude; he wanted a wife of his own, normality, trips to Nairobi, conversations, but something held him back—that legacy of loneliness, those violent losses, those gems which allowed him to indulge himself in his father's last command and wish, and perhaps something else. He felt like a crazed man who had inside himself another person, crouched in a corner of the brain, sane and waiting, watching the insanity, letting it boil, and holding off until purpose was revealed.

Some years later he would begin collecting passports and papers, and years of preparation later he would make that first sojourn down to Durban where, clumsily, he would dispatch that poor man in the toilet of the bar. In between, for years, he felt split in half, confused, held together only by Wemba's care.

Unlike the doctor, he did not want love. It would be impossible. Just another desperation he wouldn't add to the jumble. But a great purpose: yes, that. Inside him, cold as stone, waiting, was this other thing.

When at last he knew, he told Wemba, "We're going to keep a few cobras again. Not many. But I want to experiment, so we're going to put the lab in order."

Wemba was pleased. The period of inactivity and silence ended. His master, he somehow knew, had made a momentous decision.

Quentin insinuated himself into Nairobi once more. Mr. Rhamadi knew him because of the annual sales of the diamonds—ever increasing in value. Now Quentin went to Biashara Street, shopped and learned the city. In time he found what he wanted: two young thieves for hire. Over a two-year period they stole identity papers at the airport, in hotels, wherever careless tourists put down purses or stopped at counters to make purchases. It would be years more before Quentin would use the items, making up his crude, bogus passports and visas with them, crafting new signatures and numbers, adding photos, and constructing a specific plan. The thieves were teenagers, drifters of the city who came to an ironic end: they both found jobs, prospered, and later worried—with great irony, Quentin thought—that their former employer might tell on them or blackmail them in some way. One became an aide to the local judge. The other finally owned and operated a cinema. Some of the items they stole grew outdated, so that Quentin had to discard them. Once, he picked up a British passport himself—conveniently left beside Mr. Rhamadi's cashbox by a previous customer. It was a bold swipe. The blood rushed to Quentin's temples, and his hands trembled in his pockets afterward.

Years again. Waiting and preparing.

"I do not understand how you will use the venom yourself," Wemba said to him one day in the lab.

Quentin kept silent, knowing that Wemba had been thinking on this. It amused him to let the silence gather because Wemba, he supposed, had some theory he would eventually reveal.

"Would you take it into your own body?" Wemba finally asked. "That is what I think you will do. To make you immune, so the fate of your father will never be yours."

"Something like that," Quentin replied.

"I do not understand immune exactly," Wemba confessed. "But it is like the drinking of blood, I think. You take your enemy's strength, correct?"

"Sort of," Quentin said. He knew that mystery was far more powerful for Wemba than any real explanation. Mystery, in fact, was everything: it was the nature of god, the magical quality of the fate the natives suffered and knew so well, and the curiosity which kept Wemba's loyalty in this strange placed filled with restless, solitary, inscrutable foreigners. For Wemba, the laboratory was mystery; so were the great snakes, the marriage of the doctor and Mary, the majestic coma, and these new seemingly purposeful duties to which they now attended.

After a year of following the doctor's notes, Quentin found a workable compound. Wemba dutifully snared some rodents and a baby bushbuck for a test Quentin conducted in private: he touched the compound to the noses of the animals, and they died almost immediately.

More preparation, then.

Quentin started frequenting the library during his trips into town. He studied the world out there on the periphery, its slow encroachment, its merchant mentalities.

He watched the city change. Colonel Sanders' Kentucky Fried Chicken. American items in the supermarkets. Blue jeans in the shop windows. A thumping music from the storefront loudspeakers. *Playboy* on the newsstands.

Once, he watched a young Kikuyu in a green suit standing in the rain waiting for traffic to pass out on the boulevard. The cheap dye in the suit ran away from his legs in rivulets, mocking him, creating a green puddle around his shoes. The rain seemed to wash away his store-bought identity. His face showed his naked embarrassment, yet there he stood, unable to cross between the passing cars, trapped on that cement island. Not many years ago the noble elders of the tribes strolled down these same streets, observing the sights, then retired to their villages again in the knowledge that there was not much to see. The city was clearly, to them, a failure of existence: a place the helpless came to die. Later, as the years passed, more and more of them came into town during the long drouths; they banked up locusts and tiny fires along the curbsides, eating their meager meals out there beyond the hotel verandahs. Then the younger ones came to get jobs and to buy their cheap new clothing. Then a generation of newer ones yet: small boys, begging among the cars, asking shillings for nothing, sleeping in doorways at night. On the outskirts of the city a mud town of corrugated tin and lean-to huts grew up, not so stark in Nairobi as in Leopoldville or Lagos or elsewhere, but the end of everything free, in Quentin's opinion, and anything remotely wild or noble. These were barnyard creatures now, not upright figures on an open landscape.

It was a world, everywhere, Quentin felt, to which one didn't accommodate. It sickened. And it could never be turned back with a few of his mother's soft cultural amenities, with piano lessons or Russian novels or a few intelligent pieces of architecture; it had to be fought and destroyed, if possible, because its hideous, plastic, loudspeaker values were too pervasive.

A great mission, then, and great purpose: one which would make all his solitude meaningful.

22

The tour started badly.

The first city visited by Olin Lockridge, Charlie Hazo, and all the agents and engineers was Kinshasa. Their first hotel was nineteen floors tall, but its elevators and its air-conditioning system didn't work. The mighty Congo River—everyone failed to call it by its new name, the Zaire—was at floodtide, so the city swarmed with refugee farmers who slept in the streets. A curious new fever was loose in Brazzaville across the river, so no one went there to eat at the good French restaurants. Insects flew about in soft, dark, whispering clouds. A smell of sweet decay rode the air. Except for trips out to N'Djili Airport, most of the taxi drivers were on strike.

"Clearly," Jamie told the Professor, "our killer will have more sense than to come here."

"Let's use the time to announce our heavy-machinery salesman's schedule," Charlie said. "We'll lay out the publicity. Then we'll move on to Salisbury and Nairobi."

On the second day of their visit, Lockridge suggested that they should stay longer because he felt he was doing good business. The suggestion was delivered in his usual speaking style—many halts and silences—but he showed Jamie an order for over a million dollars worth of earth-moving equipment. Jamie tactfully suggested that they should continue their whirlwind tour and that Olin could send out follow-up salesmen later.

Then, on the third day, the marine sergeant driver broke a man's arm. It seemed only an annoying minor incident, at first, a skirmish after an argument about a parking space beside the hotel, but by nightfall it had erupted into a diplomatic problem.

Officers in three different kinds of military uniforms called on Jamie that evening. Money was paid, apologies were made, yet the sergeant was still asked to leave the country.

"Our group only plans to be here for another two days," Jamie told the delegation.

"What exactly is your business?" asked the officer whose uniform was dark green in color.

"We're just accompanying Mr. Lockridge who is doing business with your government," Jamie replied, trying to sound official.

"You are a very funny, amusing group," the officer said. "Your men are armed with weapons—which is illegal. They talk on little radios to each other. Also illegal. And you have a marine with you—a dangerous one—who is only a sergeant, but who is under no one's command. Unless, of course, many of you are military spies—also illegal."

"Our papers are all in order," Jamie insisted.

"You are troubled by the possibility that someone may kill Mr. Lockridge, you tell us, but naturally we could easily protect any businessman ourselves. In my opinion, not only should your sergeant leave— all of you should."

"We'll stay two more days," Jamie said firmly.

When the group left Jamie's hotel room, Charlie Hazo came in and sat in a chair across from Jamie—who stared out the window toward the gleaming, wide bend of the river.

"Well done," he told Jamie.

The sergeant appeared at the door. Behind him, brushing out her hair, stood Stella.

"Am I expelled from the country?" the sergeant asked hopefully.

"How in hell did you break a man's arm?" Charlie wanted to know.

"I thought he was pulling a knife, so I just grabbed him a little. His arm sort of came loose in my hands. It broke at the shoulder—just sort of came off. I'm sorry."

"He did have a knife," Jamie inserted.

"You were arguing over a parking space, and a man's arm came off," the Professor repeated.

"Yessir."

Stella sat down on the ottoman near the window, crossing her long legs as she continued to brush out her dark hair. The men watched her movements.

"That officer wants *matabiche*—more bribe money," Charlie said. "I think you'll hear more from him tonight."

"He sounded like he was really concerned that we're illegal and shouldn't be doing any of this," Jamie replied.

"I listened to his speech from the next room, and it sounded pretty good," Charlie said. "But all he wants is more money."

Late that afternoon Jamie met with the hotel manager, a minister from the government, the three men in different military uniforms, and the victim of the marine sergeant who wore a sling and seemed to be genuinely in pain. Marlboro cigarettes and Pepsi were served, and as the Professor predicted more money was paid and the matter appeared settled.

"Government parking only behind the hotels," the manager kept saying, and everyone smiled at each other.

While this took place, Stella and Charlie packed and went out to the airport for a flight down to Zanzibar. They planned to conclude the J.J. Barney investigation, tend to Stella's last embassy chores, and spend a few days together.

They gazed out of the window of the plane as it took off, Stella leaning across the seat so that her breast rested warmly against the Professor's forearm, watching the maze of La Cité below, those soggy black slums in the river's bend.

They were both tired, so slept side by side on that night flight back to Zanzibar, their arms entwined, their breaths close. Having kept busy with arrangements and details for the tour, they felt the continent's heavy fatigue; it was one of those times when weariness makes nothing matter.

For days they hadn't touched or made love or scarcely talked. Now they crumpled together, folded into their separate dreams, as the plane's steady roar took them in its undertow. In Charlie's dream he saw the face of a man he didn't know, a man with dark eyes, green of tint, irises deep as pools.

They got off the plane in the middle of the night, staggering in their sleepiness, and Stella hung onto his arm for support and laughed at how he couldn't hold her up. The island fragrance was all around them: clove and salt air, overpowering. They somehow found the only taxi outside the airport, its driver slumped over the wheel, and made their way to Stella's house, creaking in the windsong breeze which rises just before dawn, where they stumbled inside and made their way to bed.

Thousands of worn-out miles.

He could smell her perfume and—beneath that—her oils and body scents. Tired as he was he didn't sleep now, though, and he lay there feeling at home again, at home among her stacks of magazines, beside her wheezing little bedside clock, in the slant of moonlight which fell across the bed. His hand moved across his face: a tiny bead of perspiration, a row of craggy lines, and that indenture in his forehead. He felt weighted and depressed, yet, as always, even as he drifted down, he gave himself his own special pep talk: steady, don't, hold on. And he felt that he had lived so long, seen so much, that he was like the earth itself: his body and his mind had seasons, rejuvenations, and new stirrings of life. When he felt so god-awful cynical, a new naiveté always arrived; when he moved toward loneliness, he managed to love someone—often as not this strange collector of idiocies at his side; when death came near, he felt his pulse quicken and his life accelerate.

The continent of death always threatened him back to life.

Steady, hold on, keep awake.

The bullet in his face. Amazing, even now, that he had fought off the final sleep. In the war there was also this overbearing weariness; you wanted to drift into slumber, to zip yourself into your all-weather bag forever. You thought of the enemy almost kindly, at times, thinking, here I am, put me to sleep, help me out of this place forever, please, and your bones groaned against your skin. You were out there to die and your body prepared for it, getting sleepier, dragging you down, growing drunk on you so you couldn't last.

He remembered the chopper trip along the coast. The beaches of

Vietnam were not unlike those of Africa that day: white sand, occasional villages strewn out behind the trees, a deep green sea. But someone below them had opened fire and he remembered rifle shots striking their metal guard plate underneath: ka-whong! ka-whong! like faraway intrusions on a sleep already gathering inside him. His pilot let out a string of curses. Charlie only pulled his flak jacket tighter into his crotch, protecting his wonderful scrotum, he recalled. Never mind arms, legs, shoulders, or any other part or extension.

His pilot was flying escort along the white beaches of the coast north of Da Nang. They were doing another small recon intelligence run, and Charlie, the expert, called the Professor even then by his younger officers and men, was seeing what he could with those sleepy eyes which wanted only to close and see no more. And ka-whong! Someone on that strip of beach below actually had the audacity to shoot at them, to disturb their American dream, to violate their special version of the nightmare ride. The pilot, annoyed, turned back to get a look at their antagonists.

"Little bastards!" the pilot yelled. He said it with all the confidence of a man piloting a first-class death machine armed with rockets and cannon. Those were mere savages down there on the edges of the jungle. Mere savages with mere rifles who were taking potshots.

The bullet that got the pilot somehow came through the instrument panel—the only unprotected wall on the helicopter. Making its way cleverly among the wires and punching through the dial of the altimeter, it filled up the pilot's plastic face shield with bright blood, as if someone had suddenly sprayed it from the inside. Charlie, not thinking of crashing, not thinking anything, wadded that flak jacket into an even tighter protective ball and squeezed it between his legs. And they didn't exactly spin down and crash. Instead, they settled like some exotic Asian butterfly onto the beach, just floating down—or so it seemed until the impact broke Charlie's ribs and arm and caused him to piss into that tightly balled jacket held in his crotch.

In a state of ebbing consciousness, then, he was dragged onto the beach. Rough hands all around him, pulling him by his broken arm, but he didn't even care. He wouldn't open his eyes, he decided, and either recognize or admit any of this.

Talk and laughter all around him. He heard a distant explosion and knew it was the chopper. Inside him, inside his sleep, something was still partially awake, listening and comprehending.

He heard the click of the pistol.

He actually heard the shot being fired into his head.

A dazzling pain: a light show, a kaleidoscope. Pain so fierce that he even prayed for sleep. But the bullet, entering at an angle, had actually spun around his skull between the skin and bone and had never entered the precious brain. Even so, he prayed.

Yet sleep wouldn't come. Something, again, said, steady, don't fade, hold on a little longer. He drifted away, floating on fear, but the voice was still present, something deep in his genes and molecules talking to him, giving him that pep talk which only comes in the lowest darkness. He would think about this moment all the rest of his life; if inner voices urge us to sleep, surely others call to us to wake ourselves, if cancer, say, feeds on our weak cells, finds a weakness and begins to eat away, then in some of us there are certainly cells which fight and reject the deformity, too.

Steady, hold on. He had been given a hasty coup de grace but a voice still called. He was picked up later by another chopper, returned and set back into the daylight of the world again. He slept through his rescue, totally unconscious, yet at the same time blinded by pain. The far away voices of his body's atoms still beckoned. And when he was finally awake, his eyes coming open in that hospital room—one of them nearest the wound drooped for a year, then fluttered fully awake on its own—he felt as though he would truly live forever. And so he seemed to; he had since then eaten meals, jogged in the winter air until his lungs burned, read books, laughed, travelled, grown tired again, made comebacks, lost all his faiths, found new ones, fallen in love once more. Scarred, he had been made whole, as if strength only came out of scar tissue; lost in shadows, he had come into the light, as if vision only came out of blindness.

Now Stella breathed evenly against his chest. The first splendid grey of morning was out there on the water of the harbor.

Pushing her gently away, he got up and went to the bathroom. There, he took out his cleanser and began scrubbing his teeth; with a moist washcloth he polished and cleaned, feeling better and better as the grating noise grew louder. Much of his naked body sagged. Flab on the back sides of his arms. But sixty years old or not, he told himself, those teeth were by god pearls.

When he got back into bed and onto her warm body, he felt wide awake. He kissed her breasts and rib cage, beginning the work of reviving her.

Hold on, steady, come awake.

Slowly, he brought her out of her slumber. Her fingernails pressed lightly against his back, tracing the scars, pushing and urging him; then he was inside all her oils and liquids. Their drowsy movement increased. Her eyelids pulsed open, closed, opened, then closed again. A deep shudder built inside him, but he wanted one for her, too, and worked for it. He felt as though she had died and entered a dream from which he had to save her. Then her eyes flared. She was wakening. He saw, deep down, her disbelief and wonder, but there it was.

At sixty years of age he had been a number of men, living many lives, slipping in and out of seasons which blent together; new missions and assignments, new acquaintances, the beach where he should have died, new beginnings and failures, the rooms and continents of change. The voices which had called him from stupor and death had always been his alone; they belonged only to his own deepest desire to be alive and called only to him, but now, it seemed, he shouted across a dark, empty water to someone else, saying, come on, steady, you can make it, and in calling out like this he was shouting loose yet another corner of his own consciousness.

23

"Maybe I've come around to your point of view," Sid told Daphne Brent when he next visited the Institute. "Our job here may be too big. My men are tired out and we don't seem to be accomplishing anything."

They were drinking gin and tonic outside beneath those giant cottonwoods. Her father, Bryan Wilton, sucked on a fat little meerschaum pipe, and the curls of smoke hung around them like a vapor in the humid late-afternoon air. Ngomo had driven two agents down to Mombasa and Malindi, so that Sid had come alone—for which he was pleased. His hope was to get Daphne alone, although his plans were vague from that point on, and he could see that old Wilton was getting tipsy, probably wouldn't last long after supper, and that anything was possible. He wasn't thinking about sex exactly. But he was still preoccupied with Daphne and suffered a mixture of desire, embarrassment, need, and perplexity which wasn't all that carefully analyzed.

She seemed generous toward him since he was admitting defeat.

"It looks simple here, but isn't," she said. "In England and America we have these enormous bureaucracies and we fancy them very complicated, but Africa really has thousands of years of natural and social complexities of its own. The natives have taboos, for instance. Whole categories of taboos—ranging from their ideas of defilement to their concepts of human growth to their feelings about sex or god or social etiquette. In many tribes they can't make a move because of all their rules and regulations."

Daphne tended to lecture, but Sid didn't care. Her voice, the soft rattling of the leaves on the trees, the odor of the old man's tobacco: it excited him, all of it. He worried about himself now. Africa had charmed him, and this woman and this outlandish place had charmed him most of all. There was a breed of English poet, he knew, who loved the exotic places; they went far afield to Istanbul or Bombay or Alexandria to sniff an atmosphere which was completely alien to those in their Dorset or Sussex countrysides, and they were not especially better men or better poets for this, he supposed, although they were definitely hooked on strange sights, foreign sounds, and the faraway horizons. He knew he was getting like this. He did not want to go back home.

They emptied the gin bottle, the three of them, and told stories as the sun went down and the forest around them grew cool and darkened. When they went into dinner, Sid remembered part of the purpose of his visit.

"You said you found an old list of missionaries and others who once traded in venom," he reminded Daphne.

"Yes, I've got it for you," she said. "But let's eat first. Before daddy topples for the night."

"I won't topple! Who says I'll topple?" the old man asked, sucking at his pipe as they went indoors.

The table was laid out with pewter, cut glass, and candles. As they seated themselves, Daphne handed Sid the list, but he was distracted by the old man's antics, the smell of the food, and the candleglow.

"This was your old list, daddy," Daphne said. "I told him he could have it."

"Well enough, they're all dead and gone," Bryan Wilton snorted, drinking on his wine as he seated himself. "A few of them did all right collecting snakes. Made enough money to get started out here. Then during the war and afterward the whole business sagged. Then started up again—with lots of new uses in the laboratories for cobra venoms. That's when we started the Institute. We were farmers, you know."

"Farmers?" Sid shoved the small list into his shirt pocket. It contained, he noticed, only six names and addresses.

"My wonderful idea was to plant and harvest from wild coffee stock," the old man went on, filling his mouth.

Daphne gave Sid Cash a thin smile. Meanwhile, her father described the wild coffee which grew on the mountain slopes, coffee so strong, he recalled, that the whole forest smelled of it after the rains. He was one of many who tried to bring it under control, he claimed, but in the neat order of plantation growing it always failed.

"Besides, it was too damn strong," the old man said, chewing and coughing at his food. "The market couldn't take it. Too strong."

They talked about the Kenyan coffee business. The old man's anecdotes and asides grew less audible as he finished off the wine. Also, he talked to his plate of food, his eyes down there in the sauce and vegetables.

"You take Kenyan coffee today and blend it—for strength, you see—with any domestic coffee in the world," the old man claimed. "But the old, wild mountain coffee itself was always too much! I learned it the hard way! It was hemlock! Market just couldn't use it!"

Daphne finally helped him from the table. While she escorted her father upstairs, Sid stepped outside again.

He tried to think of his duties. The Professor would stop in Nairobi tomorrow, stay for a day of conferences, then fly on to Salisbury where the tour would resume. I need to make a list, Sid told himself, but all the night sounds waylaid his senses, and the odors from the darkness confounded him: lily and lobelia, wet fern and moss, wild orange and star flower. He could feel the shroud of Mt. Kenya in the distance. Standing out there alone, he practiced lines for Daphne, saying, "Here, take my hand and let's walk." Each overture sounded like bad movie dialogue, though, so he gave up.

At last Daphne came through the door. The light behind her set off her hair in a soft nimbus and outlined her figure through the soft material of her print dress.

"Did you get everything you wanted this trip?" she asked pleasantly.

Remembering, he touched the list in his pocket. "Oh, sure, thanks," he said, as she brought her perfume closer.

"You'll have to excuse my father. He talks on and on."

"I could listen all night."

"And, please, I wonder if you can excuse me early this evening, too?"

"All right, fine," he said, trying to cover his disappointment. "I have to get back to the city tonight anyway."

"He'll probably sleep until noon," she said about her father. "Which means I'll have to get up early and begin the work."

They were standing beside the Jeep, he realized, and he couldn't think of a good reason to retreat back into the house. Yet he wanted to stall. He wanted to ask about her marriage, anything. He wanted to touch her. In his confusion he stammered something, not even fully aware of what it was.

"If you go on excursions," she was saying, "think of my father. If you drive out into the bush to interview handlers—anything like that— think about taking him along, won't you? He likes you. And he needs to get away from time to time."

"Take your father along? Sure, be glad to."

"So goodnight, then."

She was dismissing him, and he felt helpless. And, again, embarrassed. He could never really know anyone out here, he felt. Not the blacks, certainly, and not even these settlers who had made a life of their own; they wouldn't let him in. For all Daphne's smiles and shared looks across the dinner table tonight, she was holding him off.

He turned the Jeep out onto the dark highway, his hands gripping the wheel, and promised himself that he wouldn't bother to drive up again. Disappointed and angry, he drove back to Nairobi and put in a long-distance call to his family. Their voices were far away in a sea of static, but he manufactured laughter as he spoke with them. The daughter who used so much profanity talked longest. His wife had house repair and money problems. They talked for an hour or more as Sid reported on the case, how they were close to their objective, how Professor Charles Hazo was arriving for important meetings, how everything was going well.

The next day was a Sunday in June, getting toward the cooler, rainy period in Nairobi, a bright, brisk day for getting things done, Sid felt, but the Professor arrived just before noon with plans to leave again before sundown. The brevity of the visit indicated that affairs in Nairobi weren't as important as those elsewhere, so Sid was naturally disappointed again.

"What were you doing in Zanzibar again?" Sid asked.

"There were some loose ends on the Barney killing, but I was mainly just taking time off," Charlie said.

"Must be nice."

"Sid, don't knock yourself out. You look tired, so slow down. If it happens we catch our man, it will be because we get a break."

The advice confirmed Sid's suspicion that his job wasn't all that necessary or important. Clearly, the Professor wanted to go to Salisbury where he might find some action—or, at least, the company of the woman everybody talked about.

A twitch of nostalgia befell Sid. He remembered how it was back in Eureka Springs, Arkansas, when a certain amount of prestige and leverage were associated with being police chief—even when there was no action at all. He couldn't buy his own lunch in those days. The kids caressed the pearl-handled pistol butt sticking out of his holster. Up on the mountain where the Crescent Hotel sat, a big resort constructed out of solid Ozark stone and fitting no particular architectural notion, Sid Cash was called simply, "Chief." He was twenty-six years old at that time, and the word was glorious to him. His history was enough: he had foiled a bank robbery, chasing one of the bandits into a soybean field where he had cuffed the man senseless; he had never taken a bribe; he had been elected by a wide margin; he was younger, less fat, and relatively good looking.

Sid and the Professor went to the office alone that Sunday and read through all the reports Sid's men had compiled.

"What's on your mind, Sid?" Charlie asked, once, looking up from a file folder. "You look bothered."

"It's nothing," Sid answered. But his past and present were on his mind in a way he couldn't explain. When a burglary occurred, he could sit in his cramped, cluttered little office in that hill town and probably figure out the culprit. An auto store had been robbed, say, by someone who had removed an old air-conditioner from a high window on the alley to gain access. That would be so-and-so, Sid would know. He knew everybody in town—and especially every low-life—and apprehension was easy because his locals had no imagination and few methods. Later, somehow, it wasn't enough to know only Eureka Springs. He went to Little Rock, took the tests, worked at the capitol, and was finally transferred to Washington where, eventually, he worked for Interpol. The motive was simple: Sid was more intelligent than he looked, more ambitious than anyone knew, and the world was there to be seen. He did not want to be a local. He wanted horizons—so much, in fact, that both job and marriage eroded on him; he was seldom satisfied, and only those things which he hadn't experienced or mastered had value for him. This is why Africa and the exotic assignment had come to mean everything.

They finished the folders and went for a beer and a plate of curry at a nearby restaurant. An indolent Sunday afternoon, few people on the streets. Somehow they started talking politics and Sid mostly listened.

"You have to see it this way: America is not a tribe. We don't stay home, tend our gardens, and mind our business," Charlie explained. "We're international. Sort of nomadic. We stand for the idea that our companies and corporations can go anywhere, trade with anyone, set up factories anyplace, change lives, and meddle with the chemistry of other tribes—or, that is, the smaller nations who stay at home and don't do this sort of thing. Here in Africa there are real nations and tribes. They're territorial. We're not. By definition, now, we're a race of traders and invaders."

"Do you think the killer has this sort of political view?" Sid asked.

"I've thought about him a lot. He's more than likely tribal in the old-fashioned sense."

Eating his food, Sid fell into thought.

"Do you think we have a right to be over here chasing this guy?" Sid asked, as though he sat in one of Charlie's seminars out there in the Virginia countryside.

"By our definitions of ourselves," Charlie answered, "we have a right to be anywhere. But by any tribal or nationalistic definition, we're an outlaw group—out of place."

"I haven't felt things are working here," Sid confessed. "I haven't felt anybody really wants us. Not even the British or other settlers."

"No, they like us least of all," Charlie said. "Because we've worked out a way to drain countries of their resources without even going through the colonial trouble of occupation. We don't have to put up with the tsetse fly or wild animals or anything else. We just come get the oil, the gold, and the tribal treasure."

After that long lunch Sid drove Charlie out to the airport, dropped him off early, and found that there were several daylight hours left. Sid went back to the office feeling very alone. He replaced all the reports in their file cabinets and even emptied wastebaskets down the chute in the hallway. He glanced at headlines in the office edition of the *East Africa Standard*.

Sid had enjoyed Charlie and their discussion. But he envied the Professor's career and wondered if a cop over fifty could possibly turn another direction, if he could ever join the desk out at Langley or get on the staff of the Undersecretary for African Affairs over at the State Department. The thought of returning to ordinary duty in Washington was pure dread.

In his shirt pocket he found the list Daphne had given him. The first name on it was Clare. Someone who, years ago, had lived far out on the Langata Road. There were only the barest of notes. Clare was a biologist. Others were visiting engineers, doctors, missionaries—all snake collectors from the old days. Since he knew the direction—out beyond that little row of hills which stood up like knuckles to the south of town—and had visited the national park and Masai Lodge out that way, he decided to drive out for a look.

As he left the office, he failed to sign the Day Book—which recorded the whereabouts and duties of agents out on assignment. It was another oversight, another regulation avoided. He forgot because this was Sunday, because the trip promised nothing, and because in his doleful mood such forgetting was easy.

On the way, Sid heard drums, and to make sure he pulled over to the side of the road, cut the motor of the Jeep, and listened. Sure enough, they rumbled from the foothills out there across the savannah. Ngomo had given Sid an explanation of the drums. He said that on Sunday afternoons the Kikuyu elders often got drunk on palm wine, reverted to some of the old ways, and beat the drums. Ngomo seemed embarrassed telling this, and Sid likened Ngomo's uneasiness to some modern American's feeling if, say, there was still an evangelist in the family, one of those hellfire types with the raspy voice who just didn't fit anybody's family anymore. Ngomo was a driver of cars, a city man, and his old cousins—naked, dancing, beating the drums, swigging homemade wine, and singing their incantations—were more than any man should have to explain.

The Langata Road seemed to end. There was a sign pointing directions toward the Mombasa Highway, but Sid knew he was lost.

He took a turn along a wide, frequently travelled dirt road which itself branched into other dirt roads. The clumps of thorn trees thickened. He saw, once, a pile of dead dogs. Stopping the Jeep to give this sight a careful look, he couldn't fathom it. Someone, perhaps, had been shooting strays. Shrugging, he went on.

In the late afternoon when shadows were growing long and a breeze came up, the trees seemed to whistle.

He didn't care now that his directions were confused. Those same undulating hills lay not far off, although he was unsure which side of them he was now on. Far away in the middle of a gaunt meadow of brown grass stood a solitary Masai herdsman, but he was beyond Sid's voice—and could not make himself understood even if the two men were close enough to speak.

Farther on, zebra and gazelle crossed the narrowing trail. As the sun began to set, the sky turned purple. By this time, at least, Sid had marked the western sky and had figured out the probable direction of the city. But he didn't care about returning. There was plenty of petrol, time had obliterated itself, and he wondered why he hadn't come out here in the countryside alone more often.

Suddenly, at a bend in the road he came upon a large house. Behind it, partially obscured by thorn trees and a row of gardenia bushes, stood a high stone wall; it looked like an ancient ruin. An arched bridge spanned the distance between house and compound, arcing over the high wall of the compound in a bow and joining—Sid strained to see—the upper verandah of a whitewashed stone house inside the enclosure.

The house, Sid could see at a glance, was occupied.

He circled the Jeep and pulled into the front drive.

"Hello!" he called from the front lawn. No answer.

He went to the front door and knocked. The screen door was latched, but he could see inside the cool, darkening rooms of the old house with its high ceilings. Giant ferns embraced the corners of the porch. A coiled whip hung from a peg.

"Hello! Anyone here?" No answer.

In the dirt of the side yard he came across a series of curious holes dug in rows—Wemba's mysterious game. In one of the holes, like small bird's eggs all white and smooth, lay a cluster of pebbles. He bent to inspect this arrangement and even touched one of the little stones with the tip of his finger.

It was a large house, a tile-roofed Victorian manor with tall windows reflecting the sun's last rays. Passing one of the windows as he went toward the rear of the house, Sid saw a piano. The effect of it was arresting: something stately, civilizing, and permanent. It gave him a momentary feeling of comfort, so that he laughed a short, grunting little laugh and called out again, "Hello!" Then he walked up the kitchen steps and peered inside through panes of colored glass. This back door was locked, so he surmised that the occupants had gone on a short trip, leaving the house only partially locked and unguarded. Turning, he saw a Land Rover parked near the high wall of the compound. He supposed, again, that there was another vehicle in which the occupants had gone away.

His eyes moved across the branch of a small thorn tree in the yard. There sat a monkey. It was the first one Sid had seen up close and in the wild, and he whispered his surprise, "Well, look at you."

Curiosities everywhere. Little bumps of surprise.

He strolled back out into the yard and stood quietly. The monkey chewed on something very red—a blossom, perhaps.

The compound, now, had Sid's complete interest. Its bridge was a sturdy arch built of heavy mahogany timbers, so that his footfall on it caused not the slightest vibration. As he made his way up its incline, he could see the upper verandah of the lab beyond—and, below, on the first floor, the screened-in porch which encircled the building. An odd stone structure with that porch and upper entrance, a whitewashed monument, it seemed, set off in a circled wall which proclaimed its importance. The bridge led through a bower of delicate limbs from thorn trees below: peaceful, shady, and picturesque. Then, from the middle of the bridge, he saw the yard of the compound.

Pods. Those inverted cone-shaped pods.

Something might have sounded a warning in him, yet didn't. He saw them—even in his recognition—with the same, detached, exotic interest with which he had viewed, earlier, that monstrosity at the roadside, that pile of dead dogs, or those odd rows of holes in the ground containing the smooth pebbles. He knew these housings: man-made cobra dens. Yet he felt they were empty, long empty; there were no snakes in the yard as at the Institute; there was a feeling here of ruin and of lives that were past.

"Anyone home out here?" he called.

No movement anywhere.

It was dusk now, the shadows deepening. As he stepped onto the upper verandah, the silence of evening descended. Sid stood for a moment, listening, still feeling like an apologetic intruder, then went to the wide French doors which led inside. Timidly, he gave them a try. Open. He gave his last call before entering.

"Nobody here, is there?"

Inside, a few odors: a sweet disinfectant, sulphur, some strong acid-like smells he couldn't distinguish.

The upstairs had nothing of interest: two small rooms, one of them used for storage of some empty chemical cartons. Sid followed a hallway to the stairs which led down to the lower floor, stairs which creaked underfoot as he went down.

He quietly opened a door, looked in, and entered.

When he saw that great canopy of bed draped in white netting, he felt his breath escape in a single word, "God!" Then, slowly, he stepped around the bed, peering through the gauze at that large, white figure propped on pillows and breathing evenly. He saw the body catheters. Asleep, he told himself. Sick and asleep. For a full minute he stood there trying to come to terms with the apparition, then the sickening sweetness of the antiseptic and the smell of the bedsores turned him out. At the door, leaving, he looked back. Sepulchre, he thought. A deep burial vault. Shrine.

His thoughts were still spinning away when he heard the high whirring noise of the cicadas beginning. As he made his way further along the hallway toward the lab, the insects sang a steady, dreadful note out there in the open bush beyond the compound walls. Another door. Opening it and stepping inside, he saw bright bottles, test tubes, and empty glass cages. It was a place recently in use, perhaps, but hardly very active.

Still, no associations. His mind was merely a receptacle to all this strangeness. Then, as he quietly closed the door to the lab and turned into the hallway again, he had the distinct feeling that he was being watched. His mouth formed another word of greeting, but nothing came out.

The study and sitting room, then. The clutter here was alive and current, the room of a real person, and Sid felt even more like an intruder who should not stay long. He didn't want to pause long at the desk reading the materials, but there, on the cover of the leather-bound diary, was written the name: Clare. All right, he told himself. The biologist. The first name on the list.

His eyes roamed the room. Many books with markers in them, partially read then abandoned. The chess board. Chess books beside it. Couch and Persian rug. Colored inks and rubber stamps. Almonds. A white man here, too, and not just a keeper for the old sick one down the hall.

At last, Sid went out onto the screened porch beyond. Dusk was settling into darkness, now, as the cicadas sang their steady noise. He took a few tentative steps. A large dent in the screen where he peered out into the yard once more at all those pods. His mind, far from adding anything together, was calm and blank—filled with thoughtless wonder.

He strolled down the porch and turned the corner.

Kali was there and came at him in a quick, curling rush.

Struck full in the face and reeling backward, Sid cried out, "Ah!" It was an expression of fright, not pain, and his eyes went wide with disbelief. It was the largest and most unearthly creature he had ever seen, the sight of it, even as it struck again, too much for him. He threw up a protective arm. It struck his elbow, hung on, filled it with stinging poison, then withdrew to strike again.

He was making another noise now, saying, deep down, "Nnnn, nnnnn." Reeling backward, he fell. Another strike, this time his thigh. The mamba hovered over him, still raised up seven feet tall, as Sid felt his face puffed out and numb. Dizzy and burning with sudden fever, he began to hallucinate, too, seeing the spinning colors of a dawn fire, a burst of orange and a streak of red which he knew in his last thoughts to be a trickle of blood back behind his eyes.

As he crawled a body's length away, another strike.

Burning images, then: a wide arid savannah, a yellow kitchen, silver deadwood, and pools of light off in the shadows of the forests of home.

A last strike. He felt its giant head attached to his neck. Then the endless sting of sleep.

The doors to the screened-in porch which led into the yard had been carefully propped open, so that Kali could make the porch his domain, too. Wemba, following instructions, had let Kali see him doing this before fleeing back inside the house and closing its doors tightly behind him. Then, as he was told, he hid in the closet of the lab. He had heard the enemy's footfall. He had heard Kali's attack, knowing full well what it was. Now, softly, minutes having passed and silence growing, Wemba came out, made his way upstairs, and hurried across the bridge again. He looked back only once at the screened-in porch as he ran, but saw nothing. Darkness was on him and the cicadas were wildly calling.

Quentin waited for him at the main house. "All finished," Wemba told him.

"Good, then go out there again and wait for me," Quentin ordered him. "We have lots to do."

"I will wait at the middle of the bridge," Wemba informed him.

"Well enough," Quentin said, and Wemba was gone.

Quentin strolled around the empty house thinking things out. At the piano he stopped, once, his fingers idly striking a chord as he stood there beside it. From the bridge, Wemba heard the chord and accepted it as part of the unholy night. Later, still standing there as the moon began to rise, Wemba heard the Jeep being driven around to the wall of the compound. He was like a thin, black statuette on the bridge, an immovable decoration.

The problem was luring Kali off the porch. It still occupied its new territory, moving down one side and back again, never leaving its kill for very long.

"Do you think it will settle down?" Quentin asked.

"It is very excited," Wemba answered.

They waited an hour. During this time Wemba took care of the doctor for the night and finished his usual chores in the lab. Quentin considered going outside, attracting the mamba's attention, and hurrying to safety while Wemba shut off the porch once more, but decided, instead, to wait longer.

At last the moon rose above the wall of the compound. Kali, who always favored the moonlight, slid off the porch, crossed the yard, and took up its position beneath the thorn tree.

Since Wemba refused to touch the body, Quentin managed to get it across the bridge and into the Jeep by himself.

They drove down to the dried creek bed where years ago the doctor had passed out beer and palm wine before lecturing the natives. A bright spill of moonlight made everything visible, so as they bounced along Quentin steered around large rocks and crags. The bog stretched out in the bend of the creek; its mud stank and here and there lily pads adorned small pools of glistening slime around its edges. There was always speculation on how deep the bog was, but once, both Quentin and Wemba knew, a rhino had floundered in it, had become stuck, and had grunted helplessly for hours before oozing through the quicksand to its death.

"Deep enough?" Quentin now asked as they both stood up in the open Jeep and peered over into the moonlit mud.

"Very plenty," Wemba assured him.

To Wemba's surprise and pleasure, though, his master drove further along the dry creek bed and disposed of the body as one might dispose of anyone who was not *mangati*—a worthy foe. Using the back of the Jeep for needed elevation, Quentin lifted the policeman and stuffed him down the chimney of a giant red clay ant hill—head first, upside down, like any traitor or truly evil spirit. This was a struggle because of the policeman's weight, and the thin clay top of the ant hill broke off in the effort, but down he went, one arm, then the other, slowly, then the thick waist, the legs, then gone. Wemba, who stood watching, his hand resting on the windshield, enjoyed it all very much and seemed to understand this insult.

Next, they drove back to the bog. Wemba waited on safe ground as his master revved up the Jeep, took aim, and sped toward the slimy bog, jumping off at the last moment as the vehicle careened into the quicksand. Again, this gave the old black man great pleasure; he had never seen Quentin do anything so exciting or with such dexterity.

Afterward, they waited for a long time for the Jeep to do something. It balanced at the edge of the bog, so gave them concern. Then at midnight it stood up gently on its nose like a ship which had slowly filled with water and was about to sink. A soft, sucking sound. Gradually it began to disappear. Then it was gone.

Quentin and Wemba walked across the moonlit savannah back to the estate. Beyond the far western horizon a swirl of black rainclouds moved in.

24

In the middle of the slum was Musika Market where each day buses and lorries from the rural areas unloaded hundreds of new arrivals. Quentin watched them come in: ragged natives, gaunt girls, burnt-out farmers with their belongings bundled under their arms, young blacks with squawking chickens lashed together, and even a few hunters out of the deep bush who looked as though they had just travelled in from the stone age. The Salisbury slum where they arrived—called Harare Location— was not very hopeful. It stretched out for miles, bordered by the railroad tracks and the Mukuvisi River, moving through block after city block of shanties, market stalls roofed with corrugated tin, and thousands of beer halls where the residents slumped on benches drinking beer out of half-gallon plastic buckets. Those same buckets, placed in alleys or side streets or between stalls in Harare, served as urinals; the ditches were afloat with brackish water and turd; a grey slime of mud covered the thoroughfares which intersected Charter Road, Ardbennie Road, and other main streets; the communal lavatories—*zwimbudzi*—were filled with mothers washing out their crying children's ears, old men scrubbing their genitals, young men smoking cigarettes in clustered groups; the shadow of the churches and missions fell everywhere; shops run by the Indians, the Jews, and the Chinese were filled with customers who shouted and laughed and gave the neighborhoods their noise and clatter.

Quentin had thought of staying out of Salisbury's hotel district as he had done in Cairo and Lagos, but had learned the impossibility of this tactic here. One did not easily move between the two segregated worlds of Salisbury. If he wanted his quarry, he would have to risk staying downtown. One could visit the slums like Harare or Mabvuku or others bordering the white man's city, but one couldn't stay out there without being noticed; one could pay for a prostitute's time or attend the street dances, but the people of the district slept six to a room, there was no place for tourists, and the police with their big German shepherd guard dogs who patrolled this maze of hovels would surely ask questions.

He stood near the market drinking tea and watching the buses unload. An endless file of new drifters, hopeful and in awe. Few would find work in the brickyards across the river. Few would ever find a decent meal of more substance than the daily *sadza*—a mushy maize preparation. Most of them would become whores or petty thieves. The lucky ones would work as janitors or gardeners or houseboys in the white suburbs such as Avondale or Highlands or Waterfalls.

Another sewer. And this one had no room for him even on a temporary basis. His sadness for the people here was tempered with caution and indecision this time.

"You want help?" a young man asked him as he stood at that stall drinking the thin tea.

"No thanks, nothing," Quentin told him.

The young man was a *va ka funda*—one of those who spoke English, who knew the white man's ways, and who made his living hustling and procuring.

"You a mercenary?"

"No," Quentin answered. "And I'll be wanting a taxi soon. That's all."

The young man's face brightened. He wore an old worsted jacket, a pair of khaki trousers, and a soiled T-shirt which advertised Budweiser beer.

"I'll get you a taxi and a good rate," he told Quentin.

"Fine, you do that," Quentin said.

Things weren't right. Better to employ such a nuisance than not. Better to leave the slum this time and stay in the downtown hotels. Even then, there was a guerrilla war going on, bandit gangs raiding villages in the north, unrest and political uncertainty everywhere, and he felt that his usual plan could go badly.

He took a taxi—at an inflated price—to the Hotel Jameson. As he paid the driver and picked up his small, single valise, he looked over into a little patch of park beyond Cecil Square. A group of police reservists— volunteers bearing the family shotguns and dressed in mufti except for the police shirts—were prodding and bayoneting loose earth around the park shrubbery.

"Looking for buried weapons," the driver explained.

It was a troubled country in its last days.

Quentin signed the register in the hotel with the name on his British passport: John Castle. Then he ordered lunch sent to his room and went up to think matters over.

He had read about the American manufacturer on a tour sponsored by the State Department. Very official and very tempting. He had made plans quickly to go to Salisbury, but now doubts crept in. He had seldom visited apartheid countries and felt conspicuous. His father had taken him on that visit to Johannesburg. The visit to Durban—the first victim, months ago—had been a thoughtless business. Now he paused.

His whole mission passed review in his thoughts.

If he hated the Americans and their rape of the continent, who did he identify with? Not the Europeans who plundered everything during the last century. They were mostly a vile lot. And so were their children, these second generation colonials who kept underpaid houseboys instead of slaves, who wore safari clothes to luncheons and wanted to be called *bwana,* who stood bragging all day at the Long Bar in Nairobi or made the disco scene in Capetown or formed endless new country clubs in Monrovia or Lusaka. A small credit was due some of them from both generations who stayed on the land, said they loved it, and endured its hardships. A few of them were tough and pleasantly eccentric. But they were mostly hopeless materialists who mined the earth, shot the animals, lived high off the cheap native labor force, and preened around claiming that their discomforts were noble. The blacks, then: no, his mission wasn't for them either. Their suffering and hardships were real and pathetic enough, but they were also easily bought off by any coin. A century ago explorers bought them off with shiny beads; the Christian missions bought them off with soup and a few useless medicines—camphor and calomel; the slavers found them as docile as domestic animals and usually willing to sell each other; traders often bought them with mere promises; and the white companies, later, bought them for salaries of just pennies a day and took from them years of back-breaking toil and all the gold, diamonds, oil, and uranium under their lands. Few natives withstood the onslaught. Only the Masai and a few stubborn, isolated herdsmen refused to come into the white man's towns and cities. Revolutions—or even strikes—were infrequent and half-hearted; the blacks might have taken their freedom from this insipid minority of Europeans at any time, but more than freedom they usually wanted salaries and beer. And when they did protest, they were easily silenced—made docile again, and as subservient to any master as they had always been to the fierce nature all around them. In 1900, the South African blacks who mined gold went on strike, so the companies brought in 54,000 indentured Chinese coolies who would work cheaper and complain less. The blacks lingered in the overcrowded towns or crept back to the bush, defeated. They endured, they waited, they suffered more, but they seldom raised a voice; few had any of the old, dark warrior blood.

White nor black, then. Quentin identified with neither. He did his work, he knew, for no one.

For what, then?

For raw, wild nature itself, he sometimes felt.

For the naked Dinka. Unlike the merchants and traders the tribe have never had a verb in their language meaning *to have* or *to own*. In that wide expanse along the northern periphery of Kenya, what do they do? They do very little. What do they produce? Nothing. What do they have? Nothing again, not even the proper language for possession. Who, then, are they? Wanderers, free spirits, close kin to the animals. They live off an arid land which is mostly hostile. They rarely murder or steal, but all mischief they appreciate—even cruelty which is taught to them by the rugged land itself—as if they understand that an amoral, whimsical, lusty, bandit detachment is almost a requisite for freedom.

The Turkana, too. Even among themselves they seem to go blind with their individualism and stark presence on the earth. Proud as leopards. Crazy with their own sense of themselves, as if some deep, comic secret was theirs alone. Up there on the frontier hunting with his father, Quentin remembered their passionate lives. One of them, tall and naked except for the razor-sharp bracelets on his forearms, his penis chalked so that it swung like a white metronome beating time against his leg, left the camp one night and ran off into the desert. The doctor asked where he was going and was told that he was lovesick, that he had seen a woman in a caravan a week before, a woman who was now probably one hundred miles away, and that he was running to find her. Another, a great specimen of man, a Turkana who was all height and muscle, spoke a language all his own—one of his own invention. He would have been a chief, but he preferred, Quentin learned, his own private, mystic monologue. Another travelled from his village each year to the shores of Lake Rudolph to do combat with the crocodiles. He had killed many, providing food for his people, but disdained help in this dangerous harvest which usually took a half-dozen strong men. His legs and arms were scarred, and a distant, dreamy, psychopathic look rode behind his gaze. What did he know of that huge collection of crocodiles around a lake, now cut off and strangely remote, which had once, years ago, been part of the Nile system? What did he know of himself and his deadly annual journey?

The Masai. Hunters, herdsmen, poets, solitaires. Even though Nairobi grew up in their midst, they disdained it. Quentin had seen a Masai warrior, once, at a pharmacy on the boulevard. Tall, arrogant, carrying his short metal spear underneath his cape although this was forbidden by law, he was ordering quinine for his fevered son. Trading beads the pharmacist really didn't want, but accepted. But this was a rare exception, for they stayed out on the savannah, grimy with dirt and stained with that dull red dye, as alien to the culture of cities as the Amish living alone with the old ways in America. Twelve-year-old Masai boys guarded their scrawny cattle with fearless dignity; if a lion charged, they had learned to fall away with its onrush, planting that little metal spear in the ground, so they impaled it, killing their killer, at least. And behind their eyes the creature announced itself: yes, you are from this century and know much, it said, but I am from that wilderness before time, I know what you have forgotten, in my blood runs something fierce which you have tamed out of yourself, and which of us, tell me, is more complete, which is smarter, who is the true man?

In a few isolated, remnant tribes Quentin still saw it.

The Pygmies, dwarfed and different, living deep in the impenetrable middle jungle where no civilized man would want to step, had this craziness so deep inside them that they even had, still, the capacity for laughter. Or the mountain people of Uganda. Out there on a wasteland which western man would consider unlivable they contend with death on a daily basis—and remain hostile to any encroaching comfort. They deal with death, in fact, like gamblers and warriors: flirting with it, courting it, savoring the near misses, celebrating the victories.

These curious, ancient tribes were dwindling, their domains shrinking. Most of the continent, now, was herded and calmed.

But Quentin, pausing before his next strike, wanted no less than a profound freedom: freedom from the estate which had held him, from his father, from the restraints of all convention, from love, perhaps from life itself. One swerves toward death, or there is no real and deeply felt knowledge. So he wanted a soul adventure, a purpose so serious, a risk so lonely and dreadful and primitive, that he could finally know himself in a spiritual ecstasy.

He didn't eat the lunch he ordered. Instead, he took a few of the raw almonds.

In the late afternoon he dressed and went out. He would stop at the obvious hotels and make a few bold inquiries about the American businessman; it shouldn't be too difficult finding him if all those government types were accompanying him. Caution and elation rode around inside him: he was in their very midst this time, at one of their hotels, moving among them as they surely suspected.

25

Over in the Ambassador Hotel that same afternoon Jamie, one of the secret service agents, and the marine managed to arrest the wrong man.

It happened that Olin Lockridge and the entourage had just returned to the hotel from the hilltop ruins at Zimbabwe. They had chartered a plane down and back at the businessman's insistence. He loved old ruins, he admitted to Jamie, because in Illinois there weren't any.

"Also," he said, "the only other ruins I've visited were Aztec. So I haven't seen old world ruins." There, he paused to consider a phrase. "Only new world old ruins."

Jamie blinked and nodded in reply.

They approached the mail desk in the lobby. Everyone was weary from the excursion which had started at daybreak and very anxious for the next shift to take over. Their concentration had faded.

Jamie was further preoccupied because he expected his daily messages from the Little Buddha and also hoped to hear from Stella and the Professor, who had flown to Nairobi to interview everyone concerning Sid's disappearance. He felt out of control without Charlie. And Stella was nice to have around: pleasant to look at, savvy, and more efficient by far in handling details than any of them. So he approached the mail clerk with questions, his thoughts not on Olin Lockridge at all.

"I'll just be over here," Lockridge told him.

"Yes, fine, all right," Jamie said, turning to the clerk.

The businessman crossed the lobby and entered a hallway, moving toward the men's toilet. One of the agents, who wore a lumpy brown seersucker suit which bulged with his communications device and his army Luger, fell in behind Lockridge. The agent's pace was slow, however, so that the businessman swung into the toilet ahead of him. At that point, another man—short, bald, yet quick of foot—cut between Lockridge and the agent, entered the men's room, and deftly bolted the door, shutting the agent out in the hallway.

For a moment, trying the door and unable to get inside, the agent stood there, his mind blank. Then he ran back to the lobby calling for Jamie.

The marine sergeant entered from the hotel driveway and saw the agent tugging at Jamie's sleeve, shouting, and gesturing wildly.

Inside the toilet Olin Lockridge was cornered by a man who wished to become a dealer in heavy equipment. He was a white Rhodesian named Hiram Davison who had failed, he admitted, at other business ventures. But he had read of Olin Lockridge's tour and in this unorthodox manner—unaware that agents followed the American—he had bolted the toilet door to assure himself privacy while he made application.

Hiram Davison had notes written out for remarks he wanted to make, so began to speak. With the notes rolled up in his hand, he addressed the American, who leaned into the urinal. It was this roll of paper being pointed and jabbed at his audience which caused so much trouble when the marine sergeant kicked in the door.

Jamie and the agent stumbled through the broken door, too. Both businessmen stood there—Davison with his notes rolled in his fist—looking amazed.

"You're under arrest," Jamie told the only stranger in the room.

The Rhodesian protested.

Olin Lockridge, true to form, couldn't get any words out. When Jamie asked him if he was all right, he could only nod yes.

Now the room filled with Indian clerks, hotel guests, and a white policeman who was shown the way by the agent in the hallway. Their voices echoed loudly off the tile, everyone talking at once. The head desk clerk wanted to know if damages would be paid.

"It is such a very broken door," he pointed out to Jamie.

"Don't worry about it," Jamie told him, and he turned back to Olin Lockridge, still trying to get an explanation.

"It was a business proposition!" the Rhodesian insisted. In the excitement, his nose began to bleed and the two agents, neither of whom wanted their seersucker suits spotted with droplets of blood, turned away.

"What do you have there?" the marine asked, pointing.

"Notes."

"Who is this?" Jamie asked Lockridge. "Do you know him?"

"I locked the door for a little privacy," Hiram Davison said, dismayed now that the room was so full of people.

"And now it will require payment," the tall clerk added.

"Clear the room!" Jamie announced, but his voice lacked authority. Confusion continued. Hiram Davison, bleeding and protesting, was put into the custody of the policeman who refused, despite one of the agent's argument, to handcuff his charge. The head clerk received a bribe, a down payment on the broken door. Olin Lockridge, content to stay where he was beside the urinal, lectured the congenial mail clerk on the ruins of Zimbabwe.

"Walls thirty feet high out there in the jungle," he went on. "For years, see, people thought this place might be King Solomon's mines." He paused, searching for yet another phrase. "But it wasn't."

Later that night Jamie phoned Charlie Hazo and went over the whole incident with him. As Charlie listened, Jamie's voice seemed forlorn and far away, punctuated with heavy static; it was as if the rushing waters of all the continental rivers boomed in the phone, and far off in the night a puny, small, human voice tried to make its excuses heard.

"Yes, Jamie," the Professor kept saying from his chair behind Sid's desk in the Nairobi office. "This time you will have to file a report."

"But why?"

"Because you might have blown Lockridge's protection," Charlie said, explaining what Jamie already knew and feared. It was a cool, rainy late night in Nairobi, getting toward midnight, and Stella was cleaning out the secretaries' desks in the outer offices, looking for any tiny note or jotting which might help explain where or how Sid had vanished.

"I'm sure none of the hotel guests understood what was going on," Jamie argued.

"A report is for your own protection," Charlie advised him. "If anything goes wrong later on, there it will be."

"It was only an eager guy wanting to do business," Jamie said. The forlorn, faraway syllables.

After the phone conversation ended, Stella came in and sat on the edge of the desk beside Charlie. He put his hand on her smooth knee.

"Nothing," she said. "He didn't sign out on the Day Book or leave a note or put anything on the dictaphone. Some of his lists—ones the secretaries say he kept—must still be with him."

"I've been thinking about Sid. I believe it might be sex. He might have found another woman."

"And run off without a word?"

"True, he wouldn't do it that way," Charlie said. "But then the Jeep might show up in, say, Zanzibar."

"In Zanzibar?"

"That's a sexy place, let me tell you."

"Is it?" she asked.

"For me it always will be." They exchanged a tired, loving look and smiled at each other. Then the Professor asked her—without any seeming guile and in an almost clinical way, "Do you have all your reproductive organs?" She looked to see if he was kidding, but he wasn't.

"Last time I checked," she said.

"Could you still have a baby?"

"Well, maybe," she said. "I'm nearly forty, and so I might have to stay in bed the last few weeks. And it might have jaundice and a strange hump on its back."

"Could it have, say, your green eyes and a scar in the middle of its little pink forehead?"

"Want to try?" she asked, raising an eyebrow. She felt she wanted to laugh and cry all at once.

The Professor looked at her in silence for a moment. "I think I want to get married, then try to have a child," he said. "Maybe with a little jaundice, maybe a little hunchbacked, but normal, if possible."

A proposal. She felt she would surely cry, but instead details and practicalities lurched into her thoughts. Would she lose her seniority and her government rating? Would she live in Virginia? What would she wear to the wedding? Perhaps one of those bright *kangas* from Pemba Island which were dyed with mimosa bark.

She slid off the desk and onto his lap. For a few seconds more they held each other without saying anything.

Outside, the rain had stopped, but water dripped beside the window ledge as steady as a clock's workings. It was as if they had said these things to each other—or something similar, something so sad and comic as all this—a thousand years ago.

26

In Salisbury it was still earlier in the evening, and the sky was tinged with sapphire light.

Quentin had already seen and heard enough.

That afternoon he had heard rumors of the story at the bar in Meikle's even before he could stop around at the Ambassador: some closely guarded American big shot had caused a furor over at the hotel. Two regulars in the bar at Meikle's were talking about it—one of them, for all the sultry heat, dressed in tweed as though he sipped his Watney's in some windblown icy pub out on the Scottish moors.

"Sure, he was guarded," he told his friend. "There's a bloody killer out there murdering the poor American tycoons, isn't there? Poisoning them! You've heard all about it, haven't you? Fellow carries a cobra on him, see, a trained pet cobra! Bites hell out of Americans and nobody else!"

"I don't like Americans," the friend of the one in tweed said.

"You don't like anybody."

"But I really don't like Americans."

"Why?"

"Because they want to be liked so much. They're like friendly rapists. While they bugger you, they want to tell about themselves, ask your health, and become pen pals!"

Quentin finished off his cider and walked to the Ambassador.

Two white policemen stood on the corner near the hotel where a group of black street musicians played their makeshift tin drums and wooden lutes. Traffic was heavy, so the sound of the instruments became noise laid atop noise, but the blacks were going at it, earning a few shillings before being directed to leave. The two policemen indulged them. Quentin fell in beside the shorter cop, the one who almost smiled at this tuneless, rhythmic ensemble.

"Is this bothering you, sir?" the policeman asked, turning to Quentin.

"No, not at all," Quentin answered. It was clear that if a citizen objected, the musicians—playing without licenses—would be sent off.

"What happened over at the Ambassador today?" Quentin asked.

"Nothing I heard of." Then the policeman looked fully at Quentin. "Are you from here?" he inquired. Clearly, he found something amiss in the voice or presence.

"I'm an executive with Imperial Tobacco," Quentin lied. "Live out on the hill."

The reply seemed to satisfy the policeman, who then had to explain his suspicion. "No offense," he said. "It's just the bombs."

"Saw them poking around a park today for buried weapons," Quentin said, mustering his stiffest accent. It was the last they said to each other before he slipped away and walked into the hotel.

The same mail clerk, still on duty, told Quentin everything. The American rich man, he reported, had been bothered in the toilet by a homosexual. Bodyguards had soundly beaten the offender, bloodying his nose, and he had been sent off to jail for a long term. One of the bodyguards had broken down the door to the toilet. The rich man was a fine gentleman who loved ancient ruins.

"How many bodyguards does the rich man have?" Quentin asked.

"Oh, many. They wear very fine seersucker suits, so you can easily see them. The same seersucker suits, but different colors: brown, blue, grey. They keep a very sharp watch because it isn't safe for Americans anymore with the Arab killer on the loose."

"An Arab?"

"Oh yes. From Palestine. They have extremely bad sentiments for the Americans."

Quentin leaned casually on the end of the mail counter. In this late afternoon period no one came asking for letters, so they talked for a long time. The clerk assumed that Quentin was a hotel guest.

"The bodyguards talk into the lapels of their seersucker suits, too," the clerk obligingly added.

"Do what?"

A demonstration followed. "Like this, see? Hello. Stand by. Repeat message, please. It is all very amusing."

"They have radios on them?"

"Naturally. Americans are fond of electronics."

"Who do they talk to?"

"To one another. And to the men upstairs."

Quentin sat in the mezzanine lounge drinking tea after this, hoping to see a seersucker suit pass by. When one didn't and as the lounge grew crowded by early evening, he went into the grill for dinner. There he had a prolonged meal of squab and potatoes, a watery custard, and brandy. The famous dealer in heavy equipment failed to show.

Afterward he rented a car. He had to get out of the city.

He drove south, alone, beyond the sight of the red lights flashing from the top of the radio tower in downtown Salisbury, and only after he travelled the open road did he recall that it was a country in the midst of war and that some danger might be lurking around. He wished he had his newly acquired 9mm pistol, and he determined to carry it with him after this—even though some precaution would be necessary at airports.

When the land had grown silent and darkness was full, he pulled to the side of the road and parked. Eventually, he went out and sat on the hood of the car—an English Ford—and leaned back against the windshield to gaze up at the stars.

The complicated heavens. They were dazzling out here on this empty savannah. His thoughts turned in a great wheel, like the stars themselves, and he let them go.

—we are light years from other possibly inhabited planets in other solar systems. We will never reach anyone else. And the impossibility of this awaits our comprehension. We are finite. There are things we cannot do. And our earth is all we have.

—the cobra was always part of the Pharaoh's headdress.

—the concept of the criminal presupposes a lovely culture with little deviancy in it, but this isn't the case. Culture has gone mad. The economic manipulation of some men by others is evil. Mankind turned into the herd is evil. A materialism which threatens identity is evil. In such a world the criminal, like the rogue prisoner in a penitentiary, is the only one who thinks of escape.

—there is the Southern Cross, my lovely constellation. And there is the Milky Way, the edge of my galaxy. Beyond, pure space, All chaotic.

—Hannibal threw crock pots of snakes onto the Roman ships. The Roman oarsmen panicked and Hannibal won a sea victory.

—the arrows of the old bushmen were tipped with cobra or adder venoms. In Bengal, the spears were tipped, and the Scythian archers of western Asia tipped their arrows, too.

—what is lawful and unlawful anyway? The law ultimately protects property and is the text of the domestic breed. It is the rationalization of the herd for all its greed and its petty values.

—the stars inside rare gemstones. Called *asterias*.

—since the first diamond was discovered in Africa in 1867, there has been only the grief of wealth and all the materialistic values in those hills above Capetown. The South Africans are a tough, mean lot. And Cecil Rhodes said that the trouble with Africa is its rivers; cut the continent in half with a railroad, he said, and you've broken its wildness. And so he built railroads. The Cape to Cairo.

—in some gems there is that hidden, secret light. The deep star which says, "You cannot know me. I am beyond you."

—inside all herds there are only commonplaces, never passions.

—I have my own sexual yearnings, of course, but nothing was fated for me. I am to live alone. As if that is written down in a great book.

—that snake pond up in Benin: a man who walks through it proves his innocence. Trial by ritual.

—snake stones: the witch doctors provide them for rubbing snake bites. The occult power, again, of precious or magical stones. Gems and mystic pebbles. All things fit together. Crazy patterns are thrown up there against the night skies where we pass. Time, the stars, the snake, finitude, and the infinity of death.

—who can understand murder which is not for gain; which is not for selfish and psychotic pleasure; which is for freedom?

He walked out into the middle of the empty highway and stretched his arms high. The beautiful purity of this terrible isolation.

On the way back to Salisbury, then, the headlights of his car searching the darkness in the bush ahead, he thought he saw a leopard crossing. It gave him some momentary excitement and then contentment.

His enemy was organized, but banal, clumsy, and mindless. Yet still they came. They wanted to find him and cast him aside like a minor irritation. In their inept way, they would keep searching, and because there were so many of them and because their greed was so strong—greater than any ideology on earth—they would probably and eventually find him.

He had to do something remarkable and monstrous.

Because they were so ravenous, so machinelike, so mindless, they did not yet believe their finitude. They didn't believe in the complexity of this ancient continent. They didn't understand primitive cleverness. They didn't even believe in death.

He would go back and spend some days among them, he decided. He would memorize their faces. After studying their patterns, he would prepare, and in Nairobi, the next stop on their tour, not here in this troubled land, he decided, he would kill them all.

27

On Monday Peter Foxx received a phone call from Hanning Wilson, the presidential aide.

"Very simple, Peter," the soft drawl said. "The President wants to know if he can expect results from your team. Quite a few weeks have passed since Cairo."

"The Professor has laid a beautiful trap. The whole long memo on it should be in your hands," Peter said.

"Yes, I've seen it. This will work?"

"Give it time. It'll work," Peter drawled back, trying to thicken his own Southern accent to match his interrogator's.

When they ended the conversation, Peter made three additional phone calls. He phoned the secretary over at Africa International where he had applied for a staff position. Next he phoned Kip Culley, who was recuperating at home, and asked him to compile a detailed dossier on Jamie Vander. It was needed, he explained, because Jamie was being considered for an important promotion.

"That's good news," Kip said. "I've been worrying about him."

"And listen, Kip, we need anything unfavorable toward Jamie, too," the Little Buddha said. "Anything that anyone could use against him. Personal or professional. We'll need to head off his critics because this is a sensitive job we're screening."

"I'll get everything I can. Is this inside the Company?"

"Can't tell anything else," Peter said. "How are you feeling?"

"Maybe a little stronger."

"Good," Peter said. "I need the dossier tomorrow."

"That soon?"

"If you need help, call the secretaries in the office. We have a military liaison man who will do the leg work for you."

"I'll do my best," Kip assured him.

Finally, Peter called a new acquaintance, a Pentagon general, and suggested that they should form a steering committee which would administer all anti-terrorist activity.

"It should have complete authority over all branches of the military and over all relevant groups in every agency," Peter explained.

"And who should sit as head of the committee?" the general asked.

"You should," Peter said. "That's why I'm calling you."

"And what do you get out of it?"

"I'll be executive secretary. You don't have time for all the details—and, after all, I'm still the one who wrote the book."

There was a significant pause, after which the general said, "You have a wonderful idea, Foxx. Let me see a memo on it."

"There's one written. And I've arranged for the idea to come from the White House," Peter lied.

These Monday morning phone calls were part of the Little Buddha's effort to place himself in some new position should the African task force fail. He meant, if possible, to install himself at the CIA, Africa International, or the Pentagon before any results on the manhunt were in.

On Monday afternoon the World Health Organization sent over its report. Peter went over it carefully, noting that in the last year more than two thousand Africans had died of snake bites. He wrote a memo requesting help from the organization in finding any unusual circumstance—where, for instance, a victim had seemingly died of cobra venom poisoning without actually having been bitten.

On Tuesday morning he worked on the budget. The task force spent as much on bribes, he discovered, as on the rest of its operation. As he made notes and added up columns of figures, he paused to consider Sid Cash. Perhaps he had run across something in Nairobi, Peter mused.

Everyone discounted the notion that Sid's disappearance was related to the search for the killer, but what if everyone was wrong? With the Olin Lockridge tour going into Nairobi, what if something extraordinary occurred? He shuddered at the thought.

Just after lunch on Tuesday—oysters and a soufflé at Chez Camille—Peter was visited by Andrea Sloane. He didn't know her, but accepted her appointment when she said on the phone that she wanted to talk about Charlie Hazo. When she entered Peter's office that afternoon, her movements—from the door to the chair beside his desk—were striking. Both awkward and elegant, he said to himself, like a water bird's. Her voice was full of cultured honey: softly British, a little song carefully sung.

"You wanted to see me about Professor Hazo?" Peter began.

"I've been wanting to contact him," she said, smiling. "It took quite an effort to discover that he works for you."

"He doesn't exactly," Peter said. "The Professor works by contract, as you probably know, for the whole intelligence community."

"No, I didn't know," she said. Peter's discomfort at having revealed this showed. "I thought he taught at a small college in Virginia."

"Of course he does that, too," Peter said, backing up. "He's a well known scholar and valuable to his government."

Andrea smiled and continued. Peter enjoyed her voice: a modulated music of correct speech, so unlike the hick squawkings of all the office secretaries.

"I have some personal documents for his signature," Andrea lied. "So I need to send them to him in a hurry. Do you know where he is?"

"Give them to me and I'll send them along to him."

"So it's a secret where he is?"

"No, not a secret. He's in Africa."

"I know that much," she said, trying another courteous smile.

"And you are—" Peter glanced at a note on the desk before him. "The wife of a former attaché. You still live in the house in Dumbarton Oaks?"

"I'm a widow," she said softly. "And, yes, in the same house."

"And you know Charlie strictly on a personal basis?"

"Strictly," she said with crisp enunciation.

Peter looked at her. She wore a long silk scarf, silver earrings and pin, an expensive grey dress—Halston, he guessed—and had the look of a woman in command. Yet in her eyes was this hurt look: the gaunt grief of a woman alone and in need, he felt, and a glimmer of pain, carefully covered over, which made her attractive.

"Would you come to dinner with me?" Peter found himself asking.

"Dinner? You want to talk about Charlie?"

"No, not at all," he answered.

She cocked her head and smiled at him: another water bird movement, both gentle and delicate. Behind those eyes of hers, her gaze said, you are young, you are rotund, you were not supposed to ask me to dinner.

"I read about you in the newspaper," she said.

"What did you read?"

"That you are a connoisseur of good food."

"Well, I won't take you for a hamburger," he told her, making her smile return. Was he interested in her because she was the Professor's woman? Because of her elegance? He had never asked anyone for a date before. Why this stranger?

"Tonight?" she asked.

It was all so simple. She would be a companion with whom he would have tea, listen to records, work in the garden, stroll in museums, sit in restaurants. He would probably read his poetry aloud to her.

Later that afternoon Peter received word that a delegation wanted a meeting. The Third World Conference wanted his team out of Africa. He scheduled them for Thursday and went back to the telephone. He asked Hanning Wilson to brief him on the Conference and its intentions. He made reservations at Le Consulat. Then he read Jamie Vander's file—with generous annotations by Kip Culley—and discovered that, once, at Yale, Jamie had been accused of cheating on an exam, but had been acquitted of charges.

That evening, moving toward their table across the restaurant, Andrea took Peter's arm. He liked the look and feel of it.

She asked him to order for her and he liked that, too. He felt in charge. He wanted to show her his Luger collection, his budget sheet, and the spot on his shoulder where the President had rested his hand.

The waiter served their opening course. Peter saw that her hand trembled.

"Did Charlie ever say anything about me?" Peter asked.

"No, I don't think he ever did."

"I wondered if he liked me."

"He certainly should like you," Andrea said with a smile.

"Few people do. I can't hide two unsightly things about myself: my big belly and my ambition. The trick is disguise. You wear the proper clothes for a bad figure, and you try hard to camouflage all ambition. But you know what they call me behind my back: the Little Buddha."

"Yes, I remember that from the newspaper."

Peter demolished his seafood salad with four or five quick thrusts of his fork. Andrea tactfully avoided watching.

"When they call you that does it mean that you're a very serene person?" she asked.

"No, it means they think I'm a fat little god. Or believe as much about myself."

"And you're not?"

"No, very mortal. And alone. I live, eat, think, work, and have sex alone."

As she laughed, her head tilted once more in that odd, wide-eyed, awkwardly graceful way. "Well," she said, "tonight you're dining with me."

"I might also be capable of a highly refined sexual act, too," Peter said, musing aloud over his empty salad plate. He seemed sincere, confident, and lost in a new line of thought. Andrea waited for him to continue. "I think I could have tea and brandy with you later," he went on. "We could talk art or music. Sitting close together on some deep sofa, turned toward one another, we could sip our drinks, then at the proper moment, ever so slightly, our knees could brush together. Sound all right?"

Andrea laughed out loud. "Oh, very refined," she assured him. Still laughing, she drank off her second whiskey in a single, sustained swallow. He tried to ignore her excess as she had gracefully ignored his.

It was a long meal and with each of its six courses he felt wonderful. Afterward, he took her home in a taxi, said good night at her door, and asked her to Friday dinner. Accepting, she put out her hand to touch him, but found only his protruding belly, so withdrew. He went back to the waiting taxi.

The next afternoon Jamie Vander arrived looking worn out from his long flight. His Ivy League tie was badly knotted, and his button-down collar was unbuttoned and turned up. He needed a shave.

"Peter," he said, putting out his hand. "Good to see you."

The Little Buddha avoided the handshake and pointed him to a chair. Jamie had clearly flown halfway around the world for a reprimand or worse.

With a small amount of ceremony, the Little Buddha opened the folder atop his desk. "You have always been first in your class," he said. "Top scholar. Tested out especially high when you were recruited for government work. Fine efficiency reports from Langley. So why are you such a fuck up?"

"I don't know," Jamie confessed. He was too tired to argue.

"Your marine sergeant broke a man's arm in Zaire. Stella Kane files all your reports and seems to do all your work. In Salisbury you arrested a local businessman and probably exposed the nature of the tour to the killer. And every time you do these things you ask Charlie to keep them off your record."

"I don't think we exposed anything in Salisbury," Jamie argued.

"What do you mean?" Peter whined, his voice growing high-pitched once again. "Every cop and foreign agent in the city knew that Olin whats-his-name was surrounded by bodyguards wearing wires and carrying weapons!"

"Our killer wasn't in Kinshasa, and he wasn't in Salisbury," Jamie said stubbornly. Only the Little Buddha's high-pitched voice, like a prosecutor's dictaphone played at high speed, kept him awake.

"How do you know that?" Peter squeaked.

"I just feel it!"

"The next report on you, Jamie, will probably say that you were the biggest failure in a failed project."

"C'mon, really? I hope not," Jamie protested, squirming in his chair.

"But I've brought you here to brighten your prospects," Peter told him. "Take the rest of today off. Get some sleep and get cleaned up.

When you go out to Langley for your briefing session with your deputy director tomorrow, I want you looking good and feeling right. Because I want you to tell them that our plan is going very well, that we expect to catch our man, and that one of our team is doing an outstanding job—and should definitely be appointed to the African desk or some other comparable intelligence apparatus on a full-time basis."

"Who? Charlie?"

A moment of heavy silence. "No, not Charlie," Peter said.

Slowly, Jamie's face recorded some comprehension.

"You want to go to work out there?"

"I want them to make me an offer," Peter said. "If they do contact me and make an offer, you will have a wonderful report from me. Savannah Blue—our African project—will be to your credit, I promise. None of your offenses will ever be noted, and I'll see that you receive a special commendation for Stella's work."

"I don't know if I should do this or not," Jamie complained.

"Then think it over. Carefully."

Silence between them as Jamie thought it over.

The sun broke through the Washington overcast and slanted through the basement window into Peter's office. It fell on Jamie, slumped in his chair, weary with jet lag, and illuminated his mop of boyish hair and the stubble on his chin.

"I've got to have a good report," he stated flatly.

"You've made the right decision," Peter told him.

28

Because the schedule of business appointments was incomplete, because Jamie wasn't around to direct the tour, and because the weather in Nairobi was rainy and raw so that no one sat in the outdoor restaurants, Charlie took Olin Lockridge and the Secret Service man named Gates down to Tsavo to see some elephants. They flew down with a local pilot in his Cessna early one morning, planning to return that night—a long day's excursion much like the one down to the Zimbabwe ruins that time in Salisbury.

It was July now, midsummer in full bloom in the northern hemisphere, but an intemperate time in Kenya: monsoons had blown up in the south, the chill of the highlands was more severe than anyone seemed prepared for, and the sun's rays were oddly cold. The Masai herders wrapped themselves double in their cloaks; they stood out on the open land like terracotta statues with their scrawny cattle; each herder's jaw seemed rigid and set, and his short metal spear stuck erect out of his tight wrappings. Across the savannah thatched roofs sent up curls of smoke, and herds of zebra and antelope moved around cautiously. Flying down to Tsavo, the men detected a low, blue line of cloud on the far arctic horizon.

Tsavo, as Charlie tried to explain to the businessman, used to be an impassable jungle. One hundred years ago explorers—among them, the

217

German adventurer J.L. Krapf—had to hack their way inland from the coast. There were great herds of elephant then, herds so large nobody tried to count their number, the largest collection of the beasts on the continent. But periods of drouth threatened them, so in the twentieth century conservationists—worrying over the fate of the elephants—began herding and transporting them into the Tsavo reserve.

"These men were conservationists and scientists," Charlie explained. "And, after all, Tsavo is about the size of Rhode Island. It had lots of grassland and thick bush with plenty of big trees. It could feed the herds, they said, and there were big, natural waterholes to defend the elephants from drouth. Everything was planned and worked out."

"Good," Olin Lockridge said. He cleared his throat, trying to say more, than a silence fell while he cogitated.

"Except now we don't have many elephants left," Charlie added.

"Why? What happened?"

They were flying in view of the Ndawe Escarpment. Kilimanjaro's snowy peak sat off to their right, the morning sun making it radiant.

"Elephants are like men," Charlie went on. "They modify their surroundings more than any other species. Tsavo became an elephant ghetto. The trees began to disappear. The undergrowth was eaten. The jungle of a hundred years ago thinned out into a few big trees and an occasional thicket. Then those began to go away, too."

Minutes later they were flying into the park. Olin Lockridge looked down on a barren plain.

"There is nothing much down there," he admitted.

The pilot decided to show them some of the old waterholes. The little Cessna banked away from the area around Kilaguni Lodge and leveled off at a lower altitude. They passed over two dried holes, the earth cracked and open, and at the third saw what the pilot wanted to show them: an indefinite number of elephant carcasses, legs and trunks and the great heads, tangled together, mired in the thick, drying mud. The tusks had been removed.

They stopped at a lodge for lunch. Lime coolers and baked chicken. The day was cool and pleasant, but the businessman was disgruntled.

"I like ruins," he said once. "I liked those Zimbabwe ruins. Better than trying to find any live—" He paused, getting the words right again. "Any live wildlife."

Charlie and the pilot nodded and smiled at him.

That afternoon they rented a Land Rover and toured the area near the lodge, where they saw a number of animals around the salt licks, but too many innocent-looking antelope and too many snorting warthogs, according to Lockridge, who wanted photos of rhinos and elephants.

At the end of the day, flying home, they did see a small herd of elephants—nine, including two calves—on that immense stretch of naked land below; it was an empty moonscape down there, pocked with craters where tall trees had been pushed over, eaten, and rotted away; water gone and grasses devoured, it was a land all used up, and that small herd looked bewildered and addled because all the horizons looked the same as in a desert.

"Can't say I particularly enjoyed it," Lockridge said.

"No, it isn't pure pleasure," Charlie allowed.

When they arrived in Nairobi that evening, a new team member had appeared—unofficially. Jack Hillyard, Sid's former boss at Interpol, had come to offer his assistance. He was on a personal vacation, but was willing to apply for an extended leave from Washington, he said, if wanted, so that he could help find out what had happened to Sid.

"I'll stay as long as my American Express Card holds out," he told Stella and Charlie.

"I'd like to go over everything we've done with you," Charlie said. "And, meanwhile, I'll clear your expenses, so consider yourself a member of the team. You're very welcome, and I can't say how much we appreciate this."

In the next twenty-four hours Jack Hillyard had agents check all patrol stations within 250 miles of Nairobi; he put out a bulletin on the lost Jeep in seven countries and had Interpol in Paris issue a missing persons circular; he agreed with Stella that a $1,000 reward should be established for any policeman who turned up hard information leading to Sid's whereabouts; he confirmed Charlie's plan to assign agents to review all of Sid's past movements and possible new working leads; he established a recurring check at all hospitals and clinics; and he set up interviews with every secretary, driver, and agent on the task force to inquire into Sid's personal interests. Because Sid's agents were spread around the continent, this survey promised to take two weeks to conduct.

"And what about the killer?" Stella asked. "Was Sid possibly his victim?"

"I can't see it," Jack told her. "The killer's pattern is public. And Sid just isn't one of his usual targets."

"Peter Foxx thinks it all might be related."

"He guesses a lot," the detective said.

On the day Jamie returned Charlie, Jack, and Stella drove up toward the Institute to meet Daphne Brent and her father. Rain poured down during the trip, and not far out of Kijabe the clutch on the Jeep failed, so that Ngomo, who was driving, had to get out on the highway, stand in the cold rain, and hitch a ride to town. Rides were slow, so there he stood, getting drenched, his palm exposed to the heavens in the way Africans beg for a lift, while the three Americans sat huddled in the Jeep. Eventually an old lorry appeared. Ngomo had to ride with its cargo of goats, but off he went, waving goodbye and grinning, happy enough with his job. Neither Charlie, Stella, nor Jack said anything. They sat there, rain rattling off the plastic windows of the Jeep's tarpaulin, their breaths steaming up the windshield so they couldn't see anything. Short of death and starvation, Charlie wanted to say, patience is the long suit of all Africans; an inconvenience like this, on the other hand, reduces most foreigners to sullen anger or hysterics. They sat there—at least for the first hour—in sullen anger. Two hours later they were enjoying conversation. Jack told them about his boyhood in York, Maine, and how he used to work on a lobster boat with his uncles and brothers. Stella told about her first dates and how the boys never looked anywhere except into her blouse. Charlie, when asked, reported that he did not have either childhood or adolescence.

By afternoon they arrived at the Institute: the three Americans, Ngomo, the other driver who had come up from Nairobi with a station wagon, and a young Kikuyu cousin of Ngomo's who simply wanted to observe the spectacle of a broken-down Jeep and Americans in distress.

They piled out of the station wagon like a family on a picnic. The drivers and the cousin went off to see the cobra pit. The investigative team and old Bryan Wilton had confusing introductions while Daphne went off to make tea. It was only later as they sat in the chairs under the trees, droplets of rain falling from leaves occasionally, that Daphne recalled her last meeting with Sid.

"We gave him an old list which we had in the files," she said. "Names of venom gatherers long out of business."

"Some of them have been dead for twenty or thirty years," Bryan Wilton put in.

"Is there a duplicate of that list?" Jack asked.

"Sorry, no," Daphne said. "And I don't even recall any names on it. Do you, Dad?"

"The missionary," her father said. "Big Protestant fellow named Whitehead. Liked snakes, airplanes, history, poetry—damn near everything except Jesus. Knew the man twenty years, and he was quite a good chap who knew about everything, but I never heard him put in a good word for the Lord!"

"Anyone else?" Charlie asked, smiling.

"Bill Clare, old biologist. Also been dead twenty years."

"Anyone on the list still alive or more recently deceased?" Stella asked.

"Not a one. You see, we'd still be doing business with them. We've run the competition to ground, don't you know?"

They all sipped their tea.

"Anything personal you can tell us about Mr. Cash?" Jack said toward the end of the interview. "Did he have anyone with him when he visited here? Did he speak of friends or anyone else you can remember?"

"I think he was something of a womanizer," Daphne suddenly said.

"Really? Sid?" Charlie inquired.

"He was interested in me. Tried to get me down to Nairobi. I think I could safely say that he would be interested in any woman."

"That's helpful, thank you," Jack said, ending the line of talk.

Soon after this Stella went off to find the drivers and goodbyes began.

"I want to assign an agent to the Institute," Jack said, folding his notepad into his shirt pocket. "If that's all right with you. This is such a key place in our investigations."

"Actually, we'd rather you not," Daphne said. "First you can't find one person, then you lose another. We've been very cooperative, but there's work to be done here, a very small staff, and during the last weeks we've spent a number of hours trying to accommodate you."

Old Wilton coughed and sputtered, not knowing what to say.

"An agent wouldn't be on the premises much," Jack explained. "But one is really required at present."

Daphne placed the tea service on a silver tray and started back toward the house with it. "Then you'll have to get a magistrate's order," she said. "And I don't think you'll get one, if we fight it. We have as many friends in the government as you do."

Stella and the drivers returned and started getting into the station wagon. The young cousin talked to everyone about the cobras.

Bryan Wilson apologized, but agreed with his daughter. "A scientist's work is bloody difficult," he pointed out. "Takes concentration. There just can't be too many interruptions."

"If you're scientists, you're also very much in business," Jack told him. "You're here by consent of the authorities, and if it takes a court order to win your cooperation I'll get one."

"You don't belong in this country," Daphne said with cool disdain. "Don't you see how it's perfectly logical for someone to be uncooperative or rude—or even to poison your nice businessman? You're all a dreadful intrusion."

"We mean to find out what happened to our friend, Sid Cash," Jack said evenly.

"You probably won't find out," she replied. "But that's beside the point. You don't want the Arabs buying up America. We don't want you buying up Africa. I know the police are probably taking your money and you feel you belong here, but you don't. So leave us alone. We've told you all we know."

"Sorry to trouble you," Jack said, turning toward the car.

Sunlight broke through the clouds. Daphne stood beside the house, the silver tray reflecting the sun's sudden brightness. She was a pretty woman, cool and collected, and seemingly too angry to raise her voice. Inside the station wagon, waiting, were the three blacks—listening with detachment to this argument of who exactly had a right to their continent.

"Good day, Mr. Wilton," Jack and Charlie said, getting into the car with Stella. "Goodbye and thank you."

The old boy coughed and snorted. They waved goodbye and turned out of the driveway.

"Dammit," Jack Hillyard said, frustrated.

"Well, she's right, you know," Charlie told him.

"Maybe so, but that doesn't get us Sid."

They drove along the road in silence for a few miles.

"Do you suppose your friend was actually a womanizer?" Stella finally asked.

"That woman was a bitch to say that," Jack muttered.

They drove along, then, for a while longer. An evening dampness had crept in. They dreaded stopping along the road for the stalled Jeep and all the other probable delays in getting back to Nairobi.

"And what do you think of what she said about American interests in Africa?" Jack suddenly asked Charlie.

"I have a lot of sympathy for the killer," Charlie said. "At least one possible version of the killer—one who isn't just a complete psychopath and who knows what real bastards we are."

Ngomo, who was driving and not seeming to listen at all, broke into laughter.

"Well, I don't care what her politics are," Jack concluded. "I want to find out what happened to Sid."

Stella, the cousin, and the other driver joined Ngomo's laughter. Stella wasn't sure why she did it, but one had to somehow recognize absurdity. As they laughed, they drove into a torrent of rain. Ngomo laughed hardest, as if he somehow knew that he and his co-worker would soon be instructed to get outside in the cold, rainy darkness and to remain with the broken-down Jeep. In a few minutes they were told exactly that while the Americans—and the young cousin, who had the advantage of childhood in his favor—drove back to the city.

29

Charlie pulled on his sweat shirt, laced his jogging shoes, kissed Stella on her warm cheek, and slipped out of the hotel suite.

He started running out Parliament Road, but eventually cut over to the Uhuru Highway and followed alongside it, the wet grass whipping his ankles, until he was well south of the city.

A long week had passed. None of Jack Hillyard's tactics had yielded results. Jamie, back from Washington with stories of how the Little Buddha was already conniving to find another job, seemed in a stupor. Few of the business appointments had worked out for Olin Lockridge, and the bodyguards seemed listless and homesick.

It was a cool, clear morning, though, as Charlie ran. In time, he didn't know how far he had run or where he was, but he could look back over his shoulder and see the tall round tower of the conference center and Nairobi's skyline. He had missed running. Now, his breath and legs holding out better than expected, he pumped along—determined to make it hard on himself getting back.

Eventually, he noted that he was running beside an English graveyard. He slowed his pace and began to see the individual markers and gravestones. It was not a well-kept cemetery: grass and weed had grown high, and many headstones had been pushed over. In time, after puffing up a long hill, he jogged inside the gates and saw, to his surprise, a human skull adorning one of the gateposts. This stopped him. He stood there, winded and wheezing, pondering the skull. The early morning breeze cooled his face and thinning hair; he could feel the body heat trapped inside his sweat clothes, and beneath that he could feel his heart tripping along, the mortality of all his inner gears and rasping mainsprings. The skull on the post looked silly: a bad advertisement for the place. As he considered this, he looked down a narrow dirt path and saw a small, withered black man hurrying toward him from a lean-to grass *shamba* at the rear of the property. The old man was naked except for a soiled loin cloth and a wide-brimmed straw hat—western cowboy style in character. His thin, bowed legs were no bigger than a bird's, and although he moved them in a painful hurry his pace and progress up the path was very slow.

"Jambo!" Charlie greeted him as he drew close. "Good morning!"

But the wizened little man hurried over to the gatepost, climbed the iron gate like a monkey, and plucked down the skull.

He was hurrying back to his caretaker's *shamba* with it when Charlie called to him to stop.

"Too embarrassing," the old man told him, shaking his head.

"How did it get there?" Charlie asked him.

"Oh yes," the little man said. His speaking style was a stage whisper, as if he kept a quiet reverence for his surroundings.

"The skull in your hands," Charlie repeated. "Who put it up there on the gate?"

"The hyenas come at night and dig up the new graves," said the caretaker, explaining part of the mystery. "Oh, yes!"

"The hyenas?"

"To eat the new bodies," the old man confided in his loud whisper. "How can I stop them? There is no wall on my side of this place, so they just come in! Oh yes! And the next morning after a burial, I go find the scattered bones. This is my hardest work! Very embarrassing, oh, yes, and in just a minute I will help you find the grave you seek!"

"I'm not looking for anything," Charlie said.

"You are not a mourner?"

"No, just out running," Charlie said. "But how did the skull get up there on the gatepost? The hyenas didn't do that, did they?"

"Oh, no, the *watoto!*"

"The children?"

"Who favor the hyenas," the old man whispered, and, then, without warning, he broke into a laugh, a high cackle.

"The children are on the side of the hyenas in this matter?"

"You are not a visitor seeking the grave of a loved one?" the old man asked again, making sure and still cackling.

"No, promise I'm not."

"The children are hyenas themselves," the old man said, laughing so hard that he had to hold his straw cowboy hat on his head. "They think this is a stupid place! Oh, yes! They believe I'm a fool for picking up the bones of the Englishmen and ladies!"

"Wait, stop a minute and talk with me," Charlie said, as the caretaker moved off down the path again.

"I must put this away," the old man said. "As for me, I'm no hyena. I have two thinkings: I have little care that the animals get some food. But, also, I would like a nice marble stone myself—not here, you see, but in a place with walls so this wouldn't happen! Oh yes!"

The old man kept moving away.

"What do you do with the bones?" Charlie asked him.

The high cackle again.

"I beat them with a stone and turn them to powder," the old man confided in his whisper. "Then sprinkle them on the graves and all around. It seems to me fitting. Oh, yes!" The thin legs splashed through a mudhole.

Charlie could only shake his head at this brief exchange. He stood for a moment longer, catching his breath, and watching the old man go. The cemetery was a shambles: briars, mudholes, tall weeds, and all the headstones tilted, lying flat, or broken. Charlie remembered Highgate Cemetery in London, where Karl Marx and others lay buried: much the same. The English fancied their gardens, but neglected their poor dead; there were always roses and lilies around their cottages, but briars in their graveyards.

The old man had gone into his lean-to with the skull.

Charlie found himself looking among the weeds, briefly, trying to detect a fine, white powder of bone, but saw nothing.

Soon he was on the road again.

A passing lorry. Then a Land Rover, swerving close. Charlie jogged off into the grass at the shoulder of the highway just to be safe.

It was Langata Road where Charlie took his morning exercise, and inside the Land Rover sat Quentin Clare, going into the city. He noticed the jogger with contempt: here was another affectation of the fattened herd. The Americans, he told himself, would exercise in hell. And that was surely an American with those matching sweat clothes and fancy shoes. Even so, he had looked too long and had driven too close.

By the time he reached the city the markets had opened, the shops had filled with tourists, and the *watu* in white jackets were opening the Thorn Tree Cafe, putting out the wire chairs and brewing the first coffee. He had been watching the Americans for another week, now, and had mostly figured out their habits and schedule. It was a crowded time: students off for the summer holiday, special planes filled with tour groups arriving daily, the hotels packed. Celebrities were in town: this tennis player, that author. In spite of the rains and the cool climate, the crowds covered his presence. The Americans, he knew, were considerably more conspicuous than he was. The bodyguards now wore khaki safari outfits, not seersucker suits. Because of the damp and cold, they had all bought matching windbreakers: maroon with zippers. Quentin found that he could spot them more and more easily in those few blocks around their office; they emerged at predictable lunch hours, signaled to each other constantly, went to the same bars after six in the afternoon when their businessman was safely tucked into the New Stanley, and almost announced their presence in their uniform dress.

At a newsstand he bought the *Daily Nation*. Both Nairobi newspapers had items almost daily on the business and activities of Olin Lockridge, the seller of heavy machinery and equipment. Clearly, a trap: obvious announcements, yet this elaborate security.

He took a seat so that he could look up Kimathi Street toward the doorway of the building where their offices were. As he sipped a morning glass of orange juice, he took some almonds from his pocket and ate them.

That jogger out Langata Road. Was that one of them?

He made mental notes again. Six bodyguards, two each for three daily shifts. The handsome woman, perhaps their executive secretary.

The young man who looked lost. The big one whose hands were so large, who wasn't with them in Salisbury. Olin Lockridge himself. The strong-arm driver, a military type. Their apparent leader: the one with the indenture in his forehead. Two pale sorts—accountants, perhaps. And the blacks: drivers and secretaries, perhaps three or four of them. He had watched them from the lobby as they came out of the elevators talking together; he had seen them together in the hotel and cafes, on the street and in bars; their faces had grown indelible.

Clearly, his quarry was too well guarded around the hotel and office. Quentin had considered the airport at length: a strike later on in their confusion as they left Nairobi, a quick attack in that last moment when their vigilance relaxed and they felt safe. But airport security made escape impossible. He had thought of disguises, a policeman or soldier, say, but had finally discarded that line of reasoning because, now, somehow, it seemed unworthy. The game required simpler, deadlier rules as it continued, and in his recent contemplations he felt strongly that it should be played as an attack, not as a deceit. Better to kill a man facing him as in that Cairo elevator than to sneak a substance into his drink as in Lagos. The refinements of personal style occurred only to those, he knew, accustomed to battle.

"Good morning, again!" the waiter greeted him, breaking his reverie. "You would like breakfast this morning?"

"No, nothing else, thank you," Quentin managed.

He walked over to Mr. Rhamadi's shop, but it was not yet open. At a nearby travel agency, he scanned brochures in a rack near the door where he could see the entrance to their building across the street. Two of the maroon windbreakers emerged as he watched.

He walked into Standard Street. There, coming toward him, was the woman and the American driver. The driver—he was almost sure of this—wore a shoulder holster underneath his hunting jacket. They were talking together as they came toward him, yet the driver's eyes seemed fixed on him. Quentin looked away.

"What do you see in him anyway?" the driver asked her.

At the last moment, Quentin looked up again to see that the driver was still watching him intently. His stomach went weak. But they passed each other without turning. The woman—a pretty one—left the scent of her freshly applied morning perfume behind her.

The marine sergeant had cornered Stella for morning coffee. She knew that Charlie had gone running again—and supposed the sergeant knew it, too, because he showed up at the right moment. They had gone to an espresso machine in the arcade. But the subject of the morning wasn't so innocent. He wanted her in his room—this morning, this hour.

"I really have the hots for you," he told her once. It was his most poetic line. Now, his last question hung between them. What did she see in the Professor, he wanted to know, who was clearly no big deal? She wanted to say something unpleasant, but, instead, she said merely, "He's an old friend."

"Did you see that guy?" the sergeant said, interrupting himself as they moved out of Standard Street.

"Who?"

"The cat with the dark eyes. I've seen him before."

"I didn't notice."

"Maybe in Salisbury. Shit, I can't remember."

"Think you should go check him out?"

"You don't get rid of me this morning that easy," the sergeant grinned.

She hurried into their office building where she quickly crossed the lobby and entered a waiting elevator, but not before the sergeant edged in beside her.

"You have business upstairs this morning?" she asked him.

"I got to make out the schedule for all the cars and drivers," he assured her.

When they arrived, he followed her boldly into Jamie's office.

"C'mon," she pleaded. "We've got work to do, right?"

"I think you like me," he said.

"You've just been away from your wife too long," she told him.

"Ain't married," he said, his grin getting broader.

Exasperated, Stella looked up to see Jamie arriving for the day. He pulled his briefcase through the door like an anvil.

"Hangover," he announced to no one in particular.

Stella offered to get him a seltzer. As she went off, Jamie acknowledged the sergeant, then waved him away.

As Stella searched for seltzer in one of the secretary's desk drawers in the outer office, the sergeant gave her a wink as he departed.

"Sometime soon," he said with confidence.

"Thanks for warning me," she told him.

At that moment Charlie came in wearing a business suit. He looked wonderful—in spite of the jogging shoes, which did, indeed, match the suit, and which were without the usual display of stripes, arrows, lightning bolts, or brand names. Stella went over and greeted him with a kiss on the chin.

"What's that for?" he asked.

"For taking a shower after your workout."

"I always do," he said, smiling and trying to figure her out.

Then he went into Jamie's office. His co-worker was bent over the desk, his head in his hands.

"I had a great run this morning," Charlie said, greeting him.

"I should have one more drink of Kenya Cane," Jamie answered. "A man needs to get his body while it's down. I could finish myself off."

"What's on for today?"

"Nothing's going to happen here," Jamie replied. "The nights are getting colder. It's a new ice age. We're going to be quick frozen and sent home, all of us, and when we get there the Little Buddha is going to be secretary of state."

Charlie recognized this gloomy patter as a kind of Ivy League drunk talk, so ignored it. Jamie Vander often reminded him of a fraternity boy.

"Lockridge got any appointments?" Charlie went on.

"Something came up," Jamie said, raising his head. "An afternoon entertainment over at the Norfolk Hotel. Some of the ministers will be there. Lockridge is invited and wants to go."

"Could be a bad situation. The thing in Zanzibar happened at a big social occasion, too."

Stella arrived with the seltzer, and Jamie thanked her. Then she went to her own office, sat down, and tried to see where things were. She enjoyed the sound of Charlie's voice in the distant room, and she felt relief that the sergeant had gone away; she was too old for heavy overtures, she felt, and if Charlie hadn't stumbled back into her life again she knew that she might have stayed alone and solitary forever. Sex was a wonderful commodity, she felt, but the marketplace was a drag.

Her desk was stacked with reports from all of Sid's agents in the field: the venom business from Mombasa to Morocco, political queries, notes on forgers and murderers, blue notices from Interpol in Paris, items from laboratories. There was no list of suspects. The immensity of Africa and the complications of the venom business alone had occupied all their time. And Sid had been the only real cop on the team, the one who pulled all this together, so that his absence made a difference. They had made progress—especially in the venom trade—but were without real leads. Many of Sid's agents wanted to go home. Two had asked for sick leave. And now there were other complications: Sid's disappearance and the problem of Olin Lockridge's daily schedule.

When the phone rang, Stella answered it. She listened for several minutes, then asked the caller to hold.

She went into Jamie's office, lifted the receiver on his phone, and handed it to him.

"It's a police official," she said. "Did we ask permission to take guards to this afternoon's function at the Norfolk?"

"I asked permission," Jamie said, finishing his seltzer.

"Well, it's denied."

Jamie took the phone and began arguing with the official. As he did this, Jack Hillyard came in.

"Lockridge can't go if our men don't go with him," Charlie said.

"But how are you going to tell Lockridge he can't go?" Stella asked.

Jack wanted to know what was going on. The argument on the telephone became louder. "At least a couple of men," Jamie barked into the phone. "You could be very embarrassed if something happened to Mr. Lockridge."

"Maybe Lockridge will change his mind," Charlie said hopefully.

"Not with prospective buyers out there," Stella said.

Jamie asked to speak with the commissioner. He waited, tapping his fingers on Sid's desk, and looking to the Professor to provide help. "With the government ministers there," he explained, "they want the military security forces to handle it. No police—and no us."

"Go tell Lockridge his invitation has been withdrawn," Charlie said to Stella. "Tell him this is a government affair—government contracts only. Tell him anything."

"He knows better."

Jamie began talking with the commissioner. His face contorted, he smiled, he shook his head, he grimaced. When he hung up, he turned to everyone and said, "It's a military matter, not a police matter. But he said for certain considerations he'd arrange for Mr. Lockridge to be accompanied by two aides—and you, Stella, if you want to go."

"Why me?"

"Because he likes your cleavage."

"Did he say that?"

"Naturally not. He said two aides and Miss Kane could attend. Maybe you're the consideration he's interested in."

"What is this?" Stella asked. "Am I giving off a heavy musk today? I had to beat away the sergeant before breakfast."

"Two guards aren't enough," Charlie said.

"One of the engineers has dysentery," Jack added.

"I guess I could go," Stella said. "I have my little Beretta."

"I don't want you going," Charlie told her. "And, listen, here's how we handle it: first, I try to talk Lockridge out of going. Then, if he goes we have the sergeant drive him over and work outside. And two regulars with him at all times. And, Jamie, you or I should go, too—one of us, at least."

"There's no announcement concerning Lockridge attending this meeting," Jamie said, trying to think while holding his aching head. "It would just be the killer's guess that he'd be there."

"Let's don't get casual," Charlie warned. "I've seen the victims."

"Let me help," Jack said. "I'll try to get a room over at the Norfolk, so I can be on the premises."

"Good," Charlie told him. "And let's not forget transportation. We may get an attempted hit while driving over there or coming back. And let's talk to the agents about special care at the hotel tonight. After we get Lockridge safely back home, we don't want to relax."

Jack promised to work closely with the Secret Service guards. Then he went into the outer office, sat on the edge of a secretary's desk, and phoned the Norfolk for a room. Impossible, he was told.

Jamie phoned the commissioner again on the other line. He announced that, yes, they would take the offer: two men accompanying Mr. Lockridge. And perhaps Miss Kane. He nodded while the commissioner explained that even this concession with the military authorities might be difficult to accomplish.

"And you," Stella said, watching Charlie, "you've got some sort of intuition, haven't you?"

The Professor gave her a glance which revealed nothing.

30

In the late afternoon a cocktail party began at the Norfolk with more than two hundred ministers and businessmen attending. Because the hotel was already at capacity, this created an overflow, and so the courtyard, verandahs, lounges, swimming pool area, and bars filled with people. Security, for all the talk, was light. Military policemen strolled among the guests, but seemed more concerned with their own presence than alert to possible provocations. Charlie, the marine sergeant, two agents, Olin Lockridge, and Jamie were there, and it didn't take long for the Professor to grow alarmed at the unrestricted flow of guests. He called the sergeant aside.

"Get to a phone and call Stella," he told him. "Tell her to get at least another two agents over here. And to come herself, if she can. Tell her it's a madhouse."

The sergeant dutifully went off to locate a phone booth. For the next half hour he would wait for an empty one.

One of the agents was Gates, who was captain of the men serving on the tour. Charlie located him minutes later.

"This is awful," Gates said. "What'll we do?"

"Just stick with Lockridge," Charlie instructed him. "And I mean stick close."

They found that they were yelling at each other over the noise.

Glasses clinked, men and women chattered, and the birds in the aviary contributed all their noises.

"I'm going after a drink," Jamie told them as he passed by. "I need one. The sergeant will have us some more help in the next few minutes."

"We need it," Gates shouted, and he went off to find Lockridge in the throng filling the courtyard.

Jamie went into the coffee lounge where he failed to win the attention of any of the waiters.

The old Norfolk Hotel had sat at the edge of a papyrus swamp on the outskirts of Nairobi. It featured a long wooden verandah where its guests could sit and view the game, comfortable in their rocking chairs and wicker settees, sipping their tea and whiskeys, as animals—even lions—came to drink at the tepid swamp. In time, the city grew around the Norfolk. The swamp disappeared and the hotel's guests changed; they were no longer rough types who came in dusty and telling stories from safaris, but gentler sorts who viewed the giant, padlocked closets in the Norfolk's rooms—closets for storing guns and gear—as quaint reminders of a more fearsome and romantic past.

Everyone around Jamie seemed to have someone to talk to; there were no lonely psychopaths in sight, no revolutionaries, and some of the younger women looked good. His only concern was whether or not he could get another beer for his hangover before returning to duty.

The sergeant, meanwhile, gave up waiting for a vacant phone booth and went to the hotel's front desk to ask if he could use their private line.

"Please," the tall British clerk told him with an icy stare. "Not here. Use the booths."

But at the phone booths even more guests were waiting their turns when he got back. Frustrated, he decided to drive back to the New Stanley for more agents. It would take less time than calling, he reasoned, and, besides, they would need transportation anyway. The trip could be accomplished, he estimated, in about twenty minutes.

Out in the courtyard stood an antique Model A Ford and an old covered wagon of the sort the Boers used in their trek across South Africa. A number of the ministers and businessmen sat in these while their photographs were made. The photographer, an Italian, had a flamboyant directing style and ordered them around like a true maestro. The ministers—almost all of Kenya's cabinet leaders in agriculture and industry—behaved with polite dignity, but the businessmen, whites and blacks alike, hung out of the windows of the car, made silly faces, and responded to onlookers who raised toasts to their display. Olin Lockridge was one of the loudest. A woman in a low-slung *kanga* and a generously filled halter won their whistles and hoots. Everybody laughed—or, pretended to. There were so many revelers on the covered wagon that the hotel's assistant manager had to ask them to get off. There were also too many inside and hanging off the Ford, but it was a sturdy vehicle, well preserved, and its axles sagged without breaking.

As Jamie entered the courtyard again—no better off for drinking two bottles of beer—he met Stella who had just arrived—although the sergeant was unaware of her presence.

"There's no security here at all," Stella remarked, looking around.

"No, none at all," Jamie agreed. "Our agents are watching Lockridge. He's over there inside the antique car getting his photo taken. There's no way of protecting him."

"Have you been drinking?"

" 'Course not," Jamie lied. "Just getting sobered up from this morning."

Charlie surveyed the crowd. The officials and businessmen having their photos taken in the antique car were being replaced by another group. Olin Lockridge was laughing and waving at the woman in the low-slung *kanga*.

"Where's Gates?" Charlie asked.

"I see him over there," Stella answered.

"Be right back," Charlie said, and he started making his way through the crowd.

While the sergeant found himself stalled in traffic and parked cars in the hotel lot, a businessman out at the swimming pool had a heart attack. Cries for a doctor went up and the second agent in the courtyard, hearing these, went to see what the trouble was. He tried to contact Gates on his two-way radio, but the crowd's noise prevented that—

although Gates and Charlie were scarcely fifty feet away. Then, the agent hurried out to the pool, looking for trouble. Was this an American, he wanted to know, and was it really a heart attack?

"Where's your other man?" Charlie asked Gates, meanwhile.

"Just over there," Gates said. "You can't see him, but he's over—well, he was standing near the aviary."

"And where's Lockridge?"

"With that woman—no, there he is: getting back into the car with the next group for another photo session."

Stella came over, smiling. "Everybody here is raving drunk," she said. "We might as well join the party."

"Have you got your little Beretta?" Charlie asked, cutting her off.

"Yes, in my purse."

"Give it to me."

"What's wrong?"

"I'm unarmed. Just give it here."

"I don't see my partner," Gates said, craning his neck. "I've got to go find him."

"Don't go anywhere. Just watch Lockridge," Charlie ordered him.

Gates tried his radio. He thought he heard a reply, but couldn't be sure.

A minister stood in the driver's seat of the old covered wagon making a speech. Around him, applauding, stood several admirers: women in low-cut cocktail dresses, businessmen who had shed their jackets. Beneath the arches of the verandah the waiters laid out trays of hot hors d'oeuvres. Overhead in the evening sky above the courtyard two giant birds—African kites—glided on the late breeze; they hovered, at times, without motion, and Stella looked up when she saw Charlie watching them.

Jamie strolled up, smiling like a guest.

Wake up, Charlie told himself. Keep alert. Stay sharp.

Because there were so many cars abandoned around the hotel and blocking his exit, the sergeant had to give up his plan to drive for help. Disgusted, he put the station wagon in reverse and parked it beside a climbing rosebush near the front of the hotel. He didn't know whether to go back and report to Charlie, to try the telephones again, or to try to find the owners and chauffeurs of the abandoned cars. He ended up sitting there behind the wheel of the station wagon, lighting a cigarette and doing nothing.

"A man had a heart attack out at the pool," Gates said.

"Where's Lockridge?" Charlie asked, interrupting them.

"The group left the old car and joined those listening to the minister around the covered wagon," Gates said. "He's somewhere in that bunch."

"We can't watch him from out here," Charlie concluded. "I'm going over and stick at his side. You, too, Gates, c'mon."

They made their way toward the covered wagon where the group applauded the minister for a final time as he stepped down. Lockridge was nowhere to be seen.

"Find that woman in the halter," Gates said. "Lockridge was talking to her."

"Go back and tell the others that we've lost him," Charlie said. "Tell them to find him quick."

At this point a waiter began ringing a silver dinner bell. Guests turned and headed for those shadowed arches, lit with decorative candles now, although the sun still illuminated the upper branches of the trees above the courtyard, where steaming food was being served. Charlie looked for Lockridge's grey suit, but not seeing it decided that the businessman had probably shed his coat like others had done.

"Where's the sergeant?" Jamie asked when the panic started. "I'll bet he's got Lockridge with him."

Charlie circled the aviary, his fingers trailing over the screen as he went around it. Inside, a cockatoo called out ominously.

Gates found the woman in the *kanga* and halter out beside one of the cottages. She was in the arms of a much younger man, a boy of sixteen or seventeen, kissing him.

"Excuse me, I'm looking for Mr. Lockridge," Gates blurted out. "In a grey suit. American. Can you help—"

"Don't know him," the woman said sharply.

Stella and Jamie fought their way toward the front of the food line, hoping to find Lockridge there. He wasn't.

"Rude," some Englishman told Jamie, who, in turn, picked up a meat ball with his fingers and ate it.

Gates's partner had Lockridge paged over the intercom system. His name was announced several times, but the noise of the crowd and the clatter of dishes and silverware drowned it out. The waiter still rang his silver dinner bell, calling diners to their afternoon snack with an unstopped enthusiasm.

"Dammit, he's nowhere," Gates said, hurrying up to Charlie again.

"Did you see him listening to the minister's talk after he was in the antique car?" Charlie asked.

"I'm not even sure he got back into the car with the second group," Gates answered. Already, they hurried over toward the Model A. "Is Mr. Hillyard here?"

"No, he's working on Sid's case," Charlie said. "Where's the sergeant?"

By this time they were at the antique car.

Charlie knew before they looked inside.

Lockridge's body was curled on the floorboard, his dead hands clutching his shirt over his chest. He had shed two bright tears of blood from his bulging eyes.

"Oh, god," Charlie whispered. "Oh, no."

The marine sergeant, still sitting in the station wagon and finishing his cigarette, had decided to return to the others when he looked across the lawn and saw, coming toward him, the man he had thought he had recognized that morning in Standard Street. Quentin was dressed in a dark suit and tie. He appeared unhurried, but deliberate as he crossed the road and started to pass beside the sergeant's car. The sergeant rested his elbow on the open car window and put out his head for a better look. Who was this person? He thought of speaking.

Quentin saw him, too. Without breaking his stride, he walked briskly up to the car. As his hand came up, the large topaz caught the light and flashed.

The sergeant had opened his mouth to say hello when a hot juice was squirted into his face and throat. He felt the blisters forming on his tongue and lips as he threw himself backward into the car.

Quentin continued across the road and entered the quiet domain of the university's grounds. He never looked back. He had mixed a new acid with the venom in order to get his most powerful dose, and he knew what he would see. The sergeant, trying to scream and making no sound, heaved himself over into the rear seat of the station wagon, his legs kicking. He fumbled for his .45 inside his windbreaker, but his hands, suddenly palsied and twitching violently, wouldn't work. He wanted to fire a shot as a warning and as a desperate announcement, but realized in his last, wild comprehension, that this wouldn't be possible.

PART FOUR

"Travel is conquest."

Old Arab proverb

31

The pistol—the modified Luger which Peter had given him—lay on the desk in the house in Virginia. The Professor's study showed signs of the new college term and his recent return: boxes of stored books had been opened, many volumes had been replaced on the shelves, the Persian slipper with its zippered top (contents emptied by those who had rented his house) was back in its place, his felt-tipped pens fanned out in a ceramic jar, his new class rosters were spread around once more, and on the coffee table beside his copies of *Foreign Affairs* were Stella's batiks, her framed photographs, and a pile of her cotton underpants.

One photograph showed her in Army uniform. She had served four years after college, mostly in Germany with her first brief assignment in Africa, then she had departed as a first lieutenant. In the photo she held up a plate of food and a stein of beer outside a rathskeller: her winnings from a bet in the World Cup match with the barman. Another framed snapshot caught her reading: mouth slightly open, reading glasses down on her nose. In another she played tennis—the only game of her short athletic career—on a court with holes in it at a frumpy resort. The photos had hung in her study in Zanzibar, but now she wouldn't go back. She was Charlie's wife. And she was growing certain that she was pregnant.

Their house was in disarray. He had always owned just a narrow, single bed, so they slept together on that—promising every day to go out and buy a new one. Their clothes were everywhere in piles. They had spent too much time travelling since returning to the States, first to his sister and nephew in New Hampshire, then to her parents in Florida. But their biggest problem of course, was the ongoing investigation into the Task Force and the events in Nairobi. They had both stayed up many nights filling out reports and making statements on dictaphone tape. The affair had been discussed on the floor of the House of Representatives, in the *Washington Post*, out of Langley, and on the executive third floor of the Department of the Treasury where it had been concluded that the Little Buddha was a controversial employee who should neither be rewarded nor reprimanded for his activities.

Not long after the Task Force was recalled, Charlie had telephoned Jack Hillyard with a suggestion. Jack was back at his desk at the Justice Department.

"Did you tell me we have no record of the killer leaving Kenya?" Charlie had asked him.

"We closed the airport and got nothing there. We screened every car leaving the borders for two weeks. And, as you know, the police and military did everything short of taking a census of the white population."

"Maybe that should be done now—or something like it," Charlie proposed. "Here's my thinking: up until the murder in Zanzibar we had a killer with what appeared to be a travel record. Using forgeries, taking planes. Then that stopped. So I've wondered if he's from East Africa and, if so—"

"I've already got a search started," Jack told him, anticipating. "Interpol in Paris gave me some funds. The police in Nairobi are already going door to door. Even so, it's a hell of a long shot—and I'm not sure they even know what they're looking for. I should be there myself."

"How long do you think something like that will take?"

"Maybe two months. But we don't have a thing, not even anything on Sid."

"Did you see Sid's wife, by the way?" Charlie asked.

"I can hardly look her in the face," Jack said. "It's difficult explaining."

"I just thought I'd call about my idea," Charlie said. "Maybe it's wrong. Maybe our man isn't from East Africa at all."

"We have to go with some hypothesis," Jack said. "I appreciate hearing from you."

"And I appreciate your report," the Professor told him. "I feel like everything was my fault and I should get blamed."

"Your idea was fine. Our execution of the trap was awful."

After that conversation, blame was distributed, but seldom accepted. Jack Hillyard blamed the events at the Norfolk that day on Sid's absence. In his report he pointed out that there was nobody in charge with police training. The Secret Service team, he suggested, could have taken initiative, but Gates and his men felt they had been assigned to as many as three commands: Peter's in Washington and Charlie's and Jamie's on the continent. Hillyard blamed the political and intramural character of the Task Force team. It was a generous, impersonal excuse that everyone favored.

Gates, who made excuses for not asserting his authority and training, was assigned to a job in Oklahoma City.

Charlie tried to protect Jamie, but eventually allowed Gates's testimony that Jamie was drinking the day and night before the catastrophe. Charlie also largely blamed himself. He should have stuck close to Lockridge, he said, and should have insisted that everyone do the same.

It would probably be years, Charlie knew, before anyone in the intelligence community asked him to accept duty again.

Jamie Vander was asked to resign at the Central Intelligence Agency. A complete list of his incompetencies emerged. He rebutted that he did not drink on the job, that only Gates was trained in personal security assignments, and that Charlie should have accepted full responsibility for the planned trap rather than passing authority elsewhere and becoming a gadfly all over the continent—especially down to his girl friend's place in Zanzibar. In the middle of August, Jamie did resign. He went to Montauk to live.

Stella pointed out that her job was strictly as an administrative assistant. She took a two year leave of absence and married Charlie in his college chapel.

Peter's status remained in limbo.

Then one morning Hanning Wilson walked over from the White House to visit.

"The President, as you know, has been busy in Vienna and Tokyo," the aide began. "But he's getting fussy about this thing in the newspapers. How are you going to play it?"

Peter noted that Hanning Wilson seemed to be dealing from a position of less than absolute strength—which determined his answer. "As I see it, the African Task Force to catch the murderer of Herman Carr and the others has been a complete success so far," Peter announced. His tone was true Southern rhetoric, almost Biblical, and Hanning Wilson's face twitched with what seemed for a moment the urge to laugh.

"Complete success so far?" he repeated.

"Yes, the trap failed. But the plan succeeded in drawing out the killer. And you should tell the press and Congress that the President made the right decision: we needed the Task Force, we still won't stand for our citizens getting murdered abroad, and if we suffer a setback or two we still won't quit. That's what we all want: a President standing firm and making the right decisions, isn't it?"

"Yes, that's exactly what we want," Hanning Wilson agreed. "We also don't want any more bad publicity or another murder while our men stand there watching."

"I see your predicament like this," Peter said. "You can't officially dissolve the Task Force because you'd be admitting a mistake. But I could let the Task Force evolve into something else. That way, the newspapers couldn't get at you."

"Got any ideas?" Hanning Wilson's twitch at last turned into a smile. He pulled out a new pipe—he had recently started smoking them—and tapped some tobacco in. Peter tried to hide his growing excitement; he knew he was on the verge of another triumph.

"I have something working with the Pentagon," Peter said. "With a particular general. Let him go unnamed for a moment. But if we had presidential approval, I'd head up all anti-terrorist activities for both the civilian agencies and the armed forces. As a kind of executive secretary in charge of hijackings, all hostage-barricade situations, all sabotage, the thing in Africa, all of it. And my name would be on the memo pads, but not on the official letterhead—at least not for a while."

"And you would dissolve this present group and get all of you out of the newspapers?"

"Absolutely. I think the Task Force should be commended. No blame should be placed anywhere—except, maybe, on Jamie Vander, who has already been eased out. Or on Sid Cash, who is probably dead. So, yes: the Task Force would be praised and dissolved all at the same time."

"Who's your general?" Hanning Wilson asked.

"Can't tell you. Until you tell me that the President goes along with the whole project."

"I think I can promise you cooperation," Hanning Wilson said. He lit a third match, trying to get his pipe going, but couldn't manage it.

"Good, then that's it," Peter said, his eyes wide with surprise.

"Is there anything else?" the aide asked, rising from his chair. He still sucked air through his pipe.

"I'd like to come to the White House for weekly briefings," Peter said, thinking fast. "Not to see the President, especially. I could see you or anyone. It's just that it looks good for me coming through the gates or up through the tunnel and all that stuff."

"Peter," Hanning Wilson drawled, "we should see a lot of each other. We should have coffee over in my office. We should go have some of your gourmet lunches. We should certainly meet occasionally at the Pentagon—maybe for racquetball or a sauna at some of their wonderful facilities. But you probably don't play racquetball, do you?"

"I play very few games," Peter said.

"But when you do play," Hanning Wilson said, getting his pipe lit, "you play very well, indeed, Peter, you truly do."

Afterward, Peter phoned Charlie's college number to give him the news. In the late afternoon after checking all his sources for his daily messages, Charlie returned the call.

"I wonder if this means I'll work again?" Charlie asked. "I've been worrying that I won't go back to Africa for awhile."

"Don't worry a bit," Peter assured him. "I'll see that you get back."

"How are you personally, Peter, are you okay?" Charlie asked.

"Fine. I'm seeing Andrea Sloane, did you know that?"

"No, I didn't. Congratulations."

There was a momentary silence on the telephone.

"She thinks the world of you," Peter said.

Another brief silence.

"Stella's pregnant," Charlie said, looking for a new subject. "Or at least we hope so."

"Your friendship has meant a lot to me," Peter said, squeaking a bit.

"Same here," Charlie managed.

"We are friends, aren't we?"

"Sure."

After the phone call Charlie felt a bemused kindness toward Peter. The Little Buddha was like one of his clever seminar students; uncertain of himself, confused by life, yet ever ambitious, hopeful and hard-working. Peter was the bright, fat kid in the first row nobody liked, the one who wanted to talk too long, the one who turned in oversized term papers and who broke the curve on exams. He was always polite with the teacher, but ruthless with his own kind; the one who studied hard, wouldn't share his notes, cheated when he had to, and won all the scholarships.

The next days, settling back into another academic year, Charlie— feeling his age, perhaps, in this new cycle—thought of them all as students of his: Jamie, Kip, Peter, even old Sid. They were all hopeful while he himself had settled into satisfactions beyond hope; they believed in personal and public victories while he celebrated survival; they sensed that life was tough, but he remembered death—in the curious way in which the great witch doctors spoke of remembering the future in their visions; they had played around the edges of disturbing shadows, but he had truly seen the dark continent.

He knew one thing: domesticity with Stella suited him very well. After Peter's phone call made it clear that Project Savannah Blue was finished, they settled into routine. She cooked for them what she had always cooked for herself: steaks and chops, salads, soups. They bought themselves a king-sized bed with dual reading lamps. He showed her his many hiding places: his college office, the safe house, even the Pentagon suite—where he arranged for them to go one Sunday afternoon. They had a picnic lunch down on the banks of the Potomac afterward beneath a cobalt sky. And on such occasions each blade of grass took on a special sheen, the taste of an apple or the movement of water across the surface of the river quickened his senses.

On a day when he had no classes he drove into the city to sign and initial the last budget report for the project. Stella's pregnancy had been confirmed, and she had decided to take no automobile trips, so she stayed out on the Lee Highway while Charlie drove down to the Treasury building.

This was late September, still muggy and hot in the capitol. Peter was beginning to vacate his offices for his new job at the Pentagon, so there were cardboard boxes and file cabinets—taped up and ready to be moved—sitting in his basement rooms at Treasury. His secretarial staff had been reduced to one. The military liaison man had gone.

"You moving out right away?" Charlie asked.

"Not for a month, actually," Peter said. He seemed melancholy and down, not at all like Charlie expected him.

"What's the matter? You okay?" Charlie wanted to know.

"Can we go to lunch?" Peter asked.

"Sorry, I can't. But if you need to talk—"

"It's Andrea Sloane," Peter said. "I don't think she wants to see me anymore."

"Why not?"

"Lots of reasons. I don't know. Can't we have lunch and talk?"

"I just can't. Tell me what's wrong."

"Oh, she's drinking too much. Doesn't know her own mind. She wants to sell her big house, but then she's paranoid about somebody buying it cheap. She wants to go back to England, then she doesn't. She says she's in love with you, then says she isn't. She says she wants more than I can give, but raves at me when I don't phone."

"Is it sex?" Charlie asked outright.

"Why bring that up?" Peter said, and his voice squeaked.

"Because you brought it up yourself, once, with me."

"Well, it's partially that," Peter admitted.

"Partially?"

"I've planned to have sex in the near future," Peter whined. "Really. It's something I've kept in mind."

Charlie wanted to laugh, but couldn't. He wanted to put an arm around Peter's shoulder, but touching was inappropriate, too. Then, in the midst of these strong feelings, a foreboding began. Charlie felt it, but couldn't fully know it. Peter seemed very vulnerable, even frail, and it had nothing to do with this move in his career or his troubles with Andrea or anything so sensible or real.

For a minute he couldn't say anything to Peter.

"She seems to be of two minds about everything," Peter went on. He had moved over to the basement window behind his desk. "So I've been staying away from her. I'm back to my old hours: staying down here until midnight getting things stuffed into boxes. But solitude doesn't work for me anymore, either. I get lonely."

Charlie sat down in a chair which contained a stack of stapled reports. He didn't know what was wrong, but his hands were trembling.

"You feeling sick?" Peter asked him, noticing.

"Don't know. I'm feeling something." An odd premonition, but of what? He didn't know.

"You probably need food. Let's go eat."

"No, I promised to pick up some items for Stella. And I've got chores at the college, so I've got to move on."

"I didn't want to tell you my troubles."

"Peter," Charlie said, "I'm pleased to listen. But I can't offer advice about women—and especially not Andrea."

They walked out onto New York Avenue together. There was a hot noon sunlight and the stifling breath of all the buses and trucks.

The uneasy feeling ebbed away, but it had been very real. A darkness at the center of things.

"I feel as though we've missed so many stitches," Charlie said. "Maybe it's Africa. It overwhelms good efforts. But I know we failed, too. We just weren't at our best."

"We'll catch that guy yet," Peter said, trying to buoy them up. He didn't sound terribly convincing.

Some dark nimbus had visited them. Now it was gone, but Charlie stood on the street corner still feeling it.

They were going their separate ways, then, saying goodbye.

"See you," Charlie managed.

"Thanks for listening," Peter told him, and they were off in different directions.

That night he remembered that odd feeling, but supper passed normally and so he said nothing about it to Stella. They indulged the passion of her pregnancy: ice cream. Then they took off their clothes and wallowed in their new bed. They compared stomachs—and concluded that hers had barely grown, that she was going to remain thin and never lose her beautiful breasts. Charlie, on the other hand, they decided, would have his late paunch forever, even in his probable reincarnation as a lion, the gut-heavy, thick-maned, scarred-up old king of the pride.

Past three in the morning that same night Stella heard his movements in the room. Her hand went instinctively to his side of the bed, but he wasn't there. Sleep weighed her down, but later she heard another sound, so made herself get up and go see.

Charlie was dressed in some old jogging clothes. Sleepy himself and disoriented, he sat at the kitchen table loading the .45 Luger.

"Where are you going?" she asked, drawing her nightshirt around her throat.

"Ah, Stel," he said absently, looking up. A half-blank smile. His thoughts were miles off.

"Are you going out?"

"No, nowhere," he said, as if he wasn't sure.

"Why the pistol?"

"Just tinkering," he answered.

"At almost four in the morning?" She came over and knelt beside him, her face turned up to his. He seemed like a sleepwalker. "Hey, no secrets, okay?"

"No secrets," he repeated, but he didn't look into her eyes. His gaze stayed on the pistol in his hands.

"You planning to shoot somebody?"

"No, nothing like that," he said quietly. If he wasn't lying, she felt, then neither was he telling the truth. She led him back to bed, helped him out of his clothes, kissed him, and tried to hold him in her arms. But he never went back to sleep and couldn't say what had stirred him into that restless fit.

A few nights later he was up again, pacing through the rooms.

"What is it? What's the matter?" she asked, padding around behind him again.

Premonition still rode around inside him, but he couldn't locate it. It was like a nightmare forgotten in the process of waking up, yet one which left a trace of fear behind it.

Stella went in search of the Luger. When she didn't find it, she confronted Charlie.

"After the other night, I got it out of the house," he told her.

"That scared me. Why did you get out that pistol?"

"Honestly, I don't know."

"You told me once that you really dislike guns."

"I do. I can't shoot at anything and hit it."

"Well, I'm glad you got it out of here," she said. "I don't like weapons around the house."

He didn't tell her that he had tucked the Luger—wrapped in its holster and shoulder straps—beneath the seat of his car.

32

Wemba, sullen and quiet, sat opposite Quentin in the Land Rover as they drove into Nairobi. He was displeased because he didn't want to leave the doctor alone at the estate and because he didn't want to visit the office of the attorney where he would be required to make his mark on a piece of paper. A demeaning business, making one's mark, Wemba felt: the proof of one's illiteracy, the admission that one's spoken word wasn't true enough, and an embarrassment in the mechanics of penmanship.

"You will be a wealthy *mutu*," Quentin argued with him. They had been arguing like this for days. During all that time Wemba had been considering how, if necessary, he would write his mark and what shape the thing would be.

To Quentin's remark he returned only a pouting silence.

"Also, the paper doesn't mean that I will die," Quentin explained for perhaps the tenth time. "It will just show—*should* I die—that the estate belongs to you."

Silence from Wemba. He showed no emotion, as if he played a mental game of hole-in-the-ground.

"Personally, I believe you will surely die first because you are old and wrinkled with many more bad habits than I have."

These insults also failed to raise an expression.

"But, also, you should do this for the doctor. Should I die, who would take care of him? The government would come take our estate. And do you know what they would do with an old man like that?"

Wemba's eyes fluttered only slightly.

"They would put him in a hospital. No one would feed him properly or turn him over. He would be a simple piece of clay, not a man."

"If the government came, I would turn the mamba on him," Wemba suddenly said, breaking his silence. "The same as before. And stuff him down an ant hole."

"There would be many men with rifles unless you had a paper with your mark on it," Quentin countered.

This prospect reduced Wemba to silence once again.

"This should be simple for you. You should do this for me because you are my friend and servant," Quentin told him. "You should own the estate because it pleases me."

After another few miles of highway, Wemba asked, "Because you are alone? Because you have nobody else but me?"

"Yes, that's it," Quentin answered.

Clearly, the old man didn't want the responsibility of the estate. Without it, he could go back to his people and live out his last days getting drunk on homemade beer and playing hole-in-the-ground. What, after all, would he do with a grand piano? Or Mary's crystal dishes?

Langata Road traffic: bicycles, lorries, and all the pedestrians with their everlasting bundles.

"Is the doctor chief or are you chief?" Wemba suddenly asked.

Quentin knew that some far-flung logic worked in Wemba's head. To the old black man it meant the difference, Quentin knew, in being able to accept what he was asked to do.

"What do you think?" Quentin asked in return, being crafty.

"I think that he is surely a sleeping chief and that you serve him as I do," Wemba said.

"Yes, that's true," Quentin answered.

For another mile or two Quentin thought about his father. Did he love and miss him? Not exactly. The doctor had been a fierce solitary presence bestowing the rituals of childhood and manhood on Quentin, but he was not a man one could love—even as much as he required it.

"You know I honor the doctor, don't you?" he asked Wemba.

"Yes, like all great chiefs and kings."

"Exactly."

They turned into Parliament Road, and Wemba, thinking gravely, had one last question.

"When you go away do you poison the enemies of your father?" he asked, watching Quentin as he drove.

It was a complex question, revealing Wemba's knowledge and understanding, and yet it needed to be answered simply.

"Yes," Quentin told him. "And so that is what this trip into Nairobi is truly about."

"I thought as much," Wemba said, satisfied.

It was as though he had made his master concede points in a debate.

The attorney's office smelled of mildewed books and musty rugs. The barrister was a tall, young, haughty, and mildly racist type who looked with real suspicion on the whole transaction; he favored any distant, white relative of Quentin's and suggested as much: someone from America or Europe who could come over, lay claim to the estate, and manage it in a proper way.

"No such person," Quentin finally snapped at him. Then, pointing to the document, showed Wemba where to sign—making him an immediate partner in ownership of the estate and circumventing any later dispute.

The attorney raised his eyebrows and watched as Wemba, with real ceremony, painted his thumb black with ink from the pen, then pressed down his mark—a smudgy seal—onto the paper. But he was not finished. As Quentin smiled and the attorney snorted, he embellished the print with two dots which served as eyes and made a little black face of the mark—a smiling, upside-down face, not unlike Wemba's own black, wrinkled aspect.

"Very fine work," Quentin said, complimenting him.

Wemba allowed a tiny crease of a smile at the corners of his mouth. Years from now if the old man lived, Quentin knew, far beyond any pride of ownership in a house and compound unlike anything in his own sensibilities, Wemba would tell of the time he went into Nairobi and made his mark.

After this they went to Mr. Rhamadi's shop. Wemba stood, statue-like, looking neither left nor right at all the shoppers who passed by on the sidewalk outside, while Quentin went in to sell the gemstones.

"I want to leave all the stones with you," Quentin told the old Indian. "In return, I would like you to pay me ten thousand American dollars as an advance against the total value."

"When do you want the money?" Mr. Rhamadi asked.

"Today. Can you get it?"

"Oh, yes, please, but I will have to go to the bank. Can you wait an hour?"

"That will be fine," Quentin said, and he dropped the velvet pouch which contained his remaining fortune into Mr. Rhamadi's palm.

On the sidewalk, Quentin asked Wemba what he wanted to do until the transaction was finished.

"Can we have an ice?" Wemba inquired.

"Have you ever had ice cream before?" Quentin asked him.

"Once," Wemba said. "Your mother bought me one. It was a year when there was so much rain and many cobras."

"Time for another, then," Quentin said, and they went over to the Hilton Hotel coffee shop where Wemba was served four large scoops of chocolate and strawberry in a plastic dish.

That afternoon Mr. Rhamadi paid Quentin in American currency and arranged to have future payments for the gems deposited in the Clare bank account. Later, Quentin and Wemba drove back to the estate and began preparing for another journey.

Wemba got a glimpse of the new 9mm pistol as it was being packed.

"What will you do when your enemies are all dead?" Wemba asked.

"They never will be."

"Will you never come home to stay, then?"

"Probably not," Quentin answered.

They were inside Quentin's bedroom of the main house: high ceilings, the old-fashioned water basin on a Victorian stand, a marble-topped dresser, and flowered wallpaper—faded near the window where the strong western sun slanted into the room. Wemba, as usual, gathered himself for a last observation or question; the silence which preceded this was a familiar one to Quentin.

"I do not think you are an angry man," Wemba said.

Quentin had difficulty replying to the compliment.

"A good warrior," Wemba added, "is not much angry."

"I have duty, not anger," Quentin answered. "And I thank you, Wemba, for noting the difference."

"And one last thing I must tell you," Wemba said.

"Yes, what?"

"If ever the doctor dies, I will put him in the ground like the Christians. But if Kali the snake dies, I will not touch him."

"Why won't you touch the snake?"

"Because he is evil. I would not touch him ever."

"Fair enough, then," Quentin said. "You can hire two boys. Have them drag Kali away."

"But what if they think him evil, too?"

"You can tell them that Kali was the pet of the house and our dearest love," Quentin said, and with this Wemba broke out in hard, dry laughter. Such subterfuge hadn't occurred to him, and he loved it.

33

A bright October noon.

Charlie emerged from the classroom building and made his way across the wide campus lawn. The autumn air was crisp, and all the elms and maples alongside the promenade had shaded into reds and yellows. Dressed in another jogging outfit, his arms filled with books and student papers, he walked over to the student union, where he bought a newspaper out of a vending machine and went into the cafeteria for lunch.

As he ate his salad he noticed that there was a conference on precious gems soon being conducted at the Mayflower Hotel. Its sponsors were the American Gem Society, the Trading Club of New York, and a London firm which was bringing over some marketing experts from DeBeers. What interested Charlie most was that Peter Foxx had been scheduled to lecture on security procedures.

He tore out the item, stuffed it into his jogging jacket, finished his salad, and crossed the campus to his office once more. On his desk were the cassettes, recently translated and transcribed for him by a colleague in the Foreign Languages Department. The cassettes themselves had been of poor quality, Hila's voice indistinct and uneven, but the transcriptions were curiously consistent; all the dying girl had talked about was diamonds, jewelry, and the gem merchant who had called himself Mr. Blue.

Since reading the transcripts, Charlie had wanted to get in contact with Jack Hillyard. But for what? Now, the newspaper item spread out on his desk beside the cassettes, he phoned the Interpol office. Hillyard agreed to meet that afternoon, so before the rush hour traffic began Charlie drove down into the city, parked his car at the garage on G Street, and walked over to the Justice Department.

Hillyard sat in his office going over a stack of circulars. When Charlie entered, the detective leaned back in his chair and made a steeple of his big hands.

"I keep walking around in the middle of the night," Charlie began. "I get wild premonitions. I see Lockridge curled up dead. And I keep thinking, well, we worked that venom angle, but we should have traced out gem dealers. Things like that."

"Small chance on gem dealers," Hillyard told him. "Just too many of them."

Charlie handed him the clipping about the conference at the Mayflower Hotel. "I transcribed those tapes from Lagos," Charlie went on. "Our man posed as a diamond salesman. And he used that more than once, as you remember. Maybe we could use it against him. Tempt him to come here."

"We're not even officially a Task Force anymore," Hillyard said.

"But we're not officially dissolved either."

"It would take a hell of a lot of planning and publicity on the mere hope that the killer might drop over to America where, so far, he has never bothered to come."

Charlie squirmed in his chair and looked out of the window. "I know all that," he sighed. "But, damn, we have to do something, don't we?"

Hillyard got up, strolled over to the window, and gazed out, too. "Sid Cash's widow is having a hell of a time," he admitted. "And Sid's office is still vacant. I can't hire a man to replace him because he isn't officially dead. Yet I know he is. I even agree with you that our killer is probably in Kenya—that he probably got both Sid and Lockridge in his home territory. Evidence points to it and, besides, I feel it in my gut. But in spite of your hypothesis we're thousands of miles away, and I can't run an investigation for the Kenyan police. And we're inactive, unofficial, and too damned public."

"This gem conference can be used to tempt our man," Charlie insisted. "It can be made to work."

"Sure, you want it to work because you feel guilty," Hillyard told him. "You're another research man who got over into clandestine work—and got burned. I've seen it before. Professors who fancy themselves spies or detectives."

"But if you have your gut feelings, so do I," Charlie said. "And I've got another hunch, an educated hunch, dammit, as good as any other."

Hillyard stared out the window, making fists with his big hands and knocking them softly together.

"The killer will know this is a trap," Charlie went on. "He knew it was a trap in Nairobi, and he'll undoubtedly know it again."

"He sure as hell knew it in Nairobi," Hillyard agreed.

"But I think he'll come here *because* he knows," Charlie argued. "The game demands it. I know I'm right about this."

"You don't know anything for sure," Hillyard replied.

Charlie twisted in his chair. He was still stung by Hillyard's accusation: true, he was just a schoolteacher, and one of those who had acquired a taste for participation.

"I just can't see it," Hillyard said, but somehow he wasn't as adamant. He folded his arms, tucking his hands out of sight.

"You want to know about Sid," Charlie said, using his strongest argument. "If you think about this, you'll go along."

As silence fell between them, Charlie sat there in a rare moment of introspection. True, true: up until this project he had gathered a few harmless pieces of information, attended a few African conferences, written some analysis reports, and talked to the usual intelligence officers. His work had been interesting—a service rendered with skill and worthy, at times, of pride. But he had crossed over into the excitements and dangers which belonged to the soldier of the intelligence community; he had exercised power within the arena; he had reminded himself that he had flown missions, taken risks, swerved toward death, and that he had been alive not just as a scholar and second-hand lecturer in the affairs of the world.

Sitting there, his head propped in his hand, Charlie's forefinger idly touched that indenture in his face. Hillyard paced the room.

"This will be expensive, if we do it," Hillyard said, weakening. "Somebody's budget will have to carry it."

Charlie decided not to answer. He was thinking, rather, of how he had lied to Stella about the pistol. And he shared none of this with her, so was, in effect, lying to her now and pulling himself away from her, however slightly, in the moment of his first real love for anything or anyone on earth. Lies, games, postures, cynicisms, masks: he had invited ambiguities. But he would play the game, too, whatever the costs, and knowing this about himself he also knew it about the killer, his distant adversary.

"Peter has his new arrangement with the Pentagon," Charlie said finally. "Maybe he can help bury the cost of the operation in some composite budget. He's good at that sort of thing."

"I'll bet he is."

"I'll also tell Peter that he's our decoy this time."

"My men will have to watch his house," Hillyard said, thinking aloud. "The hotel is easy. I know that place. But I'll have to arrange matters with the conference."

"The event will have to be widely publicized," Charlie added.

"Leave that to me. We have time."

Suddenly, they were making specific plans.

"You believe me, then?" Charlie asked. "You believe we can tempt our man one more time?"

"It doesn't matter what I believe," Hillyard said. "I'll do this for Sid. Quietly—with my own men. Everything subtle. And if we come up with nothing, who's to know?"

Stella, as Charlie soon found out, wasn't very understanding about his increased activity during the next few days.

"It's about Africa, isn't it?" she asked.

"Sort of."

"I wish they'd pave Africa," she said. "Then fly jets over it and drop hamburgers. That would settle it: the whole damned continent would belong to us and you could just stay home and relax."

"I'm glad you're not staying angry," he told her.

It was the afternoon Charlie was supposed to visit the Little Buddha and tell him about the new plan. An Indian summer day: leaves rattling in a breeze which promised continued warmth. Stella's skin had a milky sheen, and she wore her jeans with the top button undone for comfort. She had been picking up and cleaning house, but her natural disarray followed her through the rooms.

"You could tell me what all this is about," she said when he kissed her goodbye.

"Just more errands for the African desk," he told her, still lying. "With luck, they'll pay the maternity bills."

She watched his eyes until he turned away.

He walked across their lush front lawn, unmowed and green, settled into his car, reached under the front seat and touched the Luger just to make sure, then drove off.

That noon Peter had lunch with Andrea at La Ruche in Georgetown. Again, they talked about sex more than Peter wanted to.

"What are you anyway, a homosexual?" she asked after consuming the first bottle of wine.

"Possibly a neuter," he told her.

"No such thing," she replied, slurring her words a little. "One can have an inactive sex life or a puny sex drive or one can be absolutely impotent, I suppose, but everybody has sex. Even flowers and weeds, Peter, for god's sake!"

"Not so loud," he urged her, speaking softly.

"Well, I want us to sleep together. Sometime soon. How about tonight?"

"Not tonight," he protested. "I'm almost finished at the office."

"Can't you hire all that packing done?"

"I'm not just packing," he said. "I'm burning evidence from our African escapade." This failed to amuse her, so he began to eat once more. His hands fluttered from napkin to wine glass to food as he ate quickly and nervously. A plate of scallops vanished. In the ashtray beside his plate two burning cigarettes awaited him.

"You have no table manners," she said, if for no other reason than to hurt his feelings. He thought of how she must have been with the attaché, her poor late husband.

"One can have good or bad table manners in these restaurants," he said, mocking her accent and tone. "But everyone has table manners."

This didn't amuse her either. They seem to have discovered each other's thin charm.

After he had stuffed himself and she was drowsy with drink, they went their separate ways. Peter's cab driver dropped him at Pennsylvania and 15th, and Peter crossed to the Treasury Building. A guard admitted him and grinned, treating him like the celebrity of the staff as he brushed by. Peter only grunted.

His basement offices awaited him: boxes stacked, file cabinets done up in masking tape, maps and charts gone from the walls so that pale bare rectangles revealed their traces. Sitting in all this clutter was Charlie, who had arrived early.

"I used my old security badge to get in," Charlie said, as they greeted each other.

"Glad you're here! Let's go back to my private corner," the Little Buddha said, and he walked off into the suite, making his way between crates as Charlie followed.

"There's something we need to talk about," Charlie said as they went along. They walked along a corridor of stacked books, copies of *Disorders and Terrorism.*

"Hillyard and I are trying to get our killer to come here," Charlie began. "And I think there's a good chance he will."

"Well, the Task Force isn't very good politics anymore," Peter said, finding his desk and offering Charlie a stool beside a stack of reports. "And Jack Hillyard: he never was an official team member."

"He wants to know what happened to Sid Cash. We think we can lure our killer over to the Mayflower Hotel while you're giving your talk to the gem merchants."

"Exciting," Peter said, his drawl lengthening. "But our killer works in Africa, so his whole point would be lost if he started knocking off businessmen here, wouldn't it?"

"We think he'll come after you," Charlie said evenly.

"Really? Well, let's hope so," the Little Buddha squeaked. His hands folded themselves over his belly.

"Everything about you has been in the newspapers for months—all over the world," Charlie explained. "Your late-night habits, your dining out, your office routine, where you live, everything about you. And we know he studies our newspapers. He knew everything about our team in Nairobi. So he's an amateur, Peter, but a good one."

The Little Buddha, hands folded, brow knitted, didn't look too serene. He squirmed in his chair as he thought.

"It just isn't good politics," he repeated. "If anything happens—anything at all—it could ruin my reorganization of all the anti-terrorist groups at the Pentagon. We don't need to get into the newspapers again."

"You should worry about your personal safety," Charlie reminded him.

"My next career step," the Little Buddha said, being consistent, "is more important than my safety. I might as well be dead in this town as to be without power. No, Charlie, I don't think we can do this. Sorry."

"On the other hand," Charlie said cleverly, "if we *caught* the killer, that would solidify your power. You wouldn't even have to use a Pentagon general. You could put your own name on the door."

"True enough," Peter said, looking Charlie in the eye.

"And I think we've got a good chance. I think our man will show up."

"Hillyard wants to do this?"

"He needs help with the budget. Interpol can't set this up on its own."

"It would require discretion," Peter admitted, yielding to the argument.

"A lot of discretion," Charlie agreed. "So that if the killer didn't show up and the effort came to nothing, nobody would be the wiser."

"I like that part," Peter said.

"We'd use only a few men in laying the trap. Half a dozen, maybe, hand-picked by Hillyard. There would be a guard at your apartment. The hotel would have tight security the day you speak."

"A lot of people in Washington, especially the President, loved Herman Carr," the Little Buddha mused. "It would be something to catch his killer right here."

"It can be done. But, Peter, carry your pistol. I saw what happened in Zanzibar and Nairobi, remember?"

"I want us to have lunch at the Pentagon," Peter said, not

answering Charlie, his thoughts adream. "You're definitely going to be part of our new set-up."

"Peter, listen to me. The game isn't finished, and it's a tough one. In your mind, the Task Force isn't in existence anymore. But it's still very real for the killer. There's a good chance he'll come after you. I know I'm right about this."

But the Little Buddha, who lived in a world of political future tense, who preferred schemes and careers to anything else, was not listening anymore. He was projecting possible successes and failure. He was wondering, if the exercise failed, if Jack Hillyard could possibly catch the blame. He was weighing his own prospects.

"Let's just be discreet," he told Charlie once again.

"We will," the Professor answered. "But take care, Peter, really, because I'm not sure we're doing you any favors."

34

Outside the compound Wemba played hole-in-the-ground.

Meanwhile, Quentin crossed over the bridge to the lab to put his papers and luggage in order. Beside the thorn tree Kali stood erect and waiting.

At the desk Quentin picked up his latest forgeries. Inside his luggage all was ready: the 9mm pistol broken down into its several parts, the little vials of fluid, the newspaper articles about the conference in Washington, money, and clothes. His adversaries awaited him, but he wasn't afraid; rather, sadness bothered him because he knew he might not see this place again.

Quietly, he went down the hallway and stood at the foot of the doctor's bed. Familiar odors: gardenia and disinfectant. The old man's breathing kept its soft rhythms.

Then, papers in his pocket and carrying his bags, he crossed once again to the main house. He could see Wemba, squatting with his knees high, moving the pebbles of his game in the far corner of the yard. The house presented its coolness and shadow: his mother's soft presence seemed to say goodbye. Piano, tables, dark panels of doors and window sills, colored panes of glass, the familiar angles of rooms and corridors: goodbye all.

In the yard he loaded his bags into the Land Rover. His thoughts, he discovered, were already turning to the business at hand; annoyances crowded in, yet he was pleased to be preoccupied, as if all the details of the journey helped his leaving.

For only a moment he paused to glance toward Wemba, but the old black, hunched down between his bony knees, wouldn't look up and return the gaze. These last days, knowing what they knew, they hadn't bothered to speak of anything, and, now, Quentin would go without a word.

Wemba's pebbles were moved from hole to hole with studied intensity as the motor of the Land Rover roared to life and Quentin drove off.

In Nairobi, he parked on a crowded side street far away from the busy hotel district where the police paid elaborate attention to abandoned vehicles. The Land Rover, old and battered, would go undetected for weeks.

Carrying his small amount of luggage, he walked up to the main road and caught a taxi to the airport.

Inside the terminal Quentin found police everywhere and what seemed an extraordinary number of customs clerks. He bought magazines and debated with himself on which of several identity papers and passports to use, even considering, for the first time, using his real name. In the end, he stood in line with one of his forgeries in hand: Mr. Timothy T. Knight.

He removed his dark glasses, so that the agent could compare his face with the passport photo. For what seemed ages, the man stared at him. Then he was admitted to an area reserved for passengers. Hundreds of Americans and Europeans sipped the only available drink sold at the concession stand, a tepid orange-flavored liquid.

Half an hour later he sat rigid in his seat in the plane. His nerves had tightened, and he felt beads of perspiration on his body. He wanted to take out his miniature chess set and calm himself with a few problems, but didn't because he wanted no one interested in him. Why, he asked himself, all this anxiety? Settle down. But everything nagged at him: the Land Rover, the poor forgeries, this major flight—so different from the small, rattling airlines he usually departed in.

By the time the plane was off, winging northwest over the great Rift Valley, he felt ill-prepared, impulsive, and somehow wrong. This is my last trip out, he told himself. My point will be made after this. I can't go on.

He put his head back and tried to sleep. After a time, he drifted into a series of short dreams. In one, Kali entered his father's bedroom, slipped inside the mosquito netting, and settled on the old man's body. In another, he was walking across the high, glacial meadows of Kilimanjaro with his mother. In yet another, he sat down to play the piano for guests at the estate house. The chandeliers were lit. Wemba had dressed in a red velvet jacket. Everyone wore tuxedoes, sipped wine from long-stemmed glasses, and waited for Quentin to begin playing. But there were no keys on the piano and the soundless room began to grow dark.

Four days before the beginning of the conference Charlie received a phone call from Jack Hillyard which helped confirm their intuitions and hopes: an independent South African gem dealer named Knight had mailed in one of the preregistration forms indicating that he would be in attendance at the Mayflower Hotel.

"Except for known executives this is our only registration from Africa," Hillyard said, not able to keep the excitement out of his voice.

"What about a man using a color in his name?" Charlie asked. He tried to keep his voice low, so that Stella wouldn't overhear. In vain, he also tried to reach the volume dial on the stereo set, so that music could give him cover.

"No way to be sure, of course," Hillyard went on. "But I put a quick trace on Mr. Knight. Nobody at the address he gave. Nobody in any of the South African associations or the diamond trade ever heard of him. Could be an obscure investor, even so, but I—"

"Would our killer mail in a preregistration form?" Charlie interrupted.

"He had to. It's a closed meeting at the hotel except for registrants. But let me finish. I also traced Mr. Knight's travel. Nobody by that name took a flight out of South Africa. But Mr. Knight—same name as we got on the preregistration form—flew out of Nairobi. He went to Rome, then to Amsterdam, then to Boston."

"He's already here?"

"According to immigration."

"Damn," Charlie said, getting excited. He could see through the hallway into the study where Stella sat reading, her glasses pulled down on her nose, as usual, and her long legs tucked under her and wrapped in a mound of blankets.

"I even checked Boston's large hotels," Hillyard went on. "Didn't get anything, but didn't expect to. We've lost him for now. My guess is that he'll switch identities—except for his appearance at the conference—and that he plans to leave the country under another passport."

"Suppose he's already come to Washington?" Charlie asked in a near whisper.

"That's my guess," Hillyard answered.

"You told Peter all this?"

"Yes, just what I've told you."

"He needs a full-time bodyguard," Charlie said.

"That would be three shifts of trained guards daily. We just can't do it. Too much expense and too much exposure. But our killer will be at the conference, right? And, meanwhile, we've got Peter's apartment under guard and the Treasury Building has its own tight security, as you know."

The more Hillyard talked, the more Charlie worried.

"I think we've got too small of a force," he argued. "Now that you've got a definite lead on Mr. Knight, don't you think we should expand? What about the metropolitan police?"

"The Little Buddha wants everything low key," the detective said. "No police, no FBI, no competing groups."

"We've miscalculated all along," Charlie said, beginning to fret. "Better to add more men."

"Interpol can't afford to hire guards," Hillyard said. "If the Little Buddha won't hire guards to protect himself, that's it. My guess is that we'll catch Mr. Knight at the conference—right there in the lobby of the Mayflower Hotel at the registration desk."

"I don't like it," the Professor said.

They made plans to phone each other by noon of the next day and hung up. Trying to control himself, Charlie strolled into the study, bent down, and kissed Stella's perfumed neck.

"Sorry about all the business," he told her.

"Mmmm," she replied, not looking up from her book. An empty dish, its ice cream all spooned out, sat beside her on a table.

"I'll be busy as hell these next few days, too," he went on.

"Okay," she answered absently, and he said no more.

Charlie went out to the kitchen and stood in the glare of the harsh flourescent lights. Excitement pulsed in him. Milder adventure than this suits most men, he told himself. When their petty jobs weigh them down they usually turn to narrow little psychological vices. Sometimes they cheat on their wives or set themselves afloat on raging rivers or travel to foreign lands, but their therapies are usually conventional. Few have to go to Africa. Few get into games like this. Few of them go on those darker journeys which are forms of suicide in thin disguise.

He hated himself for keeping things from Stella, yet had to. One sets the soul on risky trips and hopes it comes back intact, he told himself, and I've got to do this. With the promise of the firstborn, he knew, he had entered a wonderful and mystic cycle: he wanted to live, to preserve and nourish. He was pleased that he would soon be a father. Pleased with Stella, the house, the new king-sized bed. But darkness seemed to be needed to confirm the sunlight; if I visit it often enough, he told himself, it might take me in and never let me come back. But I need it, I want it: all its risks and guilts.

He began to worry about the Little Buddha once more, but Stella called him to bed.

"C'mere," she beckoned when he reached the bedroom. She waited beneath a mountain of blankets and quilts, her arms outstretched for him, her cotton underpants atop her slippers there on the floor.

Later, though, when she was sound asleep, he slipped out of bed and dressed. Quarter past eleven: early. His worry had turned into dread and certainty because there was a time when the Little Buddha was alone and exposed, a vulnerable moment, and Charlie felt that, under the circumstances, responsibility was his alone.

Quentin strolled around the vicinity of the White House and the Treasury Building for perhaps the tenth time since his arrival in Washington. A busy area in daytime: beyond the south lawn of the mansion a group of demonstrators with placards made a small protest against oil

273

companies, at the east gate convoys of vans delivered food and beverages for a party being given by the President in the evening, and outside the Treasury Building secretaries and young executives hurried along to their next appointments.

All day rainclouds had gathered and threatened. At times, Quentin waited in his rented car for the downpour everyone seemed to expect, but the dark skies would give way to the light, then darken again later on. Mostly, Quentin walked and studied the Mall and surrounding neighborhoods. He picked his way among landmarks, trying to get a feel for the place, but the city seemed foreign and as lifeless as a museum: the hedges perfectly trimmed, the memorials and walkways clean and bright, everything in such order that he suspected he was being watched.

He fretted over the proximity to the White House, for the street where he knew the Little Buddha would travel, walking to the cabstand, was within easy range of the President's security force—about which Quentin knew nothing. This concern led him to others and caused his general anxiety to return; perhaps something had happened in Africa, he kept thinking, perhaps the death, at long last, of his father; and things weren't right here.

In Lagos and Zanzibar it was as if his victims had appointments for their own deaths; they waited for him, it seemed, and invited him into their presence. The game, then, at those times, had been at its best: the quarry had challenged him, but he always had an acute sense of what to do.

Now, curiously enough, he seemed unsure—and the game seemed finished just as, before this, his political and his personal obligations had seemed to end.

He wished he had not come. The grey sky overhead seemed like an omen. Although he walked around and watched, his timing seemed off and his instincts misled him, he felt, as once they had served him.

Observant these days as he slowly prepared, he nevertheless thought about cycles. He considered going back to Kenya and trying farming—coffee, say, or sisal, or some paying crop which would allow him to keep laborers and pay good wages. Surely the drouth years were ending. And, surely, too, he could enter into some new and healing work. He thought of his long preparation toward living: a childhood in a troubled house under the roof of the temperamental doctor, a young manhood in isolation and the preliminaries of a warrior's life, these last months in execution of his duties. The cycle, somehow, seemed complete, and he wanted to stand in that blue tint of evening, again, feeling the land whisper itself into silence. He wanted a new stanza of himself. Nothing severe. The evensong, instead, of a less troubled and happier existence.

He passed the Executive Office Building: a rococo monstrosity. Ahead lay the Reflecting Pool and the wide terraces. He calculated distances and tried to decide where to leave his car.

The Little Buddha's daily habits were all documented in magazine and newspaper interviews, and there had even been frequent mention of his most vulnerable moment: after dinner in the evenings Peter Foxx always returned to the Treasury Building, worked for another hour or two, then sometime between eleven o'clock and midnight walked from the building toward the Ellipse. There, he took a taxi at the cabstand, or, occasionally, he circled toward Constitution Avenue and a second and more distant cabstand. These streets and open spaces south of the White House were lit with streetlamps, but the atmosphere at night, as in any park in any city, was filled with shadow.

Quentin had seen his man. Two nights before this he had waited and watched. He had no clear view of the face in the darkened street, but the rotund body was unmistakable: the great belly, the short legs, the stride of an elf.

Time and place and target: all set. But he walked on, passing tourists who took family snapshots within shouting distance of that noisy little band of demonstrators. Simple, all of it, yet he worried. In the evenings these streets were curiously empty. Patrol cars passed at sporadic intervals. The White House—undoubtedly with elaborate security—was too nearby. And the Little Buddha would be in an open space so that he could run away. Nothing was exactly right.

Charlie knew that this was the time and place, too. Once Peter stepped into a taxi down at his regular cabstand, he would be whisked off into the city, so that a stranger—and an unprofessional, besides—would have difficulty following. The apartment where Peter lived was locked and guarded—by doormen, security clerks, and Hillyard's man. His phone had an unlisted number. And during the day he used a car and driver whenever he left the Treasury Building—which itself was fortified with a brace of guards who screened everyone who entered and pinned them with magnetic ID tags.

But that walk in the dark toward the cabstand: that was it. If the killer had read anything on Peter Foxx—and surely he had—then these few minutes each day could be the time.

"Three evening meetings in a row," he told Stella after supper that night. "Then I'll stay home, promise, and keep you company in the study."

"What exactly are you doing?" she wanted to know.

"If I told you," he said, "you could start another list of idiocies."

"And why are you wearing jogging clothes?"

"I'm not going to sit around in uncomfortable clothes," he said, and he held her in his arms. She smelled of cloves and a perfumed sea. Before she could ask anything else, he kissed her mouth. "Be back shortly after midnight."

"This group can't meet in the daytime?" she persisted.

"Right," he answered, and he gave her a smile as he gently pushed her away.

He drove over to the college. Using his office for his final dressing room, he buckled the .45 Luger in place, then taped it to his T-shirt so it wouldn't bounce against his body. Then he zipped the loose fitting jogging tunic over that. At ten o'clock that night he rang his message service. Hillyard had called to say there was no news.

Dressed and ready, he knew exactly what he would look like if he could see himself in a mirror: a greying, slender, slightly potbellied senior citizen decked out for the illusion of speed. All his many pretenses and limitations were strong inside him; he knew his own failures. Yet his nerve ends were singing.

35

The Little Buddha went to his office, as usual, that night, but he couldn't work. The clutter appalled him, and his thoughts bounced from Andrea, for whom, now, he had a kind of irritated affection, to his new quarters inside the Pentagon, for which he had unabashed longing.

He thought of going down to the sub-basement pistol range, but decided against it. No, not really in the mood. But the idea made him recall Charlie's warning, and so for the tiniest moment he envisioned the walk he would soon make to the cabstand. It was usually a calm stroll, his only exercise of the day, but now, briefly, he also remembered that his personal Luger was at home on the apartment workbench. No matter.

Yet he did move to his desk where the folder lay. Savannah Blue. Jack Hillyard's new items: the probable movements from Nairobi to Rome to Amsterdam to Boston.

Peter smoked his last cigarette as he gazed at the folder. Two packs today, he told himself. Awful.

The sound of thunder outside.

In the street near the Liberty Bell entrance to the Treasury Building, a man in a jogging outfit trotted by: Charlie. He had checked Peter's basement window, had found the light burning, so had correctly assumed that Peter was back at his desk. As he neared the entrance, then, where Peter would emerge, he quickened his pace. Hurrying by, he meant to spend most of his time at the far corners of the block. Occasionally, he crossed over to keep watch from the White House side of the street.

None of the White House security force had bothered him these evenings, and the frequent patrol cars had left him alone—although one, two nights ago, had slowed to give him a close look. A big affair was being conducted inside the White House tonight. Limousines announced themselves throughout the evening at the gate to the east wing. Floodlights illuminated the grounds—and made the shadows of the distant Ellipse even more forbidding.

Down beyond the south end of the White House lawn the demonstrators continued to wail. Their protest was unclear.

A bright bolt of lightning followed by sharp thunder.

He reached the end of the block, checked to see if anyone was watching his tactic, then turned around again and started back.

A usual number of pedestrians entered the block and passed by. Charlie had counted them: some three dozen in half an hour. Guests from over at Blair House or the Hay-Adams out for a stroll, he calculated, or late-shift janitors or mid-level government types.

He watched everyone closely.

A man walking his poodle: okay. A black girl hurrying to the bus stops up on Lafayette Square and an old man, weak in the knee, giving her ass a glance as she went along: okay. He felt that he was getting astute at sizing up people.

But jogging slowly along the sidewalk, a thought came to him: somebody, if I'm right about all this, is probably watching me.

Yet, how could he be watching? Where was he watching from? The street was an unadorned corridor: no bushes to hide in, no hard cover for potential assassins who might be waiting for those east wing gates to swing open. So whatever happened, Charlie began to figure, would happen down there—at the end of the block where the light dimmed and the lawns and terraces spread out toward Constitution Avenue. It would be after this lighted block. It would be there in those next hundred yards before Peter reached his cabstand: there, right there.

The next time down at the end of the block, Charlie jogged on out into the darkness. He moved along—not losing sight of the Treasury Building either—until he could see the cabstand itself. It was a one-taxi stand. If a taxi waited, others passed by—as, in fact, one was presently doing.

Jogging back toward Peter's exit spot, he felt confident. He knew it might happen—and, if so, exactly where.

If I had any sense, Charlie told himself, I'd jog right up beside Peter and take his arm. I'd say, look, I'm sorry about what happened in Nairobi, very sorry, but it's not going to happen again.

The first few drops of rain.

Charlie jogged on, fairly conspicuous, if anyone cared to notice, traversing the block over and over, waiting and watching. And his same rough plan remained: he would stay close in the event any stranger approached Peter during that dangerous stroll.

Inside his office, Peter looked for his umbrella, but couldn't find it. The increasing patter of rain on his window still hurried him along. He turned out the light, locked up, and started down the hallway toward the exit.

The demonstrators beyond the south lawn scattered and ran before a torrent of rain. The block outside the Treasury Building filled with confusion and movement, and Charlie, already drenched, stood watching with amazement. My luck, he told himself. This is when Peter will make his appearance.

A young man, running by, shouted something at Charlie—probably political and probably obscene. Placards were discarded along the curbs. And the rain came in pulsing sheets now as inside the White House grounds car lights came on and the President's guests began to leave. Movement and sound, punctuated by thunder. And, sure enough, Peter emerged from the Liberty Bell entrance, an old raincoat draped around his pudgy shoulders, and began hurrying along toward the end of the street.

"Goddammit," Charlie whispered, and he started jogging, trying to catch up and to fall in behind the Little Buddha. His hand touched the bulge of the Luger beneath his wet jogging suit—just to make sure.

Peter lurched forward at a good pace for a few yards, then—breathless—he slowed to his usual walk, as if he had given up on the weather and had decided to retain his dignity.

Charlie slowed to a walk, too, feeling extremely stupid walking along in the downpour in his running togs. Yet, as they came to the end of the block and neared the wet darkness beyond the corner streetlamp he felt his nerves and muscles tense.

Two cars from that White House traffic flow swerved in front of Peter, one of them almost grazing his protruding belly as he halted quickly in the middle of the street to let it pass. The rain blinded them as Peter lurched forward again. Charlie was near enough now that he could have overtaken Peter in ten good strides.

They moved onto the sidewalk around the Ellipse now. Charlie faked a few arm exercises as the darkness enfolded them. He could see the cabstand ahead—the lights of the taxi and distant streetlamp through the rain.

Nobody around. Charlie's scars tingled, every one, and gave energy to his pace.

Dark mirrored pools in the uneven concrete of the streets and sidewalks. Then, Charlie saw a figure coming toward Peter, just a few paces away, a man silhouetted between them and the cabstand, and he hurried to be there—to have the Luger in hand if the figure made any sudden move. It was a black man, hurrying in the rain, head down in the storm, and he passed both Peter and Charlie without altering his posture.

Halfway to the waiting taxi Charlie's breath—strong enough during all that earlier jogging—grew short with fear.

He saw no one else. Nobody.

At last, he slackened his stride and watched Peter's progress into that halo of pale yellow light, streaked with rain, around the taxi.

Safe. Had the killer seen Charlie's hovering presence? Had the premonitions been wrong? If so, he didn't care because his guilt, like the pounding rain, drenched him, and as he watched Peter struggle through the door of the taxi he felt vindicated for all his wildest imaginings and happy that he had been there again—even if just to scare someone off. In spite of this craziness, he and Stella would be all right. Better yet, he would be right with himself—at least for another night until he took up the vigil again. And, soon, hopefully, with Jack Hillyard at work, the killer would be found.

His wet hair was flat against his head.

Dripping, he felt a shiver as he stood and watched. The rain was cold, getting down into his bones and marrow.

The taxi, he then noted, hadn't moved since Peter had entered it.

Charlie took a single step forward and waited. His lips fell open, as though this needed to be remarked on. The rain continued to pour.

Then Peter came through the taxi's rear door, kicking and thrashing around. He tumbled onto the wet pavement, jerking and rolling.

From the driver's side, moving around the car, came another figure. His movements as he advanced on Peter seemed painfully deliberate, and Charlie watched as a jerky slow-motion catastrophe unfolded before his eyes.

Peter got up, stumbled, went down again, and yelled something Charlie couldn't hear.

Time, which had slowed, speeded up again, and Charlie had only a second to fumble the Luger out of his wet clothes, trip the safety, and fire. Even then, he wasn't sure of his target. The figure was at Peter's side, bending toward him, so the two men blurred together in the dark rain.

Charlie took aim and fired at—what else?—the taxi.

There it sat, big and yellow beneath the street lamp, and he boomed a .45 slug into its side.

The noise, at least, turned the attacker away.

Peter's hands fluttered over his body. He seemed to be struggling to rise and slipping down again. When the man broke into a run for the driver's door once again and the two figures were separated, Charlie fired once more.

It was possible that he scored a hit.

The attacker disappeared on the far side of the taxi. Perhaps he even fell.

Running at them, Charlie closed in.

"Peter!" he called, but only the rain answered.

Circling the taxi then, Charlie pulled up short.

Quentin Clare waited for him. He was down on one knee, his arms raised and pointing the 9mm pistol straight at Charlie. And Charlie's last thought before the pain was, no, unfair, you shouldn't have a pistol, that's not how you've been doing it.

It was a sad, pathetic, last conscious thought.

Then pain beyond pain again: the bullet tore into his chest, driving him backward and sitting him down in a deep daze. It blew into his sternum, spraying bone throughout his body, and made its exit through a lung and out his back.

Lying in the wet grass, pelted by rain, Charlie repeated one word over and over as the taxi pulled away. "Don't," he kept saying. "Oh, don't, don't," and he was giving himself his pep talk again, calling himself from a sleep that seemed inevitable, pleading with his body to stay awake, and the pain itself, loud as an alarm through his system, seemed for a moment to keep him going. "Don't, don't—"

The storm covered these incantations as it had covered the sound of the shots. Once, Charlie sensed that he heard Peter's high squeak nearby: a feeble mewing. Then rain seemed to come even harder and darkness descended.

Meanwhile, Quentin drove over to C Street.

He discarded the stolen taxi and managed to crawl into his rented car and drive off. His own pain was so intense that he doubted that he could walk, and after he had driven a few blocks away from the abandoned taxi he pulled to the curb and fumbled in his luggage for dry clothing and something to wrap his wound.

Charlie's bullet, aimed and fired too low, had bounced off the wet pavement and had entered the leg flattened out like a fist. Most of Quentin's calf had been shot away—the leg was broken—and blood was everywhere. Tearing his clothes into strips, Quentin began to bind himself tightly, gritting his teeth and rolling back his eyes as he wrapped with all his strength.

The bleeding wouldn't stop. Bandages soaked quickly with blood, so Quentin tore up more clothes. Doing this, he passed out. For a while—he couldn't tell whether it was seconds or several minutes—he lay with his head back on the car seat. Then, revived, he wrapped the leg some more, tying off his bandages with hard knots. He managed to pull on another pair of trousers, then get behind the wheel again.

Driving across the river to the airport, he tried to recall his plan, but a delirium of pain swept it from his mind. He wanted only to crouch in darkness, in the deep bush away from the hunter's next shot, and he fought to think of the hour, schedules, airlines, and the details of escape.

Cars honked their horns at him as he drove too slowly along the airport access. Dizzy with pain and nausea, he struggled to keep watching the road.

Pulling into a parking slot for rental cars near the door to the terminal, he decided to stop, rest, and think things out. His head fell back and he closed his eyes. A skycap, he decided, with a wheelchair. If he could make those few steps over to the baggage station near the entrance, he would pay a skycap to help him. The late shuttle up to New York would accommodate him without an advance ticket, then he could transfer to one of several late-hour international flights.

No, none of that made sense.

The pain in his leg caused his whole body to twist.

Short, undefined dreams invaded his consciousness.

I'm bleeding to death, he told himself.

Nothing at all made sense because of the pain, but he wanted very much to walk to that door, get on a plane, and go home. He wanted to see Africa again. There was nothing exotic about it, nothing so splendid, nothing the Americans could possibly understand or want; it was just his place, and he didn't want to die in this sad, metallic country on the wrong side of the world.

Minutes after the taxi had pulled away from the Ellipse, Peter flagged down a passing car. On the way to the hospital he held Charlie in his arms.

Peter was unhurt himself except for skinned knees and elbows which he had collected scrambling out of the taxi as Quentin attacked. He had seen—and would tell this many times, for years to come—that first stream of poison coming at him. Some of it, he would claim, actually struck him, but he was too wet and too quick. He had thrown up his arms for protection, covering himself, because suddenly he had known exactly what was happening.

Charlie had saved his life. It had been Peter's greatest moment: someone—other than his devoted parents—had cared about him. It didn't quite alter his fierce ambition, improve his disposition, or temper his bad habits, but even so, he felt, it deepened him. His reverence for Charlie Hazo, at least, would be unbounded forever.

Charlie's life hung in the balance only briefly. He survived the shock, so survived the lasting effects. Pain became his enemy and friend: it kept him from the final sleep.

After thirty minutes at the hospital Peter heard from doctors in the emergency operating room that Charlie's vital signs were strong and his condition stable, so he phoned Stella.

"No, no," he told her. "He's going to live."

"He's shot clean through? How can he live?"

"Promise," Peter said, squeaking. "Just one more scar."

"One more—" She began to laugh and cry all at once.

Peter assured her that a car was en route for her and that he would make all arrangements. Only after he finished talking with her did he realize that perhaps an hour and a half had elapsed with nothing being done toward apprehending the killer. Because he didn't have coins for the pay phone, he barged into an administrator's office and called, in order, Hanning Wilson, Interpol, the FBI, and the metropolitan police.

As an afterthought, then, he phoned the reporter Fielding Blanks, his general at the Pentagon, the Secretary of the Treasury, and, at last, Andrea. Each one, he felt, was sufficiently impressed.

"This all just sounds so unlike you, Peter," Andrea said.

"It's a rough business," he told her, and somehow his tone managed to convey that he and Charlie Hazo were equals in dangerous intrigue.

After this he went back to find that Charlie had been moved from the recovery room upstairs to intensive care.

"Nothing wrong?" he asked the doctor. "No complications?"

"No, he'll make it," the doctor said, "Shock, bad loss of blood, a collapsed lung, a busted chest, but the wound was clean as a whistle and missed the heart and spinal column. And the old guy's tough."

Policemen and two FBI agents waited to see Peter.

"Did you get the killer's description on the wire?" he asked them. They stood huddled in a wide, white corridor. The agents both smelled of men's cologne.

"Yes, and the airports and major terminals are all on alert," one of the agents confirmed. "We've got every procedure started."

"Good. I've got to go upstairs to be with my friend now," Peter told them. "I'm sure you understand that. I'll trust things to you."

They liked his dedication to his wounded companion and promised to do a good job.

Going up in the elevator, Peter couldn't help think how fortunate all this could turn out to be. Except for Charlie's pain, of course. The country would get a better operated anti-terrorist force. Appointments would be made and careers would flourish. And time would, after all, heal all scars—even those on the Professor's almost immortal body.

36

Dreams and visions.

Quentin saw himself, once, entering the terminal, moving through crowds of passive faces, and getting on a plane. It took off into the evening sky, soaring above the incandescent cities, the whole glistening seaboard of America spread out below: the symmetries of Washington, the pulsing towers of New York, and textures of endless light spreading out into the dark wastelands beyond. Great arteries of traffic blurred the neon highways. There was no true darkness below, just an endless sparkling nebula of movement, waves of light, bursts of color.

Then he knew that he was still sitting in the car, his head thrown back in sleep. He had only dreamt his escape. His leg was warm and stiff now, but caused his body to throb with fever, and beneath his feet he could feel the carpet soaked with blood, making a soft sucking sound when he stirred.

He could no longer clearly remember what had happened in the taxi with the fat little bureaucrat; he recalled turning, flashing the ring, trying to hit him with a stream of poison, but the fat arms had gone up, a raincoat had flapped between them like a shield, then the high shrieking began, the kicking, and he was gone. Quentin recalled his feeling, too, as he chased his quarry into the rainy darkness: I don't want to kill anyone anymore; I am a soldier tired of wars and weary of my own cruelty; the game is empty and finished; and only my self-protection remains, but even that doesn't matter so much.

He passed out again.

Nearby, another squad car arrived and another pair of policemen joined guards already posted at the door. They were everywhere, watching for him, but he was hiding inside his dreams once more.

He saw the savannah, wet and fresh after the rains, birds whirling overhead, the great herds in transit. In a thicket of trees naked men moved in a slow dance, their arms outstretched, circling, and chanting to the sky. A river made its way down from the far valleys, curling silver and black like a slow serpent.

Get up and go to the door of the terminal, he kept telling himself, knowing that he wouldn't.

Wemba sat at the doctor's bedside.

Sunlight streamed through the window and created its warm, dappled patterns in the room. All was in order: the catheters, the large white bed draped in netting, the familiar steady breathing from the pillow. But then something stirred Wemba to raise his eyes. The breathing became irregular and the old man moved, too weak to pull himself up, his muscles gone, yet his neck taut. His eyes opened—deep and as dark as caves—and seemed to focus.

"Quentin," the old man said, his lips barely working. It was his only word, but he pronounced it distinctly, as if he clearly saw the vision.

Wemba pulled back the netting and stared at his old master. The eyes glared for a moment, then closed again, but the doctor wasn't dead; he had resumed his sleep as if he would never pass away. The room was as real as real: Wemba's perspiration shiny on his craggy black face, the odors of gardenia and disinfectant blent together, the sunlight.

Then, as if Quentin was a camera seeing all this in silence, he receded from the room, moving down the hallway, passing the lab, the study where all the clutter of his life and mission lay around, the screened-in porch. Kali was there in the yard of the compound. Then across the bridge for the last time and into the main house: the soundless piano, the familiar vacant corridors where loneliness covered everything like dust. Beyond, then: the little raw estate set off in the middle of nowhere, the arid bush, the hills, the road into the city, the region, the continent itself turning on the greater earth which moved in space like a shining, mystic-blue sapphire.

Then back again.

Quentin lay across the front seat of the car, too weak to sit upright. His breath came in a soft wheeze.

In another dream, he followed after the legendary rogue elephant. Swaying, holding its longer tusk sideways and above the ground, it shuffled toward the Mountains of the Moon. Behind it in a long ragged file came creatures and men, Quentin among them, moving toward that horizon of unexpected snow-capped peaks which rose above the jungles and hot savannahs. Juju, the magic one. The strange, wild elephant and its entourage trekked on and on, a long, unruly column going to its distant oblivion.

In the last dream, then, which was a vision of things to come, Quentin saw the yard of the compound once more. The pods were turned over, broken and empty, and riddled with holes. Men in uniforms were everywhere: on the bridge, in the laboratory, standing at the foot of the doctor's bed in awed silence, roaming the main house. Beyond all their activity sat Wemba, his face down, staring into the dust at all his holes and pebbles. Beneath the thorn tree Kali was coiled and proudly raised up.

Slowly the men gathered on the bridge, brought their rifles to their shoulders and aimed. They spoke to each other in hushed tones and agreed to commence firing. After the first few hits the mamba coiled itself tightly, hiding its face. It scarcely moved as shot after shot ripped wounds in its flesh.

After many rounds, the men stopped shooting. But not one of them would enter the yard to make sure the creature was dead.